Shirley Smith was born in Yorkshire. For some time she worked as a headmistress in Manchester and as an inspector in South Yorkshire. Her first novel was *Dear Miss Grey*.

DANGEROUS LEGACY

When Sir Thomas Capley inherits a fortune from his great-uncle, he returns to Wintham determined to restore the family seat to its former glory. In somewhat unusual circumstances, he meets the proud and beautiful heiress, Miss Helena Steer, who has decided never to marry and, instead, devotes herself to her widowed father and her two young sisters. However, aided by Thomas's mischievous grandmother, the couple fall in love. There are many dangerous adventures for both of them, but will Helena find happiness with the passionate Sir Thomas?

Books by Shirley Smith
Published by The House of Ulverscroft:

DEAR MISS GREY

SHIRLEY SMITH

DANGEROUS LEGACY

Complete and Unabridged

ULVERSCROFT
Leicester

First published in Great Britain in 2003 by
Robert Hale Limited
London

First Large Print Edition
published 2004
by arrangement with
Robert Hale Limited
London

British Library CIP Data

Smith, Shirley, *1942* –
   Dangerous legacy.—Large print ed.—
   Ulverscroft large print series: romance
   1. Love stories
   2. Large type books
   I. Title
   823.9′2 [F]

   ISBN 1–84395–679–9

Published by
F. A. Thorpe (Publishing)
Anstey, Leicestershire

Set by Words & Graphics Ltd.
Anstey, Leicestershire
Printed and bound in Great Britain by
T. J. International Ltd., Padstow, Cornwall

This book is printed on acid-free paper

This book is respectfully dedicated
to my friend Angela Wood

1

'Depend upon it, Thomas, my dear boy, if old Ashtree says that it is seven hundred thousand then it must be so. But oh, Tom, I feel I must be dreaming!'

The old lady bobbed her head excitedly and her curls quivered in sympathy with her mental agitation. Tom's grandmother was very small and upright and her cheeks were coloured a rather deep pink. The tight little curls peeping from her bonnet owed much to the past fashion for false hair pieces and were suspiciously dark and luxuriant, but her eyes were as handsome and bright as a young girl's. One slender, mittened hand rested on the ivory head of a walking umbrella and in the other she carried a dainty little fan which she tapped on Tom's arm to emphasize her point.

'And I must say, Tom, that although it is a great deal of money, I know you will use your great fortune both wisely and well.'

'Yes. It *is* a great deal of money,' Tom replied soberly. 'And I intend to restore the Capley Estates with it and do some good among my tenants.' He turned to stare

1

through the carriage window at the passing scenery. The tranquil landscape was such a contrast to the grime of London that he became lost in thoughts of his country childhood, but his grandmother soon interrupted them.

'A fortune,' she repeated. 'Why, heaven take it, Thomas, I never thought your great uncle Silas had it in him to engage in honest toil, never mind make so much money in foreign parts. Bless me, his pockets were always to let as I remember. He was forever being dunned by creditors for his gaming debts. Poor Silas. What a scape-grace! And when he sailed away in that emigrant ship all those years ago, he was almost forgotten by us all.'

A tear glistened in the corner of Lady Lavinia's eye and she wiped it away with a dainty scrap of lace.

'And to think he made all that great wealth in Jamaica. Planting, as I heard it from Mr Ashtree.'

'And other activities possibly, Grandmama,' Tom murmured drily. His serious profile was still turned to the window, in order to get a glimpse of his family home as soon as it should appear through the trees. They were travelling down in the chaise, posting with hired horses for speed. The

2

August weather continued fine and the interior of the chaise was stiflingly hot, but they were on the final stage of their journey from London to the Capley family seat in Wintham. A second vehicle, an old carriage of Grandfather Capley's, and driven by a groom, had departed a few days previously. It carried the bulk of their luggage and Tom's recently acquired butler, Strang.

Miss Gill, a maiden lady almost as ancient as his grandmother, who was dozing in a corner of the chaise, gave a soft ladylike snore. She hadn't even pretended to know how or why their ill fortune had suddenly been reversed. It was sufficient for her to be with the only two people she had left in the world and to be secure in her position as companion to her beloved Lady Lavinia.

'But what really saddens me, Tom,' continued his grandmother, glaring at the snorer, 'is that my brother never returned to visit any of his relatives. He only ever saw you once as an infant, my darling boy. You were in your mother's arms, of course, and kicking your plump little legs about as babies do, Thomas. You were such a beautiful baby.' The old lady's fine eyes grew bright again at the memory. 'Of course, when your poor mama died ... So untimely, Thomas. No wonder your papa acted as he did. He was very unhappy.'

'Quite,' replied her grandson, in a tone which discouraged further discussion of his dead parents, because the fact was, that in less than three years, Sir William Capley, Tom's father, had squandered a double inheritance in drink and gambling debts, before inconsiderately dying himself, before any of the debts were paid off.

At his death, the young Thomas had been brought up by his grandmother, the widowed Lady Lavinia, and after a lonely student life at Oxford had worked at conserving and trying to make profitable the lands and estates that still remained to him. But it had been at a price. He had allowed himself few pleasures and no luxuries at all. He and George Gaunt, the estate manager, had sold off certain tracts of land, had encouraged the Home Farm to be self-sufficient and given employment to as many of the labourers in tied cottages as they could. Such as were turned away were given modest stipends and helped to find other positions. Capley Hall was closed down and Tom and his grandmother moved to a modest town house in an unfashionable part of London. Only Miss Gill and the groom had been retained as personal servants. For the last few years, Miss Gill had been willing to continue her duties for no wages at all, thankful to receive merely bed and board. By living frugally and with prudent investments, the young Thomas Capley had been able to survive.

He was a good-looking young man with features too blunt to be deemed conventionally handsome; his strong features and healthy outdoor complexion balanced by high cheekbones and fine dark eyes. His tall frame and broad shoulders made him seem too athletic for a member of the *ton*, but his shapely hands and aristocratic bearing, unmistakably proclaimed him as a gentleman. His sudden good fortune, coming from such an unexpected source had given him the inspiration to open up the Hall for refurbishment and to explore the possibility of restoring the Capley estate to its former greatness. He was conscious of the long history of his family and the responsibility he had to both the land and the people of the neighbourhood who were dependent on the estate for their livelihood and this had made him serious beyond his years.

He frowned slightly as the old lady broke into his thoughts once again. 'But your dear mother, God rest her, made me promise to love you and guide you, Thomas.' Here her voice became a little tremulous. 'But now,' she made an attempt at brightness, 'we are at last returning to Capley Hall, where you were born. Twenty-seven years is a long time, is it not?'

'Indeed yes, ma'am,' said Tom, gently squeezing the small hand.

'And what do you intend to do with all that money?' She was disconcerting in her abrupt question and her sharp eyes were uncomfortably shrewd as well as loving.

'Do with it? Well I . . . '

'Of course I know you will open up the Hall and I expect you will be looking for a wife and wanting to start a nursery of your own?' Her bright eyes regarded him askance. 'Shall you wish me to retire to the Dower House, my dear? No doubt you want your establishment for yourself.'

'Dear ma'am,' he said gently, 'that is for the future. For now, Strang is awaiting us and we must hope he has been able to appoint further staff and prepare some of the rooms for our use.'

They left the turnpike road and drove through Kesthorpe and on towards the village of Wintham, much of which still belonged to the Capley estate. Cottagers came out to watch the carriage pass and a few of the children ran alongside for a little way. The recent hot sunny weather had dried the deep ruts of the unmade road and they trotted along these in their bare feet, calling out excitedly at the sight of a lady and gentleman of the Quality passing by. Now, the chaise turned into the long stately drive of Capley Hall, lined with the magnificent beeches which had been planted over a century earlier and Thomas sat a little straighter in his seat.

The Hall was remarkable in that it had been preserved for almost 400 years in the style in which it had been built by a respectable wool merchant in 1412. Although grand and imposing, it had been lived in by a family who had made comparatively few changes over the years. Successive Capleys had merely added extra rooms and extended the Hall gradually as more sophisticated possibilities for comfort and safety became available. Extra wings were built on as the family's prosperity grew and grew with each succeeding century. The grandson of the wool merchant had become a lawyer in Lincoln's Inn and purchased more land, so that the estate became richer and more extensive. A subsequent Thomas Capley married one of Queen Elizabeth's Maids of Honour and had thirteen children. Later, one of them was rewarded with a baronetcy for services to his monarch. At no point in its long history had the great house ever changed hands and even in his deepest moments of despair, Tom's father had never considered the possibility of selling it. Now, the present Sir Thomas Capley was coming home at last. The horses slowed down and the chaise gradually came to a halt in front of the great historic house.

Miss Gill opened her faded old eyes and blinked in some bewilderment as the footman stepped forward smartly to open the door of the chaise. Strang, the butler, was standing in the sunlight outside the imposing portico of the massive front door. On either side of him were liveried footmen and maidservants in crisp white aprons. The rather heavy-featured housekeeper in respectable black stepped forward to bob a curtsy to Lady Lavinia and Tom as the staff were introduced.

'Welcome home, Sir Thomas. It is good to see you, Lady Capley.' Strang greeted them. He gestured to the assembled staff.

'I have managed to engage reliable local people and we are eager to serve you, Sir Thomas. May I present Mrs Armstrong, the housekeeper, Daisy, Bets, Mary Ann?'

Strang had certainly executed his commission very efficiently. An army of workmen as well as the servants had been employed in bringing Capley Hall to life again, after its ten years of slumber. The maids greeted him one by one, beaming and smoothing their white aprons. Then Jackson, the valet he'd appointed at the Dale Street house in London stepped forward.

'All is in readiness, sir.' He bowed. 'I have taken the liberty of arranging your wardrobe and dressing-room and buying some more toiletries, sir.'

'Thank you, Jackson. You see to everything,' murmured Tom. 'Now, Strang, Lady Capley and Miss Gill wish to retire to their rooms to rest before dinner.'

'Yes, certainly, sir,' said the butler importantly. 'I have already ordered the covers to be laid at six. I hope this is acceptable, sir?'

And so the staff bustled about to complete the arrangements. The house was rather silent and empty, some of the rooms still bearing traces of mustiness and neglect, but sunlight streamed through the windows, giving an air of life and optimism. Both Lady Lavinia and Miss Gill declared themselves well satisfied with the way the old house had been put about to accommodate its aristocratic owner as they made their way upstairs for rest and refreshment.

Seeing everything was settled, Tom left the house and strolled slowly across the terrace and through the garden. The orchard and meadow were richly planted and he drew deep breaths of satisfaction as he walked beyond the gardens towards the rolling parkland and an ancient stile which he remembered from his boyhood. Here, a narrow path led up a slight incline to a wood where dappled shade quivered with diffused sunlight and a stream mottled by pale green willows washed softly over smooth pebbles. This was a vivid reminder of his past and he savoured the memories of his lost childhood when life had been both innocent and idyllic. Lost in thought, he followed the winding path through the woods. He still marvelled that he should have inherited such vast wealth after so many years of penury and the tremendous effort to keep some of the Capley estates intact. The thought that his dear grandmother who had loved and helped him for all those years was here with him and able to partake in his good fortune, was almost over-whelming. He had so many plans and schemes to improve the village and farms that he remained absorbed in his reverie as he walked along the well-remembered way. The path turned suddenly into a clearing full of bright gold sunlight and there he halted in his tracks.

In front of him, galloping far too fast for the woodland ride, was a slender young woman, mounted on a spirited black stallion. Even as he watched, some branch or obstacle must have frightened the horse and it reared suddenly, throwing its rider to the ground. Instinctively Tom hurried forward. She was lying full length on the ground, her blue velvet riding habit was in some disarray and her dainty little feathered hat lay close by. Her loosened fair hair contrasted brightly with the emerald green of the grass and shone as though it had been polished. Tom caught his breath in astonishment and slowly stepped nearer. Who was she? And what was she doing here? Her eyes were tightly closed and the lashes, darker than her hair, were spread against the pallor of her cheeks. His gaze wandered from the graceful black heel of her riding boot past her voluptuously curved thigh and slender waist to the rounded swell of her breasts. He bent over her drinking in her delicate pale beauty and as he stood stock still, staring wonderingly at the beautiful stranger, Tom gradually became aware of another presence close by in the bushes. The leaves rustled ominously and then parted to reveal a pair of extremely elegant black Hessians, skin-tight beige pantaloons and a smart blue coat which was very close fitting and had obviously been tailored exclusively for the exquisite young gentleman who now stood before him. The heavy eyelids were lowered and the thick sensual lips turned down disdainfully as the tall, slim personage

11

glanced sneeringly at Tom's own clumsy breeches and tough country boots.

The fine gentleman now spoke softly without looking at him, 'Who are you?' he said carelessly. 'And what're you doin' here?' His languid tone was carefully calculated to insult and Tom answered civilly but coldly.

'That, if I may say so, sir, does not concern you. And I might beg the same question of you.'

'I am Percy Davenport of Davenport Place. I pray you, leave us. I am known to this young lady and she is quite safe with me.'

'Pardon me, sir. I think she is not.'

Tom looked again at the figure on the grass and unconsciously moved nearer to her as though to guard her, staring at the intruder. The exquisite gentleman now raised his heavy-lidded eyes and looked directly at Tom for the first time, frowning threateningly at him. His right hand tightened on his silver-headed cane until the knuckles grew white.

'Take yourself off, you peasant,' he said through tight lips. 'If you refuse to go I shall thrash you.'

'Pardon me, sir, but I think you will not.' Tom said again. He squared his broad shoulders and his firm chin jutted aggressively, but the stranger was again staring fixedly at the young woman on the grass. Without taking his eyes off her he fumbled in his purse and threw down some coins contemptuously. 'On your way, yokel,' he drawled.

Leaving the coins gleaming on the grass, Tom now stepped forward clenching his fists and closed with him. As they grappled and panted, Davenport's fine clothes became more and more dishevelled, his breathing more and more laboured. Tom who was regularly used to going several rounds with the 'Cheapside Fox', a famous retired boxer, was breathing evenly. Hours of practice had made him joyfully alert in the ring and very light on his feet. Seizing an opening, he struck his opponent in the ribs and then delivered a truly punishing blow to the chin. The fine gentleman crashed down slowly and heavily onto the turf and lay still for some seconds before sitting up slowly, holding his head in his hands. The expression on his face was of the utmost hatred and malevolence as he glowered up at the young man who had just knocked him down.

'You'll pay for this, you cur,' he snarled. Then he got to his feet rather unsteadily and disappeared into the woods without a backward glance.

But Tom had already turned away to look

again at the young woman lying on the ground. As he walked towards her, he noticed a piece of crumpled paper caught on the grass and instinctively he bent to pick it up and thrust it into his coat. Then he knelt by her side and scooping her up in his strong arms he began to carry her along the path to the bank of the stream. As he walked, he gazed straight ahead, concentrating on walking carefully, so as not to jolt his beautiful burden, but after a while he had the uncanny feeling that her eyes had opened and that she was looking up at him. He risked a downward glance at the tantalizingly demure eyelashes and curved red mouth. It was a very shapely mouth with full generous lips, a mouth Tom felt, that could be firm and proud, or even tender and loving depending on her mood. He was acutely aware of the soft warmth of her body under his hands and the rise and fall of her breasts as she unconsciously leaned against him. He laid her carefully on the grassy bank, then he went over to the stream and soaked his neck cloth in the clear water. As he splashed the pale face and soaked the fashionable curls framing her forehead, she let out a shocked gasp and two very blue eyes opened wide to glare into his face. She pushed the wet cloth away and sat up, arranging her skirt more modestly and

14

patting her damp hair.

'Pray do not . . . Do not soak me in any more cold water, sir,' she gasped. 'Who are you? Where have you come from?'

'I am Sir Thomas Capley, madam and this is my land.'

She looked puzzled and then said slowly, 'My horse took fright and ran away. But I thought Sir Thomas Capley lived in London.'

She was already looking better and the colour had now returned to her cheeks.

'You were injured from your fall, so I carried you here to this stream.'

'Injured?'

'Yes. Just below your ear.'

'And so you found me?'

'Yes. In the clearing over there.'

'That is quite a long way off,' she frowned.

'But you are not heavy,' he said. He was eyeing her with some amusement and as his gaze slid over her she saw his rather mocking expression change to one of open admiration. Helena was well used to the adulation of the opposite sex but there was an intensity of expression in his dark eyes which made her want to look away. She bent her head in order to dab carefully at the cut below her ear and her colour deepened.

'Madam,' said Tom softly. 'That is the wrong ear.'

'Then why did you not tell me which one?' she snapped.

Tom reached out and held her by the nape of her neck as he took her hand and guided it very gently onto the scratch. 'There,' he said. 'Though to be sure, it is a very trifling cut.'

'That may be so, but it is bleeding, sir.' Helena removed the handkerchief and showed him the small red stain.

It was very pleasurable for him to feel the soft warm curls at her neck twining through his fingers. Pleasurable and very sensual. He was reluctant to let her go. 'I shall get more water,' he said.

'No. Please keep it for your own wounds,' she said hastily. 'You too have a cut on your cheek. Did your horse run away also?'

He didn't answer, but remembering the fine gentleman and becoming aware of his bruises, rubbed his cheek thoughtfully.

'Sir. That is the wrong cheek,' she said at last.

'Then my wound must also be trifling.' Tom smiled at her. His usual expression of rather brooding seriousness was transformed instantly into one of youthful amusement and their eyes locked for what seemed a long moment. Helena was the first to speak.

'You say it was not your horse?' she persisted.

'No, I must have scratched myself,' he replied smoothly.

'Goodness. What a strange habit. To scratch yourself until you bleed.' Helena was unable to resist a smile at his obvious discomfort. 'Still, I owe you my thanks, sir,' and she stood up gracefully.

'For what? For carrying you over here?'

'Well,' she said carefully, 'for your kindness and care of me.'

She was beginning to dislike his very direct eyes and the forthright way that he questioned her. In all her dealings with the opposite sex, Helena Steer was used to being in control. Now, under his intense scrutiny, for some reason, she felt at a disadvantage. She smoothed out the skirt of her habit and held herself erect and Tom noticed she was taller than he had at first realized. She retrieved her hat and turned her head as though to leave as the church clock began to strike. She held the hat in her hand and glanced back at him under her eyelashes, her expression full of mischief.

'Good gracious, five o' clock. I shall be late home and just look at my hair.'

As she raised her arm to tuck in the stray tendrils, Tom stared at her shapely figure with

17

such frank appreciation, that she lowered it immediately and flushed with annoyance at herself.

'It is fortunate that I do not have far to go.'

'How far?' he asked.

'Just to Wintham Rectory.'

She gathered the folds of her skirt over one arm and turned into the leafy path.

'And you, sir? Do you have far to go?'

'No. Just as far as Capley Hall, madam,' he said shortly, in a tone that forbade any further questions.

They walked on together in silence. Helena wondered what had happened to her brother, Richard. The note had definitely said four o' clock. No doubt he had been delayed. The fall from her horse had shaken her somewhat and she was glad of Tom's courteous assistance when she had to negotiate the old stile.

'This is where our paths divide, I shall be on my way and I thank you sir.' She raised her eyes to his and gave him her most brilliant smile, which was always successful in enslaving young men, but he merely nodded politely and turned to go on his way.

And so they parted. After fifty yards, Helena paused and turned back to watch him. He was striding rapidly towards the Hall on his long legs, without a backward glance.

He could be anyone — a gamekeeper, gentleman farmer, some countrified squire or even a labourer. His unsophisticated clothes belied his high rank and educated voice, and he'd seemed very matter of fact about her injuries, but what was worse, he hadn't even bothered to ask her name. How dared he soak her in cold water and ruin her hair like that? She must look an absolute fright. Truth to tell, Miss Helena Steer had not been seriously hurt by her fall and in fact had managed to enjoy the short journey in the strong arms of her rescuer. During the brief walk across the grass, she had taken not one, but several sly peeks at him and liked what she saw. Despite her dismay at being soaked through, she noticed what a very personable young man was bending over her, his strong smooth throat bare and with the sun shining on his wide shoulders and crisp dark curls. This was a lonely place, but yet his air of virile strength had not seemed threatening. Indeed, it was oddly comforting, especially when his long fingers had held her so gently at the back of her neck . . . It had sent little shivers of pleasure down her spine.

Miss Helena Steer, famous heiress and star of the County set, frowned as she watched him go. How could he be so lacking in common civility and address as to resist the charms of Wintham's first beauty? In all her four and twenty years, she had never been quite so mortified by such a lack of response from the opposite sex. She walked on thinking angrily that he might at least have offered to escort her home and she hurried through the little wicker gate which led to the rectory garden. She needed to summon her maid and change her clothes before dinner.

Helena came from a long line of respected and principled clergymen, but she herself had been adopted by wealthy childless relations when she was a very small child. When her guardians died, within weeks of one another, Helena had become an heiress in her own right, but had chosen to return to Wintham and care for her widowed father and two young sisters. There was a son, Richard Steer, who'd made his life in London and they scarcely ever saw him, but this didn't stop him from begging her for money when he needed to keep his creditors quiet. Recently, this had happened very frequently and she had fully expected to meet him this afternoon and hand over yet more money to him.

The memory of her fall had now almost disappeared, although it was unfortunate that her horse had taken off, because she knew that Stubbs would be disapproving of her going out riding alone. Still, she had to admit that it had been quite an adventure, meeting the handsome young Sir Thomas Capley. Something she *might* tell her sisters at dinner. For the moment though, she must order her maid to prepare a bath and re-curl her hair, after she had spoken to the groom, of course. A lad would have to be sent out to hack Blueboy home, but with any luck he would be grazing safely somewhere and not have come to any harm. She walked round to the stable yard to find Stubbs. He was grooming one of the mares and greeted her request with his usual taciturn disapproval of anything to do with young women, but he was respectful as always.

'Yes, ma'am, I shall send young Joe. Only hope as the horse will be found unharmed, Miss Steer. The reverend and myself don't hold wi' young ladies riding unaccompanied, Miss Steer, as you well know.'

'Quite so, Stubbs.'

Helena had ceased to listen and merely held out one slim foot for Stubbs to pull off the tightly fitting riding boots, so that she could change into her shoes and prepare for dinner.

Meanwhile, remembering the elegant Percy Davenport, Tom had paused in his walk and he drew out the scrap of paper from the inside of his coat.

> *Dearest Helena,*
> *I shall be in Capley woods at four.*
> *Please do not fail me.*
> **R.**

Frowning, he returned the note to his pocket and made his way thoughtfully back to the Hall. He had a sudden vivid image of the young woman in the woods, her mischievous smile and the sensuous feel of her soft curling hair. Unaccountably, the day seemed no longer to be quite so bright.

And as she hurried up the wide staircase, the object of his brooding thoughts almost bumped into her young sister.

'Why Charlotte, what a start you gave me. Did you not arrange to go to tea with Miss Carty today?'

'Indeed, yes, Helena,' said Charlotte in her rather breathy young voice. 'But Eliza and I saw Mary only very briefly and returned early so that she could keep company with her dear mama who was indisposed. But Helena,' she breathed excitedly, 'the most famous news! Mary has had it from Mrs Radford that Capley Hall is occupied again. By Sir Thomas Capley, no less and his grandmama, Lady Lavinia. Mrs Radford is reckoned to have caught a glimpse of him and has pronounced him handsome, but very serious-looking and

22

quite romantically rustic in his dress. There are servants and gardeners everywhere at the Hall. Tomorrow Mrs Radford is going to leave her card. Perhaps we could also call on them, Helena. Do you think?'

Charlotte waited breathlessly for Helena's reply.

'We shall have to see what Papa says,' said Helena shortly. 'Meanwhile I must find Rose and change my clothes.' Helena did not see any point now in describing her adventure in the wood, but went up to her room, reflecting that quite a few female hearts would be set a-fluttering when they came face to face with her rescuer.

Emerging in good time, she made her way to the dining-room to check that the arrangements were such as would please her father. Since his wife's death, Francis Steer had come to depend more and more on his daughters and in particular, Helena, who seemed able to run the house effortlessly in spite of her youth.

Now as she surveyed the lovely old room, with the silver glittering and winking on the white linen napery, Helena sighed and wondered where Richard would be spending this evening. Safely, she hoped. With luck he would be within driving distance and she would be able to see him again before he went back to London. Since Richard had left home to take up a life of gambling and dissipation, the Reverend Steer did not like his son's name to be mentioned, but this didn't stop Helena nurturing a great deal of affection for her weak young brother and she continued to hope that he would return.

Naturally, the conversation at dinner was all about the owner of Capley Hall and the intriguing gossip which was circulating in the small community. None of the sisters had any memory of ever having met the young Sir Thomas Capley, but the Reverend Steer recalled that Tom had been at Oxford with Squire Arnold's son and he'd pronounced him a capital fellow, although inclined to be solemn and rather too bookish. Their father also said that several of the more elderly ladies must remember his parents and would recollect the small but formidable dowager, Lady Lavinia. They would all be agog at the rumoured fortune that the young man had inherited from the disgraceful Great Uncle Silas.

At this, eighteen-year-old Charlotte and sixteen-year-old Eliza were so excited that they could hardly eat.

'Do you know, Papa?' Charlotte breathed. 'Tomorrow, we thought we might call and see if they are at home. Or must we wait to meet

Sir Thomas and his grandmama at Mrs Radford's garden party on Saturday?' she asked uncertainly. 'Mary Carty will certainly attend that event, if her mama's health is somewhat improved, that is,' she finished in a rush.

She was aware that the Reverend Steer was giving her a rather quizzical look over his wine glass.

'I am quite sure that her mama's indisposition will prove to be a minor obstacle in the path of Miss Mary Carty's pursuit of the Capleys' acquaintance,' he said quietly, but his irony was lost on the two younger girls. 'There can be no objection to your paying your respects, my dear, if Helena will attend you. For my own part, I shall wait to see them at Divine Service on Sunday. Perhaps I should take as my text an appropriate reference from the Holy Bible, although perhaps the 'Prodigal Son' would not be very apt for Sir Thomas, I think.'

Only Helena smiled at his wry little joke, knowing how sadly he missed Richard and how eagerly he would welcome that particular prodigal were he to come home. The maid cleared the dessert dishes and the young ladies withdrew to drink tea, leaving Francis Steer to a solitary glass of port. Helena only half listened to the younger girls' chatter because her thoughts were still on her brother, Richard, and the encounter with Sir Thomas Capley. She wondered fleetingly what Percy Davenport had been doing on the Capley estate. She knew him of old, to be a dangerous libertine and a man who was quite ruthless where women were concerned. She frowned at the thought of the danger she might have been in if she'd not been rescued. Then she smiled as she acknowledged to herself that she'd been delighted at the way Sir Thomas Capley had dealt with him.

By bedtime, Charlotte and Eliza had discussed every aspect of Tom's appearance, possible character and matrimonial prospects with various eligible young ladies in the area.

'And what are *your* thoughts, Helena?' asked Charlotte at last. 'Do you have any inclination for his acquaintance?'

Remembering the dark eyes and disturbingly direct questions of the gentleman she'd met in the woods, Helena replied slowly, 'We shall have to see. I daresay we shall be meeting him at the Radfords' and in the coming fortnight the Kesthorpe Assembly balls will be starting their autumn programme, so perhaps he will attend some of them.'

With that exciting thought they all retired to bed and, as she floated between waking

26

and sleeping, Helena's last thoughts were of the dark eyes probing hers and the strong arms enfolding her. What really disturbed her was that she could not get his strong face and unusual eyes out of her mind. And those arms! She had never been held so close by a man before and it was not just the experience of his arrogant male strength, it was the memory of his fingers on her neck, tangling softly in her hair, which thrilled her so much.

He was still in her thoughts the next morning which dawned very bright and sunny, bringing with it serious decisions about what to wear. The girls spent much time giggling and whispering over their clothes but at last, Charlotte and Eliza decided on similar dresses of sprigged muslin with matching pale-blue shawls and ribbon sashes. Helena wore her favourite summer walking dress of pale yellow with a band of deeper gold at the hem.

'Another fine day,' Charlotte said happily. The sun was indeed very warm and the younger girls were in such good spirits that they seemed unaware of Helena's rather quiet mood as they unfurled their parasols and set off on their walk up to the Hall.

They were met by Strang who received their cards graciously. 'Sir Thomas and Lady

Lavinia are receiving callers in the morning-room, ladies,' he said, with a dignified bow and ushered them in.

Mary and Mrs Carty, now remarkably recovered, just as Francis Steer had predicted, were already present. Fanny and Mrs Radford were sitting very decorously on small mahogany chairs and Lady Lavinia looking completely at ease, murmured something to Strang about refreshments for the new arrivals. Tom was standing by the window and glanced up when the visitors were announced. He wished there were more gentlemen, but with the exception of the refined and quiet Mr Radford, he was the only male present.

He stepped forward to greet the three young women who now entered and his gaze encountered Helena who returned his stare, totally unabashed. So, she was his neighbour, Miss Helena Steer. She looked a vision in her pale-yellow walking dress and matching bonnet, even more beautiful than he remembered her in the woods, although her nose was a little too long for classical beauty, he decided critically. He scowled suddenly as he thought of the contents of the note, but she was still looking up at him with the devastating blue gaze that he recognized from their first encounter.

'Lady Lavinia, Sir Thomas, may I present my sisters, Miss Charlotte and Miss Eliza?' she said politely.

The butler closed the door behind them and Tom collected himself sufficiently to seat Charlotte and Eliza and to lead Helena purposefully to the sofa under the window. He looked down at her and again he caught the provocative glint of mischief. Today her eyes seemed to have flecks of turquoise and the whites had the slightly blue sheen of perfect health. It was obvious that she had quite recovered from her fall. She looked absolutely radiant. As he recognized again, the slightly mischievous smile, he noticed for the first time, an intriguing little dimple at the corner of her mouth which came and went when her eyes began a smile, which her lips completed.

'We are delighted to welcome you back from London, sir,' she said softly. 'No doubt we may expect you in the future at some of our modest assemblies?'

He merely nodded, his eyes still deep and clouded as he thought of the note he had intercepted. Aware of his scrutiny, Helena, confident and smiling, graciously accepted a glass of lemonade from the maidservant. Her heart was beating somewhat faster than usual, but outwardly she was assured and secure. Her two young sisters meanwhile, looked round shyly with obvious awe at their grand surroundings.

For Strang had worked a miracle already. The furnishings which had been shrouded in dust sheets for over ten years were now completely refurbished. The beautifully moulded ceiling had been repainted and gilded, the huge fireplace cleaned and polished. Over all was a distinctively masculine air of quiet elegance, which was more than matched by the young man at her side.

If the morning-room was an exercise in taste and refinement, so also was Sir Thomas Capley. Gone were the rustic breeches and plain neck cloth. They had been replaced by a deceptively simple blue coat which fitted his muscular frame to perfection, without a single wrinkle to mar its perfect tailoring. A pair of yellow unmentionables were fitted into his immaculate black boots. The fashionable shirt had an elegantly tied cravat that looked as though it had taken hours to achieve and his dark curls, arranged by Jackson in the carefully careless style made popular by the Prince Regent, had been dressed to shining perfection.

Lady Lavinia, her bright eyes observing every aspect of her grandson's encounter with their beautiful neighbour, was agreeably accepting the proffered invitation from the Radfords and remarking how truly lovely the young ladies looked nowadays in their gauze and muslin dresses. She herself was dressed in a style popular ten or so years ago with a tight corset and a rich silk dress which had a rather unfashionably full skirt.

Under cover of the restrained conversation among the rest of the company, Tom spoke to Helena softly but directly.

'This is yours, I think,' and he handed her Richard's note. 'I cannot tell you how relieved I am to notice that you appear none the worse for your riding accident, Miss Steer,' he said ironically.

'And I, that your self-inflicted scratches seemed to be completely healed, Sir Thomas.'

She raised her chin and gazed back at him defiantly, too proud to tell him about Richard.

His shapely mouth tightened a little before he continued steadily as though she hadn't spoken. 'I was most surprised by the presence of a . . . gentleman of your acquaintance who was trespassing on my land, Miss Steer. Perhaps he is well known to you, in which case I would be obliged to have his name?'

There was no mistaking the insult implied in his mocking voice. Helena's cheeks flushed a little, but her eyes didn't waver. How dared he infer that she was meeting someone clandestinely in his woods, when she planned to meet only her own brother? When he'd carried her so strongly in his arms, she'd been foolish enough to enjoy it and had almost been tempted to confide in him, but now some demon of rebellious pride and arrogance gripped her and she was determined not to explain or apologize.

The elusive dimple appeared at the corner of her mouth as she smiled as provocatively as she knew how. 'Certainly not, Sir Thomas. Honour would forbid me to compromise my reputation by giving a gentleman's name.'

Still his probing eyes held hers as he said contemptuously, 'Indeed so, Miss Steer. Any lady who is of influence in the lives of two young sisters, ought to be above reproach.'

He was challenging her pride to the limit and Helena was even more determined that she was not going to justify her actions to this objectionable man. The little dimple disappeared and her dignity now became icy. She looked across the room to where Charlotte and Eliza were still chatting to Lady Lavinia and the Cartys.

Then she said deliberately, 'It appears I must rescue your grandmother from my sisters, or she will be exhausted.'

She stood up purposefully and he rose

immediately and gave a slight bow, his face expressionless. 'Of course, Miss Steer.' He watched her go, conscious of his own mixed emotions of fury and disappointment.

Helena maintained a dignified silence as they took their leave of Lady Lavinia and the rest of the company, which was not lost on the observant old lady, but the younger girls never even noticed the constraint between Sir Thomas and their sister. They were full of excited promises to meet on Saturday at the Radfords' garden party.

2

Mrs Radford's garden was all that was fashionable and very much in the style nouveau. It had been landscaped from plans devised by the great Humphry Repton himself to give an impression of natural beauty, which in fact was very structured. No expense had been spared to develop the garden as a tasteful extension of the house and everything in it had been calculated to give a calm and refined atmosphere that was modelled on nature. This didn't mean wild nature, however. The picturesque grounds were planned to provide a stunning dramatic background for the cream of Wintham society when the Radfords entertained.

Elinor Radford was fully aware that socially she was not of the Quality, being a merchant's daughter and not born into an ancient family. Nevertheless, her father's money had bought her an expensive education and one most calculated to enhance her chances of finding a suitable husband. Mr Edward Radford was a wealthy banker, so she was able to use their combined fortunes as well as her own excellent taste to provide the elegant and luxurious lifestyle that they enjoyed. The graceful Palladian residence with its exquisite symmetry and proportions, was the perfect setting for the soirées and lavish dinner parties at which she excelled. She worked tirelessly to establish herself more firmly into polite society and to provide opportunities for Fanny to meet suitable young gentlemen and at the same time to introduce accomplished young ladies to Fanny's brother, Frank.

Mr and Mrs Radford were well liked and not just tolerated in Wintham. Mr Radford's refined manner and quiet friendliness and his wife's generous but never vulgar hospitality, had made them perfectly acceptable to the local gentry. Seventeen-year-old Fanny was all that a refined young lady should be and young Frank was at present doing well at Oxford. Both of them had friends in the village and were part of a group of young people which included Mary and Alfred Carty and who met each other frequently.

Although the morning had been rather misty, by the afternoon it was brilliantly fine and sunny and pretty parasols were being unfurled all over the garden to protect delicate female complexions. Windows and doors were open and tables had been set up in the drawing-room for such gentlemen or older people who preferred cards to strolling in the garden and admiring the flowers. Many of Edward Radford's influential clients and banking colleagues had travelled up from the City with their wives and the whole place was a kaleidoscope of colourful dresses and smart costumes. Servants circulated with lemonade and small cakes for the guests who were all well mannered and very much in the mood for all the Radfords' lavish hospitality. Even Francis Steer had been persuaded that he must attend and was soon in conversation with Miss Gill who hung on his every word and proved to have been flatteringly attentive to his last Sunday's sermon.

Charlotte and Eliza saw Mrs Carty and Mary as soon as they arrived and went to greet them. Meek little Mr Carty had been bullied into thinking that they must be present as early as good manners would permit and the three of them were seated outside on little wrought iron chairs where they could see and be seen. Alfred had already sought out Frank and Fanny and they had disappeared into the gardens away from the formal reception, but Mary had been ordered to stay with her mama and papa. Helena greeted their hostess and then conscientiously went forward to make herself agreeable to Mrs Carty and her daughter.

'And how are you, feeling now, after your indisposition, ma'am?' she asked.

She knew that Mrs Carty was able to rule the whole household by means of these minor illnesses, which prostrated her for as long as it suited her purpose. She could lie on her day bed with hartshorn and water whenever she needed to avoid some unwelcome duty, or when she wanted time to plan an alternative which suited her better.

'Oh, tolerably well now, thank you,' Mrs Carty replied, with the habitual invalid's sigh of resignation. 'Of course, you know, all mothers make sacrifices for their little chicks and dear Mary and Alfred would have been so disappointed to miss the garden party. Such a fine day for it,' she said with a brave smile. 'And Mary is looking so well I could not deny her this pleasure.'

Helena recognized only too clearly this planned self-interest on the part of Mrs Carty. Mary was a pretty if insipid looking young lady who was now twenty years old. Her coming out had not resulted in the hoped for offer from any of the eligible young bachelors who had been so assiduously encouraged by her mama, but now Mrs Carty saw no reason why her dear little Mary shouldn't catch the eye of Wintham's most eligible man of all, Sir Thomas Capley.

For her part, Mary was pleased and relieved to see her young friends. Pleased because she knew she was looking her best in a new dress of sky-blue gauze which ended in a froth of pale-blue frills. It had a matching parasol and suited her pale prettiness to perfection. She was relieved because she felt that now her friend Charlotte had arrived at last, there would be some respite from her mama's repeated whispers of advice on her appearance and deportment.

The two hours before their departure for the party had been spent in tortured and lengthy preparations. Mary had been coerced into lying down for the whole of the morning with Mrs Carty's own cure-all for nervous agitation, a compress of vinegar and lavender water applied to the temples. Then her curl papers had been removed and she had submitted to the dressing and arranging of her rather fine and mousy hair into the modish arrangement that her mother had seen in the *London Ladies' Magazine*. The maid had done her best, but Mary's sparse locks had not borne even a passing resemblance to the illustration on the fashion plate. Her mama had insisted it should be done again, so the elaborately decorated ribbon bands had been duly taken off and her hair dressed for a second time before the expensive gown was put on.

The only good result of poor Mary's torture was that her normally pale cheeks were flushed becomingly with resentment and pain and her rather small blue eyes were sparkling with the unshed tears of her frustration. She gave an almost lyrical welcome to Charlotte and Eliza and the three girls immediately left the terrace to wander in the garden away from Mary's mama. They immediately met up with Fanny Radford and Mary's brother Alfred and soon other young people joined their group and with much chattering and laughter began to plan an excursion to nearby Averthorpe-on-Sea.

'I think we should ask Mama to accompany us,' Frank said seriously. 'It is only an hour's ride to Averthorpe and if we set off early in the morning, we can have a whole day for the picnic.'

'And we all know why Frank is suggesting that,' Alfred laughed. 'Mrs Radford will let us have the carriage and will provide a splendid picnic box with everything to make us comfortable. We shall be dining in as much luxury on the sands as though we were at the Radford residence!'

Frank grinned at this, but Fanny immediately joined in saying quietly, 'I am persuaded that Mama would be more inclined to consent to such a large mixed party, if she were to be present. Mama likes everything to be so correct, you know,' she finished, blushing a little.

Charlotte and Eliza nodded. 'Papa will agree to it if Mrs Radford is going with us,' Charlotte said. 'I think that Frank should ask her tonight. The weather seems set fair and it ought to be planned soon if we are to take advantage of it. Do you not think so, Alfred? One fine day is all that is needed to make our outing a success.'

She gave them her most winning smile and Frank was only too eager to agree to anything that she suggested. The others all seemed keen and enthusiastic with this idea and they gradually split up into smaller groups as the girls discussed the outing and gossiped among themselves while the boys went to look for ices and lemonade.

Helena was pleased to notice that there was as yet no sign of Sir Thomas. She knew that in such a small community it would be impossible not to meet him and that she must treat him civilly so as not to give rise to gossip. Crossly, she thrust away the memory of his handsome face and shapely lips, of the warm strength of his body as he'd carried her in the woods and his contemptuous expression at their last meeting. What did she care if he was now the most sought after bachelor in the neighbourhood? She was not going to give him the satisfaction of knowing that she found him so attractive. She hoped against hope that he would not turn up at all.

As it was, the drawing-room was crowded, not just with Wintham gentry, but also with notables from the nearby market town of Kesthorpe, so she was able to greet quite a few friends and acquaintances in a short space of time.

'Helena. Good afternoon.'

She turned to find George Arnold at her elbow. Squire Arnold's son was a tall, slender young man with the fresh open face and good colour of a country gentleman, used to outdoor pursuits and rural sports, but equally at home in the more formal atmosphere of the garden party or the Kesthorpe assembly rooms, and quite at ease with young ladies. It had been tacitly assumed for some years by his parents that he would be a good match for the beautiful heiress Helena Steer, and it was their fondest hope that one day she would accept their only son and join the two families by marriage.

For her part, Helena liked and respected him, and his frequent and regular proposals had over the last few years, become almost a joke between them. She felt at ease chatting to George and as she had her back to the house, heard but did not see the arrival of the guest of honour, who was announced with much ceremony by the Radfords' butler.

She noticed with some amusement several of the young ladies taking notice of their mamas' instructions on the importance of deportment, as they sat a little straighter and simpered more winningly at their companions when they heard the name, 'Sir Thomas Capley'.

Still retaining her dignity, she turned coolly as her hostess introduced Tom to various senior members of the company. She was almost prepared to ignore him, but that proved impossible because within a few minutes, he came up to greet George Arnold.

'Good afternoon, Miss Steer.' He glanced from Helena to George and back again, but his particularly warm smile was reserved for George.

'My dear fellow,' he said. 'It is so good to meet you again after all this time. Our days at Oxford seem long gone, but I remember you well.'

He clasped George's hand warmly and Helena moved almost imperceptibly sideways towards the balustrade at the edge of the terrace. She was, as on their first meeting, acutely aware of his uncomfortably direct gaze and deliberately turned away as though absorbed by the view of the garden.

The next moment he was by her side.

'How fascinating this particular view seems to be to you, Miss Steer,' he said in a low voice. 'Have you never observed this part of the garden before?'

His eyes were mocking as though sensing her discomfort.

Helena tilted her sunshade defiantly and returned his gaze, feeling decidedly less cool. In its shadow, she looked up at him crossly.

'Of course I have. I was merely giving you an opportunity to renew your acquaintance with Squire Arnold's son and some time to enjoy speaking to an old and valued friend.'

Tom continued smoothly, 'And is he another of your swains, Miss Steer? I feel I must congratulate you on the number and quality of your conquests.'

He gave her a challenging look which angered her all the more because she had to acknowledge to herself how attractive she found him.

'No. He is not one of my swains as you call it, sir, and if he were, I would certainly not mention it to another gentleman.'

Helena now felt at a distinct disadvantage and very conscious that she was on the defensive. She gave him a very cold look from eyes which were now like blue chips of ice, forcing Tom to recognize a sudden unexplained attraction for her, within himself, which was absolutely impossible to bear and which left him feeling almost helpless as Helena continued to glare up at him angrily.

Fortunately they were interrupted by Mr Radford wanting Tom to talk to yet another local worthy and Helena excused herself to stroll across the terrace and gaze with pretended interest at a classical urn. The next time she caught a glimpse of him he was talking to Mrs Carty and Mary. Both of them were listening intently to his every word and gazing at him with open admiration as though mesmerized by his conversation.

Helena was only too pleased that he was concentrating on someone else. She told herself that Sir Thomas Capley was merely a tedious and rather intense local landowner who was over-zealous in his interest in her private business. She gave an impatient flick of her parasol and walked slowly down the steps holding the sun shade to disguise the angry heat that she could feel flaming her cheeks. She stepped along the winding gravel path breathing slowly to calm her rapid heartbeat and went on until she came to a pretty little arbour set into the high hedge. Here, roses climbed over a rustic arch and tumbled picturesquely round a wooden seat. Bees buzzed lazily, absolutely sated by the nectar of so many blooms and even the birds seemed to be hushed and temporarily asleep in the still warmth of the afternoon. A peaceful spot and one far enough away from the disturbing presence of Sir Thomas Capley to give her some opportunity to calm her ruffled temper and think out what she could do about her brother, Richard.

When she'd received his note the other day, all the messenger would say was, 'This 'ere's from a gennelman name o' Mr Richard Steer. Thankin' you kindly, ma'am, he sez there's a shillun for I when I gives you this into your 'and, ma'am.'

When she'd questioned him more closely, he just repeated what he'd already said, word for word. She finally gave him the shilling with a sigh and he was away. The note was in Richard's handwriting and it had appeared genuine enough, but Richard seemed not to have bothered to keep their appointment. Oh, Blueboy, she thought. Why did you have to choose that afternoon to misbehave?

Thoughtfully, she plucked a rose from the many which cascaded down over the arch and breathed in its sweet scent. What scrape was Richard in now? She wondered where he was and what had happened. Obviously, something serious. He couldn't bear to face his father's gentle disapproval and would have to lean on Helena for support as always. It would of course be money for his gaming debts or tradesmen's bills. She frowned and wondered what it would be like to have a strongly supportive man, one whom she could lean on when she herself had troubles, one who would be always steadfast and reliable when she needed him. Would she ever meet such a one? Lost in her thoughts, she rested on the rustic seat absently tucking the sweet smelling rose into the bosom of her dress as she breathed in the fragrant air and gradually became calm again.

The peace was not to last for long. George Arnold, feeling rather *de trop* as Tom was fussed over and lionized by all the young ladies and their mamas, followed Helena along the path and chose that moment to articulate his often repeated proposal of marriage. Helena good humouredly prepared to refuse him gently as always, but to her dismay he went down romantically on one knee before her, as though this time he was determined to be taken seriously. His face was set and he seemed more than a little put out by the promptness with which she rejected him.

'Dash it, Helena,' he said in an aggrieved tone. 'I haven't even started yet.'

'Well, do not,' she said firmly. It sounded more curt than she intended, but she felt this was neither the time nor the place for a passionate declaration.

'But I am about to make you an offer,' he protested.

'I know,' said Helena. 'It is useless. Please say no more, Mr Arnold.'

George rose reluctantly to his feet. A large patch of grass stain had appeared on the immaculate beige of his pantaloons and his normally good natured expression had turned to one of frowning resentment.

'I must say, Helena, you might let me speak. You know my ancient pa instructs me to get on with our engagement at every interview I have with him. Why can't you let a fellow declare himself?'

'I won't give my hand where I cannot give my heart,' she said stiffly. 'I would like to spare you the pain of rejection, Mr Arnold.'

'And for pity's sake stop calling me Mr Arnold in that missish way,' he snapped, chagrined at the ruin of his nether garments and dreading the silent disapproval of his valet. 'Damme, Helena, there's no need to 'Mr Arnold' me. I've known you all my life and Sophie's been a good friend to you when you needed her.'

Helena flushed a little. It was true that his elder sister had helped tremendously in her coming out year. She had organized Helena's first formal ball in London and had even come over to the rectory to organize a coming-out party that would have been quite beyond the capabilities of Francis Steer and his kindly housekeeper. She was the one person whom Helena felt she could turn to in a crisis, and the only one in whom she had confided about the odious Davenport. But now her head was beginning to ache and much as she liked George, she wished to be alone. She had indeed known him in her childhood and thought of him with no more than sisterly affection. She was certainly used to more respectful approaches from the other young men who professed to be in love with her. She must be a natural born old maid, she decided, because so far, she had never felt any stirring of romantic interest for any of them.

She gazed out across the garden while George paced up and down in front of the rose arbour. The lawns and well-stocked garden beds offered no soothing respite from this difficult situation. Helena felt angry with herself for having chosen this particular spot which had given him his ideal opportunity to propose to her again.

When he'd first approached the Reverend Steer to ask for Helena's hand, Francis Steer, not being as worldly wise as the Mrs Radfords of this world, had said vaguely that he must ask Helena herself.

'I cannot answer for her, dear boy, she will come to her own decision. There is no telling what young ladies think about anything nowadays,' he said sadly. 'And she has no mama to speak for her, or give her any advice, you see.'

He turned back with some relief to composing his sermon for the following Sunday and so George had taken this to mean that her father had no objection to his making Helena an offer. This he did quite frequently and usually there was no rancour in her regular refusals, but just at this moment, her mind was in some turmoil.

The fact that she'd known George Arnold for some time, didn't blind Helena to the fact that he was an attractive and personable man, popular and well liked by all the young ladies in the neighbourhood. Not as brilliant a match as Sir Thomas Capley, perhaps, but very presentable all the same, and heir to considerable lands with a fortune to match her own. She knew that there were half-a-dozen young women in the area who would be delighted to accept him. He regularly spent time in London with a fashionable set of dandies his own age and was a wild enough young blade to be intriguing to the opposite sex. Helena knew from his sister, Sophie, that his stated adoration for her had not led him so far to keep away from the pleasures of London life, or the pursuit of his bits of muslin when he was up in Town, but it was assumed that once married he would settle down to respectable family life. She was always somewhat piqued that he never gave any tangible sign of this great love he purported to feel for her and she had an ignoble suspicion that he was merely obeying his papa's instructions to 'get on with his engagement'. Meanwhile, George stayed secure in the knowledge that if Helena accepted him, he would be comfortable and easy with her as a wife. If she continued to refuse him, well, he'd obeyed the squire's wishes and could turn once more to his other pleasures and pastimes.

Helena looked at him speculatively as he continued to pace and turn in front of her. He wasn't as handsome as Sir Thomas, whose dark good looks she found so unsettlingly attractive. He was equally as tall, but more slender and with lighter colouring than Sir Thomas Capley. He'd obviously dressed with great care for the occasion and the fact that his pantaloons were ruined she knew would be a cause of great regret to him. He stood in front of her again and scowled.

'Dash it, Helena, you know I love you to distraction, don't you? Can't you give a fellow some hope?'

At that moment, Helena observed over his shoulder, Sir Thomas Capley himself, slowly approaching with his aged grandmother on his arm and on a sudden mischievous impulse she immediately gave George her most brilliant smile, which left him completely bewildered.

Taking the red rose from the bosom of her dress, she presented it to the bemused young man and said sweetly, 'Yes, there is always hope as long as life exists, George.'

Then she ordered him to circulate among the other guests before he compromised her reputation by remaining with her any longer in such a secluded spot. With that, he had to be content and he departed wearing the rose in the button hole of his expensive jacket, just as Tom and his grandmother came slowly along the gravel path to the rose arbour.

'Oh is that Miss Steer over there?' Lady Lavinia exclaimed artlessly. 'Over there, my dear,' she said again, as Tom didn't answer. She gave a sly smile before continuing, 'What a beauty she is to be sure, Thomas, and quite a glass of fashion. Such charming company her sisters are, my dear, and Gill was very much taken with Parson Steer's sermon on Sunday. They say Helena's coming out was quite dimmed by the death of her guardians, although she was left very wealthy you know. She had several offers and Squire Arnold's son is still dangling after her shoestrings. She seems determined to devote herself to helping her father in the upbringing of her young sisters however, which is very commendable is it not? But as to the brother, well, from all accounts, he doesn't appear to be up to snuff at all. Continuously dipped at cards, you know. A very rackety young man, I fear.'

Lady Lavinia clutched her grandson's arm and paused for breath. She held her diminutive sunshade further away from her face the better to observe Miss Steer, who as though unconscious of their approach, was posing attractively in the bower with yet another red rose. In front of her was Benjamin Hallam, a handsome young soldier who had recently acquired a lieutenancy and had been in love with Helena for the whole of the summer.

'What a successful party it is, and how fortunate that the weather is still so fine,' Helena remarked to him, conscious of the steady approach of Tom and his grand-mother.

'It's always such a pleasure as well as a privilege to be able to partake of Mr and Mrs Radford's hospitality, is it not?'

'Yes indeed,' agreed the young Benjamin, tongue-tied by her beauty and the heady feeling of being so near to his beloved. Then, recovering his wits with an effort, he went on, 'A last pleasure for myself I'm afraid, Miss Steer. Alas, the 86th departs for Spain on Wednesday and I have to rejoin my regiment.'

'I suppose you will be gathering comforts and mementoes from your dear mother and sisters to take with you on such a hazardous undertaking,' Helena said in an unexpectedly soft and kind voice.

'Yes indeed,' Lieutenant Hallam said again. Then he blushed and gulped. His Adam's apple bobbed up and down in a convulsive movement as he plucked up the courage to say, 'I would deem it a great honour, Miss Steer if I had some trifling object of *yours* for a keepsake to take with me on my journey.'

Seeing that Tom and Lady Lavinia were still out of earshot, Helena turned to the young man and smiling prettily, breathed in the perfume of the red rose.

'Unfortunately, I have no such trifle about me at the moment,' she murmured.

'I . . . I . . . would be delighted to receive the rose you are holding,' he stammered, hardly able to meet her amused glance.

'In that case, please accept it with my wishes for a safe and successful campaign,' she said gracefully, handing it to him.

Aware that Sir Thomas had now almost reached her, she mimed movements of gracious condescension, on purpose to be noticed by Tom and the old lady. She allowed the young soldier to kiss her hand and hold it for a moment longer than necessary, which created a pretty tableau for her approaching audience of two. Then she dismissed the lieutenant very kindly and he departed, triumphantly carrying the red rose as tenderly as though it were a newly born baby.

Helena turned as though catching sight of Tom and Lady Lavinia for the first time.

'Oh, Sir Thomas! Lady Lavinia.'

She glanced up at him with a carefully assumed expression of surprise, but in spite of her acting ability, she was unable to feign the widening of her deep-blue eyes and the involuntary dilation of the dark pupils as she noticed once again his athletic frame and strong muscular thighs, enhanced by the fine, close-fitting clothes. He looked so tall and strong, standing outside in the open air and much against her will, Helena found it difficult to take her eyes off him.

'Lady Lavinia, how are you enjoying the garden party?' she asked politely.

'Oh my dear, we've been made so welcome, and Tom has met so many people and renewed acquaintance with so many more. Is that not so, Thomas?'

He merely gave a polite nod of acquiescence and continued to gaze broodingly at Helena, who was aware that she was looking her best and was determined to appear as an incorrigible flirt, just to let him know that she cared not a fig for his opinion.

Lady Lavinia looked from one to the other very keenly. Miss Steer was now looking away from him, gazing across the parkland as though she could see something interesting in the distant view. Her grandson was glaring at Miss Steer as though he could kill her. Neither of the young people spoke a word. In the bright sunlight, the face of the Dowager Lady Capley was seamed by a myriad of lines and wrinkles, but her eyes were as bright and alert as ever. She viewed them both shrewdly through these wise old eyes and making a swift judgement, closed her sunshade with a decisive snap and moved purposefully towards the rose arbour.

'And now, dear Tom, I feel a trifle weary and must sit in the shade and rest awhile.

Perhaps Miss Steer will like a walk round the lake. It is reckoned to be most pleasant and has a romantic island with an abundance of wild birds. So very soothing to be near water,' she continued, noticing the expression of outraged anger on her grandson's face. 'Especially on such a hot day,' she went on, aware of Helena's heightened colour and tight lips. 'Do you not think so, Miss Steer?'

'Why, yes, ma'am,' Helena replied, forcing herself to appear unconcerned by Tom's presence, but inwardly, she was in turmoil.

He meanwhile, altered his expression to one of neutral politeness.

'Should you care for a stroll down to the lake, Miss Steer?' he asked calmly, and taking her silence for agreement, offered his arm. Helena took it and walked with him further along the gravel path. She almost forgot her feelings of dislike for someone she judged to be so arrogantly critical, in the pleasure she felt at his nearness. Even without turning her head to look at him, she was conscious of his pleasant male smell, could catch the play of the light in his dark hair and feel the strength of his arm. Her hand, resting on the sleeve of his jacket, was light and graceful and yet her senses were so heightened that she felt that each of her fingers was engraved on his flesh.

They rounded a corner and the beautiful

green countryside was laid out before them. The garden had been designed to blend in with the surrounding landscape and the trees and shrubs round the lake had been chosen carefully to add variety of colour and foliage. Although it was man made, the whole effect was one of stunning natural beauty.

Helena was still very aware of his nearness and the strength of the muscular arm beneath her hand. Trying to find a topic of conversation, she exclaimed in rather a strained voice, 'How tastefully Mrs Radford has ordered the planting.'

'Yes, it must require an army of gardeners, but I'll wager it will have brought work to the neighbourhood.'

He sounded interested and impressed by the way that the Radfords had developed their estate, and in the next five minutes she discovered a new facet to the character of Sir Thomas Capley, that of his love of the countryside. His concern over rural poverty and the well-being of his tenants was obvious.

'There is such a problem for the poor in country areas,' he went on, rather earnestly. 'I have similar plans of my own to develop the grounds at Capley Hall.'

'But not at the expense of the magnificent beeches, I hope,' she said quickly. 'It would be such a shame to do away with them in order to follow the present fashion for the picturesque.'

'No of course not, but I am very concerned at the needs of the poorer labourers,' he said, 'and I want to create employment. However, you may rest assured, the beeches shall remain utterly safe with me.'

He turned to her for the first time and gave her his open smile. A smile so unaffected that as she returned his glance, Helena felt as though she were drowning in the depths of his sparkling dark eyes.

Then he stepped back smoothly so that he was standing behind her and said very softly, 'Is that a kingfisher, over there in the reeds, Miss Steer? Can you see it?' He leaned towards her pointing to the island.

At first she was unable to pick out which bird he was indicating. He leaned even closer to her and at last Helena recognized it. There was a flash of turquoise blue and white as the bird dived towards the lake. Diamond droplets hit the surface of the water and ripples spread outwards as the bird surfaced again with its prey caught in its beak. He continued to stand behind her as they both watched, fascinated. Helena felt suddenly comforted by his strong close presence and wished it might last forever. She gave a long sigh. Her heart was pounding and she knew she should go back to the party, but strangely, she lacked the will to make the decision. She took yet another deep breath and forced herself to turn and suggest to him that they should return along the gravel path, back to the house. He was so near that she could feel the warmth of his breath fanning her cheek, and was acutely excited by his nearness.

'Perhaps we should go back to the garden party,' she began to say, but at that moment her foot encountered a treacherous patch of mud and she slipped sideways.

Tom caught her immediately. His arm was like an iron bar around her waist and he steadied her elbow with his other hand. They were now so close, she could feel her heart pulsing against the stuff of his coat. Her breasts felt swollen under her thin dress and seemed to be pressing painfully against him. She lowered her eyes to look at his mouth which was almost touching her own, and exhaled raggedly as the moment lengthened.

Then, very slowly, he drew back and waited for her to look up at him. Her eyes were once more deeply shadowed with violet, almost unbearably soft and luminous. Her yellow bonnet had fallen onto her shoulders and hung about her just by its ribbons. One of her pale kid shoes was covered in mud. It struck Tom how vulnerable the proud and beautiful

Helena Steer looked as she lay helplessly in his arms for the second time. He was agonizingly aware of her soft yielding body against his, and the full, slightly parted lips so near his own. They stayed that way for a long moment before Tom released her gently and, taking out a handkerchief, bent down to wipe her shoe.

Looking down at him, Helena noticed the close curling hair on the strong young neck and felt the warmth of his hands through her thin shoe. She thought how humble the strong and arrogant Sir Thomas Capley seemed as he bent before her and she felt a tremor of excitement at the thought of his powerful body and the strong circle of his arms.

He stood up. 'The best I can do for your shoe I'm afraid,' he said regretfully, 'but I seem to have removed most of the mud. May I escort you to your sisters, Miss Steer? Perhaps you would care for some refreshments?'

She recognized the change of mood immediately and walked very decorously back with him along the gravel path. As they passed the rose arbour, they noticed it was now quite deserted. In spite of her earlier fatigue, Lady Lavinia was at present on the terrace with the other ladies enjoying the refreshments and observing minutely all that was going on.

Helena found Charlotte and Eliza in the drawing-room, still discussing their jaunt to the seaside with Frank and Mary. They didn't appear to have missed her and so far no date seemed to have been fixed for the proposed seaside picnic.

Much later, when he was escorting his grandmother from the party, Lady Lavinia remarked innocently, 'Good gracious, Thomas. There's young Martin carrying a red rose. And is that Henry Clifford with one in his coat? And George Arnold? What a lot of young men seem to be wearing a red rose today, to be sure. My word, Thomas, you seem to be the only one left out of the red rose stakes!'

Her grandson glowered at her blackly, his lips compressed with annoyance and he made no reply. As for Lady Lavinia, noticing his angry look, she kept her expression perfectly serious, but her eyes sparkled with repressed laughter as she took her seat in the carriage.

3

Even their father seemed to have enjoyed the party and for a few hours, the younger girls talked of nothing else. The clothes, appearance and romantic interests of all the unattached females in the neighbourhood were remarked upon and discussed at length and the single young gentlemen received the same treatment, but in rather less detail because Charlotte and Eliza laughingly paired them off, theoretically at least, with various of their friends.

'Helena, did you see how particularly Alfred Carty was attending on Fanny Radford when the cakes and ices were served?' asked Charlotte.

'And I thought he was your admirer, Charlotte,' said Eliza slyly.

'Not at all,' said Charlotte firmly, but blushing all the same.

'But I noticed that Sir Thomas Capley was extremely courteous to all the ladies, perhaps more so to Fanny Radford and Mary.'

'I expect her mama would no doubt like to think so,' murmured Eliza mischievously. 'Mrs Carty told Papa that Sir Thomas has promised to attend the first Kesthorpe Assembly ball in September. That should be excitement enough to last everyone until Christmas!'

'He is very handsome, Charlotte. If he asks me to stand up with him at the ball, I shall say, yes,' giggled Eliza. 'What about you, Helena? He is sure to ask for a dance with you.'

Helena's thoughts and feelings were on other things, however. For the moment, she'd dismissed the intriguing Sir Thomas Capley from her mind and thought only of her brother. She'd still had no word from him and her anxiety for his safety was rising by the hour, but while she was so preoccupied with her own thoughts, the conversation had moved on and the other two went on to discuss the proposed picnic at the seaside. No date had been set and once Francis Steer learned that Mrs Radford was herself going to chaperon the young people, he lost interest in the chatter and retired thankfully to his study.

Helena was still only half listening when her maid, Rose, came in and told her quietly about a 'rough sort', who had hung around the rectory all day. Finally, when asked by Stubbs what the devil he wanted, he'd said that he had a note for the lady of the house, but would entrust it to no one but herself. Helena's heart leapt when she received Rose's whispered message and she prayed that the note would be from Richard, saying where he was. After her disappointment in Capley woods, she was at a loss about how to make contact with him. She thought he might have returned to London, but no one knew his address. Her only hope was that somehow he'd managed to stay in the area without anyone seeing him. But how would that be possible in such a small place where the presence of every stranger was noted? I'll soon find out, she thought. Pray God he'd come back to try and make amends with Papa. One thing was certain: she knew that her father would welcome him with open arms, given the sadness of the last few years. After their mother had died so suddenly, Richard had got in with a fast set of young London Bucks including Lord Robert Thursglove and the Honourable Percy Davenport, whose lives were entirely devoted to gambling and whoring. Helena felt powerless in the face of such friends as these and had no strong hopes of influencing her reckless young brother from a distance. If only she were a man, she thought. Then she could go to London herself and rescue him by force, if necessary.

Shaking her head at such unrealistic thoughts, she left Charlotte and Eliza to their needlework and gossip and hurried to find Stubbs who was still in the stable yard keeping a stern eye on the 'rough sort'.

The man sat on a wooden block near the pump with his hands clasping his ankles. His head was bent but he looked up at Helena's approach. He wore the rough breeches and strong boots of a farm labourer, but the kerchief round his neck was bright like that of a gypsy and his long dark hair was tied back in a black ribbon.

While Stubbs gazed in open disapproval, Helena spoke to the man courteously.

'You have something for me, I believe,' she said in her usual forthright manner.

He was not the same man who'd brought Richard's previous note. He looked like a tinker and when he spoke, his voice had a definite brogue.

'Yes, a note, madam, so I have. To be put in your fair hand alone, lady. But I'd wish to be private, so I would.'

He gave a meaningful scowl with his bright blue eyes at the hard-faced Stubbs.

'Yes, of course,' said Helena. 'Leave us, Stubbs, if you please. This person and I have private business.'

She knew that in Stubbs's opinion,

well-brought-up young women couldn't possibly have business with roughs like that. As a family man, he strongly disapproved of the Reverend Steer's gentle handling of his daughters, especially herself who, he opined was positively wayward. She waited as he turned on his heel and stumped sullenly into the tack-room. Once there, he cuffed the unfortunate stable lad and gave him whispered instructions to follow the lairy cove who was with the mistress and to inform the gamekeeper at the big house of the ruffian's presence in the district. Pearson, the gamekeeper, would ensure that Sir Thomas Capley was made aware of any potential poacher who might be trespassing on his land. He gave a satisfied grin to himself as the lad nodded.

Meanwhile, Helena turned eagerly to the stranger.

'Quickly,' she said. 'Have you a note from Richard Steer?'

'Indade I have, madam,' he smiled, and, fumbling in the band of his dusty wide-brimmed hat, produced a small folded paper.

'But first, beggin' pardon, lady, this is yours for a small fee.'

But Helena was prepared.

'Yes, yes,' she said impatiently and pressed a coin into the eager brown hand.

Helena,
I shall be at Bentick barn at nine tonight.
Be there for me, I beg of you.
Richard.

She read the note quickly. It was definitely written in Richard's spidery but elegant hand. What was it this time? she wondered. Cards, as always, or some worse problem, perhaps? Richard had never seemed the sort of young man who would lose his head over a woman, but she supposed that his immaturity could make it possible for him to be a fool for love. Perhaps she was doing wrong in constantly helping her brother with money, but she had so much and Richard was always so pathetically grateful. Every time, he vowed that he wouldn't ask again and that she was an angel. Perhaps one day he would have the strength to come home and ask forgiveness from his father and her worries would be over. She hoped so, but she knew that their father would stick to his strict religious principles and wait for Richard to make the first move.

The Reverend Steer was not a wealthy man, but he was very comfortably off, being a gentleman farmer as well as a cleric. Besides Wintham, Mr Steer had a second living at the nearby market town of Kesthorpe, where the twice daily London stage halted at the White Hart and the Steer family collected their letters. The combined populations of the two parishes was only 350 persons and the unwanted parsonage was at present let to the widow of a clergyman. But the Glebe farm brought in a decent income and was profitable as well as providing for all the needs of his household. One day, Richard would inherit all that his father owned. With a modest lifestyle and a good marriage, her brother could live quite comfortably in a safe rural community where he would have all the status and respectability of a country gentleman. If only he could be persuaded to leave his present way of life, that is.

But that was for the future. Just for the present, she must think of a way of slipping out after dinner without being noticed. It would be dusk around that time and she could wear dark clothes to make herself less conspicuous. Lost in thought, she failed to notice that the tinker had silently disappeared. Stubbs had noticed however, and gave young Joe a nod and a jerk of his head to tell him to follow.

She hurried back to the house and was met by a very worried housekeeper.

'Oh madam,' Mrs Chantry puffed as she hurried to meet her. 'Reverend Steer's feeling unwell, miss. It's one of his backs as I understand it. He won't want no dinner, Miss Helena. He's gone to lie down. Shall I make him one of my possets, Miss?'

Francis Steer often had an inflammation of the back and it was only eased by bed rest and one of Mrs Chantry's special possets of warm milk and ale.

When she returned from the sick-room, Charlotte met her at the bottom of the stairs waving a book of musical duets.

'Jane Clifford has copied these for us, Helena, and I'm so much obliged to her,' Charlotte beamed. 'After dinner, Eliza and I are going to practise them together. Perhaps we could play for you and Papa later, if he's not too poorly, of course.'

This was even better than she'd hoped. As soon as dinner was over, Charlotte and Eliza made straight for the pianoforte. Now Helena had only to conceal her intentions from the sharp-eyed maid.

'I shan't want you until bedtime, Rose. I intend to write letters in my room while Miss Charlotte and Miss Eliza are practising their music. Please wait for me to summon you when I'm ready.'

Rose smilingly bobbed a curtsy and hurried to join the housekeeper in the kitchen, very pleased at the idea of a pleasant and relaxed evening with her knitting and a gossip.

Helena, with a purse of money hidden under her cloak, waited for the long case clock in the hall to strike eight and then slipped out quietly. She was sure no one had heard her but still, she glanced back at the rectory as she hurried through the wicket gate and passed along the lane which led to the open fields owned by Parson Steer. His farm and herds produced everything that was needed for the rectory household. He kept the accounts meticulously and when she was alive, the brewing and dairy work had been supervised by his wife. Now a bailiff organized the farm and the dairy while Helena ran the house and servants.

As the light faded gradually, a pale moon appeared above the trees and Helena unconsciously quickened her pace. She had kept to the path by the hedge where it was dry underfoot and reached a narrow lane with palings on one side. Here was the boundary of the Capley land. Sir Thomas Capley had so many fields, they had individual names such as Bentick, Clore Hill and the Lime Plantation. This was Bentick and as she went through a gate in the palings, Bentick barn loomed in front of her.

The heavy door groaned and creaked as

she pushed it open and stepped inside. There was a soft diffused lamplight, but she couldn't make out its source. As she slipped hesitantly into the middle of the fragrant barn, she glanced round eagerly, trying to see Richard in the darkness.

Then she whirled at a sudden noise behind her as the barn door swung closed, blocking out the pale moonlight. Thoroughly alarmed, Helena tried to make out the figure facing her in the shadows. It wasn't Richard, but she was spared any other guesses because the Honourable Percy Davenport placed a lighted lantern on the floor.

'Welcome, Helena,' he drawled in his soft mocking voice. 'What a pleasure it is to meet again like this.'

Helena shivered as she remembered the first time she'd encountered this rake. It was at her coming-out ball when she'd been too green to notice how assiduously Percy Davenport had attended her. Always he'd used Sophie's presence to lend respectability to his pursuit of her and it was only by the merest chance that Helena had escaped the ruin of her reputation. He had cunningly pretended that he was escorting her to meet her brother for an evening at Vauxhall Gardens and then had virtually had her abducted and delivered to Lord Thursglove's town house where he at once proposed marriage as an alternative to the disgrace which would follow after she had spent the night with him.

It was only by good fortune that Richard himself had been visiting Lord Thursglove and had been admitted by a servant before Davenport could go further. The would-be seducer had passed it off as a joke, and the three of them had returned to Sophie's together. But Helena knew it was no joke. Davenport was desperate to marry money and, as she grew a little older and wiser, Helena discovered that he'd attempted to seduce more than one innocent young girl who was in possession of a fortune. She hated and despised this man for the vile character that he was, but fortunately was able to avoid occasions where they would meet. This didn't prevent him from exerting his evil influence over her weak young brother, but she felt powerless to change things. Now she faced him bravely from behind the lantern although she was trembling and sick with apprehension and loathing.

'Where's Richard?' she demanded, more boldly than she felt. 'I was to meet him here and — '

'And you've met his friend and mentor instead. Just one of my little ploys my dear, to be alone with the woman I love.'

He smiled at her displaying small sharp teeth and Helena realized with a stab of fear, the danger she was in with this unscrupulous villain in such a lonely place.

'Where is he?' she repeated. 'I received a note from him asking me to meet him in Capley woods but he never came. Then I had this note promising to meet me here. For pity's sake, tell me where he is.'

'All in good time, my dear,' he said, still smiling infuriatingly. 'The note was also mine, but written by dear Richard. I knew that the disdainful Miss Steer would refuse to meet me unless I used a little subterfuge, but unfortunately I was thwarted by other circumstances on that occasion. Richard is with friends in London, at present, and is in very good hands.'

The smooth way that Davenport said these words and the wolfish smile that accompanied them did nothing to reassure her, but perhaps a softer approach would be more sensible.

'Please tell me where he is and when I may see him again,' she said, almost humbly. 'I am anxious to know how he is and what his life may be like. We miss him and want him to return home. My father is overwhelmed with grief at the rift with my brother and feels that life in London may be harmful to his health. Richard has never been very strong.'

This last statement seemed to afford Davenport even more amusement and he began to snigger openly at her anxiety, but his mocking laughter was cut short at this point as the barn door burst open to reveal Sir Thomas Capley.

'Oh Miss Steer. Well met,' he said sarcastically, taking in the scene in front of him. 'And with your lovesick swain again. Is there no end to your stratagems?'

Helena stared aghast as Percy Davenport spun round to face his tormentor. Tom stood four square in the doorway and, in spite of his languid tone, had the air of a tightly coiled spring.

'Once more, you are trespassing on my property, madam,' he said, staring at her coldly. 'How dare you set my gamekeeper worrying and put me to the trouble of intercepting the go between of your tawdry liaison?'

'Go between?' Helena echoed faintly.

'Yes. The vagrant who was brought before me this afternoon and confessed to being the carrier of your romantic messages.'

Before Helena had time to reply to this latest insult, Davenport made a sudden movement as though to take something from his belt.

'And you, sir,' Tom continued, glaring at him. 'Perhaps I did not thrash you sufficiently the last time we met. I must finish the job now.'

He stepped forward purposefully, a dangerous gleam in his eye, but Davenport was quicker off the mark this time.

'Hold hard, Capley. I am the Honourable Percy Davenport, in case you were not aware of it. You will have a lawyer's letter about that violent attack in due course,' he snarled. 'Meanwhile, madam' — and here he made an ironic bow to the silent Helena — 'here is my card. If you wish to hear more of a certain person, you may contact him at this address.'

Skirting cautiously around the still threatening figure of Tom, he disappeared swiftly into the dusk leaving the other two to glare at each other.

Tom was the first to recover.

'I am utterly bored with these repetitive situations,' he growled angrily. His eyes were deeply black in the gloom of the barn. 'Young ladies who ought to know better should not arrange assignations with dangerous rakes and then expect to be rescued when things go wrong. You do not want danger, only excitement, is that it? Well, you deserve to take the consequences.'

He took a swift stride towards her and, as Helena raised her hands instinctively to protect herself, he grasped them roughly and pinned them behind her back. Holding her easily he kissed her long and hard on the lips.

When he raised his head, he was smiling, but without humour.

'Am I right, Miss Steer?' he jeered, as he released her.

'No you are not,' Helena flamed at him and, raising her arm, she gave him a stinging slap across the cheek.

The effect was almost ludicrous. He stepped back just as swiftly as he'd moved forward. Even in the dim light, the marks of her fingers could be clearly seen against the white anger of his face.

Helena's immediate reaction was one of dismay and regret at what she'd done, but his next words soon dispelled any natural impulse of sympathy or concern for his feelings.

'By God, madam, you shall pay for this,' he growled, putting his hand up to his cheek and touching the red mark left by her sharp smack.

At the ridiculous melodrama of these words, her natural humour and common sense took over and she laughed out loud.

'Oh no I won't,' she retorted spiritedly 'Because I shall have nothing more to do with you, sir.'

Drawing her cloak about her she pushed past him with her head held high and hurried off into the dusk towards the safety of home.

Entering noiselessly, Helena crept up to the privacy of her room. The fire that Rose had made earlier in the little grate had almost gone out but she managed to coax a flame and lit the candle on her desk. There were no sounds of music from the drawing-room, so she supposed that Charlotte and Eliza had finished their duets. She sat down at the writing desk and looked at the card given to her by Percy Davenport. It was plain and to the point with just his name in a bold Gothic script and then two addresses. One she knew was the family seat at Miston, roughly fifteen miles north of Bath, where she had been brought up. The other must be his town house:

Vernon House
Vernon Street
London

She wondered if this was where Richard was staying. Percy Davenport had described himself as Richard's 'dear friend and mentor' but she knew from past experience that he was neither. His friendship took the form of plying Richard with cheap brandy and encouraging him to gamble with money he didn't possess, as well as other excesses that she could only guess at.

After further thought, she decided that she had no choice but to write to Richard at this address and she might even be able to visit him, if only she knew for certain that he was there. Perhaps a 'shopping trip', for instance, and if she took Rose with her, there should be no problem.

As she sat lost in thought in the darkening room, there was a tap on the door and Charlotte's breathy young voice called softly, 'Helena? Are you there? We're quite ready to play for you now, if you wish to hear us.'

Helena snuffed the candle and went downstairs. For the rest of the evening the girls played and chattered lightheartedly about the problems they'd had with the fingering and Eliza's tendency to play rather too many fancy flourishes and trills, so neither of them noticed that Helena was quieter than usual. She was busy planning in her mind how to accomplish a visit to London to see her brother. She would try to persuade him to come home, even for a short while. Money was not a problem, but she knew that her father wouldn't approve of her travelling on the stage coach. It would have to be a private vehicle, and preferably with another respectable female as well as her maid.

At least I have the wherewithal to travel in comfort, she thought, and was still wrestling with the problem when the two younger girls declared themselves to be quite fatigued with the duets. Rose was summoned from the kitchen and they retired to bed, but before she went to sleep, Helena wrote a brief note to Richard promising to visit him in London. In the morning, she would have to risk sending it to Vernon Street and hope that it would reach him.

The first ball at the Kesthorpe Assembly Rooms was due to take place on the second Tuesday in September and although she was anxious about her letter to Richard and impatient for a reply, Helena felt she also had to give some time and attention to her sisters.

Charlotte and Eliza were immersed in their plans for the ball and talked of little except what they'd wear and how many partners they might have. Helena thought with a pang about their mother and how much help and advice she would have been able to give them if she'd been alive.

'Mary Carty says that George Arnold's

eldest sister will be attending the ball,' Eliza announced. 'Captain Malpass is at present serving abroad with his regiment, but Sophie and James are visiting with Squire and Mrs Arnold.'

After twelve years of marriage to an army officer, Sophie had developed into a dashing young matron with a wide circle of London friends and acquaintances. Helena supposed Sophie's gift for making friends stemmed from the nomadic life she led as an army wife and the long days she had to spend without her husband. She looked forward to seeing her old friend and exchanging some lively gossip with someone she was so fond of, but she was definitely not looking forward to seeing the insufferable Sir Thomas Capley again. The pride and arrogance of the man were beyond belief, Helena told herself. Then, she had a sudden mental picture of his bent head and strong young neck when he'd knelt so humbly to clean her shoe and then the even more disturbing memory of his kiss. She remembered vividly the firm pressure of his warm lips on hers and admitted to herself that he was also a dangerously attractive man. If they met again, as she knew they must, she resolved to be cool and distant with him.

Tuesday evening was fine but rather cool when Helena and her sisters entered the

Assembly Rooms. Francis Steer had begged to be excused from attending his daughters — the chill which had settled on his back a few days ago was now nearly better but he wasn't in the mood for company. Mrs Radford and Fanny had called round personally with their carriage to take them all into Kesthorpe and Helena knew her father would be happier left at home.

The ballroom was already crowded and Helena was obliged to greet various friends as she ushered her young sisters to the top of the room. Squire Arnold and his wife were there, presiding over a little family group which included their daughter-in-law, Sophie, and their young grandson, James.

George immediately asked Helena for the first dance and showed absolutely no concern or embarrassment about her latest refusal to marry him, in spite of appearing so disappointed at the time. In fact, George had an air of quiet confidence about him this evening as though something had happened to set his mind at rest. Helena felt intrigued by his subtly changed demeanor and wondered idly what it was that was making him appear so pleased with the world. Then the Master of Ceremonies asked for those present to form a set for 'as many as will' for the first country dance. With so many people, the set was a long one and she had little chance of conversation with George, but they felt the ease of long acquaintance and both took pleasure in the dance.

When they had performed all the figures and she had time to look around, Helena caught sight of Sir Thomas Capley just entering the ballroom with a small group of people who were not known to her. Probably his Town friends, she thought. She felt her heart beating faster, though why it should, she didn't know. It wasn't surprise — she knew he would put in an appearance at some time this evening. Perhaps it was the memory of their encounter in Bentick barn and the hard way he'd crushed her mouth with his own. He hadn't seen her yet. Good. She was pleased that the next figure involved turning her back on him because this gave her time to calm her rapid breathing and to hope that her face wasn't as flushed as it felt.

As she and George moved further down the set, Helena stole another glance at Tom. His black evening clothes and formal white shirt served only to enhance his air of outdoor energy and quiet strength. In spite of her dislike of him, Helena had to acknowledge his handsome and personable presence. All the ladies present gazed admiringly at him as he led Lady Lavinia to a seat near the other elderly ladies and he was pounced on immediately by Mrs Carty who had the blushing young Mary in tow.

'Why there's Tom,' George said. 'Over there with Mrs Carty,' he went on, as Helena made a point of pretending that she hadn't noticed Tom's arrival.

'He seems very friendly with the Cartys,' she said after a pause. Then she changed the subject.

'How well Sophie is looking, George, and what a fine boy James has grown into.'

'Yes he is,' George agreed. 'Quite the young gentleman, nowadays.'

During their return progress up the set, Helena realized that Tom had not only seen her but was staring at her in what she felt was a rude and pointed way. Raising her chin slightly, Helena gave him a cool unfriendly nod of acknowledgement, which was barely polite, and thereafter ignored him until it was time for George to escort her back to her sisters.

Sets were now forming for a quadrille and young James was asking his mother if he could be allowed to dance.

'Please, Mama,' he begged. 'You know I love to dance and I've no one to stand up with.'

Helena hesitated. He was a graceful boy,

tall for his age and his young face was alight with eagerness.

'I'll be happy to be James's partner,' she said kindly to Sophie, who gave her a grateful smile and went to fetch James's gloves. She ordered her son to keep them on while he was dancing with Miss Steer and to remember everything that had been told him by Signor Dario, the dancing master, about the correct way to treat a lady. Helena smilingly allowed him to lead her to a corner of the room where circles of four couples were being formed ready for the dance. She already knew two of the other dancers in their set and smilingly introduced her young partner, who was flattered at the attention and praise he was receiving for being allowed to partner the beautiful Miss Steer. James was a good dancer and naturally light on his feet. He was able to anticipate every figure and never faltered in any of the steps. Helena began to relax and enjoy the dance which had always been one of her favourites. She glanced round once or twice for her sisters and saw Charlotte dancing with Henry Clifford. There was no sign of Eliza but she supposed that she was in one of the more distant sets. James made polite conversation as he had been taught by the dancing master. He wasn't the least bit shy and told her animatedly that he was going back to school later that month.

'I expect your mama will miss you,' Helena said.

'Oh no, Miss Steer,' he reassured her kindly. 'For you know, my mama will want to visit her Aunt Maria Malpass in London. They always buy dresses and hats when she visits Aunt Malpass,' he went on ingenuously. 'And she brings back ribbons and trimmings for Grandmama Arnold. Then they make things,' he added vaguely. Helena smiled at him. An idea was already forming in the back of her mind, which might resolve the problem of visiting Richard. By the time the quadrille was over, she had decided to engineer an invitation to London with her friend Sophie.

It was inevitable that she should eventually come face to face with Sir Thomas Capley at some point in the evening. No sooner had Master Malpass escorted Helena back to his fond mama, when George joined their group and of course brought Tom with him. Helena had the presence of mind to make some small talk with Sophie about James's skill on the dance floor, but she knew that eventually, she would have to turn round and be drawn into the general conversation which would include the arrogant Sir Thomas. What was she to say to him, she wondered? Her feelings for him were still very confused. The strong attraction she had felt at their first meeting had been terribly muddied by the encounter in Bentick barn. She felt that his pride and the patronizing way he had treated her would be obstacles in any social situation and she felt particularly threatened at the idea of dancing with him. She sought to avoid it by first not giving him eye contact and then by accepting eagerly when George requested another dance, but it was useless. George, and Sophie were quite oblivious to her lack of enthusiasm and seemed in fact to engineer a situation where Tom was almost duty bound to request her to dance. The musicians struck up again and he asked stiffly if he might have the honour of her hand in the waltz.

Good manners compelled her to accept the offer and with a small curtsy, she allowed him to lead her onto the floor. Here he surprised her by proving to be an experienced dancer, very light on his feet and seemingly able to perform the steps without having to think too much about it. As he guided her into the first gliding steps, Helena concentrated on the dance and kept her eyes firmly fixed on the diamond pin winking in his cravat as she adapted her steps to his. As she relaxed into the rhythm of the dance, she noticed that several young ladies whose mamas had forbidden them to waltz were in a huddle and watching her with undisguised envy. Indeed one or two of their mamas were watching too, but it seemed they mistook her lowered eyes and lack of conversation as quite becoming modesty. Only Lady Lavinia seemed to have an inkling of the tension between the two of them as she remarked to another of the elderly ladies, what a handsome couple they made, to be sure!

In spite of herself, Helena started to enjoy the dance. The music swirled, rose and fell in the subtleties of strict waltz tempo and Helena felt an echo in the swish and swirl of her skirt each time they spun round. She could feel the hardness of her partner's thighs as they moved against hers and he guided her into a turn. Although neither of them spoke, each was conscious of his strong arm round her waist and the confident clasp of his hand on her own. In the warm atmosphere, she was acutely aware once more of the attractive male scent of his skin. Her right hand rested very lightly on his arm and yet she could feel the powerful masculine strength of him through the fabric of his sleeve.

Tom glanced down at her. Her gaze was still lowered and the dark lashes that he found so seductive were spread like miniature fans against her soft cheeks. He had an insane desire to shower her with expensive jewellery to see if such stunning natural beauty could be further enhanced by artifice. An emerald necklace to contrast with the dazzling whiteness of her bosom. A ruby tiara to bring out the burnished gold of her hair. Fine diamonds for her delicate ears. He looked at the white-gloved hand resting on his arm. He was sure she wore no rings. What stones would compliment those graceful fingers he wondered? Appalled at these thoughts, his clasp on her hand tightened involuntarily and, startled, Helena looked up at him for the first time. They both started a polite remark simultaneously, then each smiled and relapsed into silence again as the dance ended and he escorted her back to where her sisters were sitting, still without speaking.

Eliza and Charlotte pronounced the first ball of the season a great success. Neither of them had danced with Sir Thomas and indeed, he seemed to have vanished into the crowd during the supper interval. They were cheerful nonetheless and made several jokes about what might have happened if they'd had a chance to charm Wintham's richest resident while dancing with him.

'Alas, he never even asked me to stand up with him,' said Charlotte, pretending to be mournful.

'But that doesn't signify,' said Eliza in a

lofty tone. 'We both had our country dance programmes full and at least Helena was honoured with a waltz.'

Helena refused to be drawn. She was busy with her own plans and didn't wish to think about the disturbing pleasure of waltzing with Tom. She had agreed with the Arnolds that once James was settled in at Rugby, she and Sophie would travel to London in Squire Arnold's coach for a visit to Sophie's Aunt Maria Malpass. The journey would take two days but accommodation would be arranged for them and Helena's maid, Rose, along the way.

She was pleased that at last she was going to take some action to resolve the problem of her errant brother, but when she thought of the evil Davenport and how effectively the virile Sir Thomas Capley had dealt with him, yet again, the elusive little dimple appeared at the corner of her mouth. She couldn't help smiling to herself with quiet satisfaction.

4

When she discussed her plans with her father and sisters, Francis Steer readily agreed to Helena's visit to London. He considered that it would do Helena the world of good to be away from her responsibilities for a little while and enjoy a change of scene. He had now fully recovered from his chill and was able to continue his duties in the two parishes and get out regularly to visit his farmlands.

'I fancy you've been looking a little peaked lately, my dear, and some distraction in the company of the Malpass family is bound to raise your spirits,' he said.

If she felt a pang of guilt at her father's obvious love and concern for her and her own intention to deceive him, Helena quickly stifled it and set about making her preparations. Her sisters insisted that they were very capable of coping without her and in fact would welcome the experience of supervising the household for a change. The visit was to be for two weeks and while Helena was away, Charlotte and Eliza would take turns at writing to her to send news or express any worries they might have in her absence.

The housekeeper was given hundreds of instructions regarding the meals for her father and sisters and Helena emphasized the necessity of making specially light and nourishing suppers for the Reverend Steer if his back problem should return.

'As though a body could pass by on the other side, when the master's bent double with his old problem,' the housekeeper confided in the cook. 'And upon my soul, there's only one woman who can prepare the right posset for the reverend's back and that's Betsy Chantry.'

'And please make sure that there is always a fire in the study before my father starts to write his sermon,' Helena instructed. 'For you know how abstracted he can be when he is concerned by the problems of his flock and he will sit writing until his back is rigid, without even noticing. It would be quite distressing were he to take a chill while I'm away.'

Mrs Chantry confided darkly to the housemaid that although there were some as could tolerate damp sheets and nay, even put them on their masters' beds, she, Betsy Chantry, was not one of them. She always kept a good fire and could be trusted to guard the reverend's health with her life, while his eldest was away in the City.

Stubbs likewise, had strict orders on the care and exercising of Blueboy and of allowing only the two docile mares to be available for Charlotte and Eliza to ride.

'I'm sure I knows my duty, miss,' he said with his usual disapproving expression, 'and I've never thought of Blueboy as a suitable mount for a lady. Madam may rest easy that the two young ladies will not be allowed out of the grounds on any mount that Edward Stubbs would consider to be too lively for them.'

Helena checked the still room and larder, the wine cellar and the linen press, before declaring that everything was in order and that Charlotte and Eliza would be able to manage the domestic arrangements. Then she and Rose sorted out the clothes she would need for London.

Fanny and Mrs Radford had promised to look in at the rectory and give any help that was needed and the girls themselves urged Helena to enjoy her visit and not to worry about them.

'We will have our own pleasures,' Eliza said eagerly. 'We're promised for the Radfords' picnic you know, Helena, and this must take place soon while the weather is set fair. Mary's mama may be giving a small luncheon party for Frank, Alfred and the others, before they return to Oxford. We're certain to receive an invitation to keep company with Mary and Fanny,' she added ingenuously.

'I hope you will visit the theatre and see the latest plays, Helena,' urged Charlotte when their father was safely out of the room. 'It will be so interesting to hear an account of the first actors and actresses in London. They say that Lord Byron gives unstinting praise to Mrs Jordan in her role as Miss Hoyden in, *A Trip to Scarborough*, and of course, for her Shakespearean roles,' she added hastily, as Francis Steer returned. Helena heard the unexpressed longing in the young voice. Charlotte had never visited London and Helena was conscious of the fact that some effort must be made to give her young sister opportunities to meet a wider circle of young men. If only Mama were here, she thought, Charlotte would have a much less restricted life. She resolved to arrange a visit to the London theatres for her sister and to give her an opportunity to choose some fashionable clothes at Madam Monte's establishment.

'I've heard there are some excellent concerts of sacred music in St. Mary's,' suggested Eliza. 'And Helena, be sure you visit that milliner in Bond Street where you had your green straw. Perhaps you may find one like it to match your new blue silk,' she added, and blushed, because to own a smart straw hat was the dearest wish of her own young heart.

Helena made a mental note that whatever else she did in London, she must find exactly the right straw bonnet for her youngest sister. She felt a little ashamed at the way she'd led them to believe that she was only on pleasure bent, but she was aware that it would not be easy to contact Richard and it would be even more difficult to persuade him to leave the life he was leading for the quiet of the country rectory. Above all, she was determined that Davenport would not have the chance to renew their acquaintance while she was in town. She was sorely tempted to confide in Sophie, whose quiet good sense had always impressed her. However, one look at the red-rimmed eyes and drooping mouth of James's fond mama after his departure for Rugby, made her reconsider and she realized that for the time being at least, she would have to fight her own battles and to act as independently as she always did. In any case, she thought, as she and Rose packed her boxes and valise, it would be time enough to tell Sophie if it became necessary. Meanwhile, least said soonest mended.

Her father had proved surprisingly cheerful at being left to cope without her and had merely requested her to try and find a copy of the Abbé Simenon's book of sermons for him if she should chance to visit any bookshops. 'And don't worry if it's not in translation, Helena,' he said seriously. 'I'll be more than content if it's in the original French. It will serve as exercise for my old brain to puzzle out the good man's deeper thoughts, rather than wrestling with the increases and decreases in the Glebe farm milk yield, or potato blight in the two acre field.'

Noticing the slightly harassed expression on the face of his beloved elder daughter, he added diffidently, 'But please don't get into a taking if there's none available. Enjoy yourself, my dear. It can't have been easy for you having to take the place of your dear mama when you are so young yourself.' He looked wistful as he added, 'And who knows who you may meet in the big city?'

She knew he was thinking of Richard as he said this, but she kept her plans to herself. She'd called at the White Hart to see if there was any mail, but Richard predictably, hadn't replied to her letter.

Rose had managed to close the valise by the simple expedient of seating her large bottom on it and strapping it closed before it could burst open again. A basket of essential refreshments and drinks was produced from the kitchen by the cook who was not to be outdone by the housekeeper's standards of care. She described to Mrs Chantry the excellent contents of her hamper, containing as it did, not only the cold meats and hand-raised pork pie and cakes, but starched linen and crystal drinking glasses for the bottle of wine.

'Madam and her friend won't lack for sustenance on their journey,' she boasted. 'Not with the victuals I've packed up for 'em.'

Helena's writing case, suitably replenished with fresh notepaper, was carried down to the hall and Helena put on her travelling dress and matching pelisse of deep-green silk. She tied her bonnet firmly under her chin and turned to kiss her sisters who, now that the moment had arrived, were suddenly less confident about their ability to cope without the person on whose strength they had come to trust and depend. With many last-minute hugs and reassurances, Helena said goodbye to her family and prepared to depart.

Now the Arnolds' carriage was at the door and the luggage packed. All the farewells had been said and they were off at last, through the village and towards the turnpike road which would lead eventually, to London.

The two friends were rather quiet at first, each thinking their own thoughts. Helena knew that Sophie was missing James and she herself was content to let her mind wander to her most recent encounter with Sir Thomas Capley. What a surprise to find he was such a skilled dancer. She thought of the smooth way he had guided her round the ballroom and closed her eyes, imagining once more, his comforting arm around her and the firm clasp of his hand before he had so coldly relinquished her at the end of the dance, and his early departure. He'd probably still been feeling angry with her. No doubt he'll never forgive me for slapping him, she thought. After all, why should he? He had the pick of the young marriageable girls and she herself was rather mature as unmarried females went. She'd always envisaged getting married when she was younger, but now, perhaps it was never going to happen. Perhaps she would never meet the right man.

New ideas chased themselves round in her mind. Surely Sir Thomas Capley must know that she was not playing fast and loose games with men? And yet, he had accused her of arranging meetings with 'dangerous rakes'. He must by now have been told that she had her own fortune and was not in need of a rich husband. He appeared so disdainful and superior and yet she had felt instinctively his genuine concern and care for his tenants when he'd spoken of his plans for the estate. She deeply regretted now her behaviour in the barn and the humiliation she'd inflicted on him by striking him across the face like that. But then, she argued with herself, no gentleman had any right to forcibly impose his kisses on her. Perhaps in different circumstances, she might have enjoyed the pressure of his mouth on her own. She gave a little shake of her head to try and banish such thoughts, and opened her eyes.

Gradually, as the calm of the countryside unfolded with all its green fields and neat farms, Sophie's spirits recovered. In spite of her anxiety, Helena couldn't help being entertained and diverted by her friend's sarcastic and amusing observations about her friends and neighbours as Sophie chatted humorously about Wintham society. Rose had her eyes fixed firmly on the passing scene, but Helena could tell by the twitching of her maid's lips that she was enjoying it, too.

'And that poor little Mary Carty,' Sophie was saying. 'What a milk-and-water miss she is, Helena. When is she ever going to stop trailing after her mother?'

'Her mama is very particular about the company she keeps,' Helena excused Mary. 'None of her beaux have so far come up to scratch in spite of Mrs Carty's best efforts.

She would dearly love a good marriage for her darling daughter. But Mary is no cipher, Sophie. I think if she met the right one she'd soon come about and make her own match, without her mama's help.'

'Perhaps she feels that Sir Thomas Capley is the right one,' Sophie persisted. 'She seemed to be very taken with him at the Assembly Ball and he did dance with her, as well as yourself, of course,' she said, because his close embrace of Helena in the waltz had not gone unnoticed.

Helena glanced away quickly and looked out of the carriage window. She had no wish to think about Sir Thomas Capley, especially in connection with Mary, or any of the other young women if it came to that, she thought.

The gesture wasn't lost on Sophie and she said teasingly, 'Well, I wondered as you continue to be a maiden lady, Helena, whether you had marked him out as your own?'

They both laughed, but Sophie was serious. 'Don't be too tardy in the marriage stakes, my love. There's no want of freedom in the married woman's state if she has the right man, but there can be a lifetime of enslavement in the role of dutiful daughter.'

No, but suppose, I never meet the right one? Helena thought. A country parsonage was hardly the setting to attract the sort of man she could admire and respect, let alone love. Even if her fortune was tempting to the fashionable London set, she could hardly impose country house parties and fashionable entertainment on the unworldly and ascetic Francis Steer. No, it must be in the hands of fate, she decided. She would either meet with true love and marry, or remain unwed. She thought again of Sir Thomas Capley. He was single and undeniably attractive, and now possessed a significant fortune. Any woman could be excused for losing her heart to him. She remembered his deep eyes and the hard pressure of his body. She wondered what it would be like to enjoy more gentle and loving caresses with him.

Then she dismissed this thought as Sophie suggested a short break and an exploration of the excellent hamper. Helped by the buxom Rose, they managed to do more than justice to the cook's picnic and the rest of the journey to Oxford passed pleasantly enough. As darkness fell, they were pleased to stop at the Crown and step into the private parlour which had been arranged for them. It had been a very early start to their journey and a long time since they had enjoyed their lunch in the coach. They were able to do more than justice to a succulent collation of roast ham and some slices from a noble side of beef, washed down with a mellow wine. Tired and satisfied, they retired to bed.

The journey the next day was increasingly smooth as the roads became gradually more maintained and the toll gates more regular. Helena looked out of the window rather dispiritedly. She felt no particular enthusiasm for London. To her mind, the much vaunted excitement of the capital seemed to be overstated and rated far too highly, particularly by ladies of fashion. Even in her coming-out year, she had not enjoyed life in the great bustling city and had often longed for the security and stillness of the rectory. Now as they got nearer to the centre, she felt almost deafened by the noise and frenzied activity on the streets.

It was early evening. Postmen ran from door to door, porterhouse boys were busily despatching home deliveries of pewter mugs with small beer for customers' suppers. Tired and drooping little sweeps with huge brushes on their frail shoulders trudged back to miserable lodgings. All sorts of loud and unlovely shouts by piemen, flower-sellers and broad-sheet vendors competed with the bells of the dust carts and the cries of apprentices putting up the shutters on their masters' shops, or kicking a piece of butcher's offal along the muddy road. Ragged urchins with pinched, unnaturally pale faces stood mutely with hands held out, begging and not daring to go back to whatever place they called home. Others ran shouting at the side of the carriage, offering to hold the horses, lay straw for the ladies' feet, mind the luggage, or perform any other task required by the gentry, while various painted ladies with bold eyes lurked in doorways idly observing them.

There were huge wagons and drays, pulled by powerful horses whose feet were covered in long hair which was spattered with mud and dung from the filthy streets. Every time one of the carts got stuck or locked wheels, the commotion was added to by the furious raucous shouts of the drivers on their way to Smithfield or Billingsgate. Hackney cabs with bad-tempered cabbies bore well-heeled passengers out of the City towards the more fashionable West End and when they had to stop for a few moments, some of the street women would immediately sidle up to importune the fine gentlemen inside before being threatened by the driver's whip.

They made their way along Cheapside towards Holborn and eventually Oxford Street. Gradually the noisy stinking roads gave way to quieter more ordered streets where all the houses seemed to have clean sashed windows and pedimented front doors. They all had area steps and iron railings and there was an air of well-ordered gentility.

They had now reached Aunt Malpass's luxurious house in Brompton Square and the name of the house was engraved into a brass plate by the front door. When her brother had done the Grand Tour, he had stayed at a place in Tuscany called Villa Alba and she had been so taken with the name she decided to use it for her own house. Here, in the select London square the signs of affluence contrasted strongly with the noisy City centre. Wealth and prestige were evident in the quiet streets and large houses, all with steps leading up to the imposing pillars of massive doorways. The carefully planned streets were well swept and free of bustle and commerce.

Maria Malpass met them at the door herself, smiling and nodding with pleasure.

'Welcome, my dears, I've been listening for the carriage these two hours. Come along in, my dear Miss Steer. You're so welcome.'

'Helena, if you please, ma'am,' Helena said, holding out her hand and lowering her cheek to be kissed.

'And how is the little man?' Miss Malpass asked, turning to Sophie with yet another beaming smile.

Sophie's eyes threatened to fill up once more at this reminder of her son's departure for school and the older lady hastily went on to ask about her dear nephew, Jack. Sophie assured her that Captain Jack Malpass was well and happy and they both looked forward to his next leave. So, while the servants bustled to take the luggage up to their rooms, Helena and Sophie were ushered into the drawing-room for gossip and refreshments. In the next few hours, Helena understood perfectly the bond of love and affection which existed between her friend and her aunt by marriage. Elderly, she might be, but behind her comfortable plump exterior dwelt an extremely alert mind and an acute intelligence.

'I've planned one of my little soirées for Wednesday,' she beamed at them. 'Just a simple little supper with friends, but company all the same. I hope you will enjoy it, my dears.'

They were made more than welcome and the next day was taken up with exchanging visiting cards among the numerous acquaintances of Aunt Maria Malpass and her niece. There was a card from George Arnold, paying his respects and begging to be allowed to call while his sister and Helena were staying in Brompton Square, but no suitable chance arose to seek out Richard, and Helena chafed inwardly with frustration.

On the second day, however, there was an unexpected opportunity to put her plan into action.

Miss Malpass appeared at breakfast wearing a strange strip of fabric wound round her face and head. She waved all offers of breakfast aside rather sadly and confided in Helena and Sophie that she would have to visit Mr Thurkstone to have a painful tooth extracted. By eleven o'clock, Sophie and her aunt had departed in the carriage to consult with the dentist and get the offending tooth seen to.

Helena assured them that she and her maid would take a hack and have a pleasurable morning in Bond Street sightseeing and shopping for trinkets to take home to Wintham.

'Well if you're sure, my dear,' said Miss Malpass in a rather muffled voice and she seemed very relieved when Helena declined to accompany them for even part of the way in the coach.

'Very well, Wilkes will order you a hackney cab when you're ready, Helena. Goodbye then, dear. We'll get off for the dentist now.'

Once she and Rose were ready and dressed to go out, the butler stood on the steps of the

Villa Alba and gave a particularly strange and shrill whistle. As if by magic, a hackney cab clip-clopped up to the door and the horse stood snorting gently as the driver waited for their instructions. Wilkes opened the door for them and Helena now had to plan quickly so she decided to take Rose into her confidence.

She said casually, 'I've received some knowledge of Master Richard, Rose. We may perhaps divert our trip to Bond Street and seek out his lodgings.'

'Very good, Miss Helena,' the maid said impassively, and Helena gave the cab driver the Vernon House address, her heart pounding nervously. She put on a cool front for her maid and, as they approached the Honourable Percy Davenport's town house, she allowed the driver to go a little way past before she ordered him to stop and instructed Rose to wait in the cab.

'Wait here please,' she said, and walked boldly up to the green front door. The rap with the clenched fist in a brass gauntlet, which served as a door knocker, brought an instant response. An extremely dignified personage immaculately dressed in sober black, answered the door with the utmost disdain.

'Yes, madam?' He bowed but with the superciliousness of a confident butler in charge of a fine gentleman's London establishment.

'I'm enquiring for Mr Richard Steer,' Helena replied firmly.

'Indeed, madam?' the butler replied, with a scarcely disguised sneer. 'He is not known at this address, Madam.'

'Then where may I find him?'

'My master is not at home at the moment, madam, but I'll enquire within,' he said loftily.

Helena waited on the doorstep with extreme unease, feeling exposed to the rude stares of anyone who might be passing by and very aware that although the Honourable Percy Davenport was not at home at the moment, he might appear at any time and add to her embarrassment and discomfiture.

Finally, another of the servants arrived. This time, the first footman, whose powder-blue livery did nothing for his florid complexion and heavy legs, but at least he was more friendly.

'Mr Steer is not here, madam,' he said rather unnecessarily. 'However, he has left a forwarding address where he may be found,' and he held out a silver tray bearing a piece of paper, which read: 35, Pegasus Mansions.

Helena took it and placing a coin on the tray, which was graciously received by the footman, she hurried back to the cab and directed the driver to the address on the paper.

Pegasus Mansions was in a very different part of town and was not nearly as grand as the title suggested. It was, in fact, a sordid tenement in an evil-smelling back alley. Even their driver looked askance as she alighted from the cab and went through the scarred door, prepared to climb the dingy stairs which led to number thirty-five.

'Old 'ard, my lady,' he warned. 'Them's rough coves in there. Belt yer 'ead in soon as look at yer,' he added, as Helena turned her clear gaze upon him.

'I better go wiv yer, miss,' he continued. 'These's rum places for a lady on 'er own.'

He summoned a ragged urchin from a murky doorway and handed him the horse's reins. He slipped a nose bag over the horse's head and told the urchin to ''old him on a loose 'un and let 'im take 'is oats.'

Leaving Rose in the cab, once more, Helena climbed the steep rickety stairs to number thirty-five, which was on the fourth landing. From the many blank doors that she passed, came mysterious sounds and unidentifiable smells. A baby cried out and she heard a muffled curse. Heavy snoring came from another of the anonymous doors and the sound of a woman sobbing as Helena and the driver passed by hurriedly. At last she stood hesitating at number thirty-five. There was no sound from the other side of the door, so she knocked gently and after a pause, went in.

The room was shocking in its sordid disorder. There was a smell of stale food and an unmade bed with a mass of tousled bed linen. A small filthy window without curtains let in a little light and underneath the window there was a plain wooden table full of the debris of a meal.

In a shabbily upholstered chair, slumped forward with his head among the unwashed wine glasses of last night's supper, was her brother, Richard.

Helena darted forward impulsively towards the drunken figure lying among the mess on the table.

'Richard,' she said. 'Oh Richard. What are you doing here? What's happened to you?' she asked, in a shocked voice. Her breath caught in a sob as she noticed how white and thin his young face had become and how tense were the wasted knuckles clutching the soiled table napkin.

'Wassamarer? Wha' is it?' he muttered.

'Richard. It's Helena. What's happened to you? What are you doing in this place?' she asked, in shocked tones, and she lifted his head from the table and cradled it against her shoulder.

'Oh Helena. Hello, dear Sister.' He opened his dull eyes very briefly and gave a mirthless smile. 'Pegasus Mansions, dear Sis'. Last resting place don't yer know for humble servants of cheap Spanish brandy and all those in hock to Jonah Rudd, may the devil take him.'

Then he closed his eyes and slumped forward again.

Helena looked round helplessly and encountered the bland gaze of the cab driver who was standing in the doorway.

'Maybe we should be going, lady,' he said uneasily. 'This 'ere's no place for the likes of them that values their skin. I'll wait for you on the landing, ma'am.' he whispered tactfully, and withdrew.

Helena took in the squalid room and the threadbare dressing-gown which her brother was wearing and then pulled up the second rickety chair to sit close to him.

'Richard, what is it?' she asked urgently. 'What are you doing in this place when your papa and sisters are missing you so much and want you back at home?'

He opened his eyes again, this time managing to raise his head unaided.

'I know it's a devil of a place, Sis', but it's all I can manage, deuce take it. Even here, I don't know what I'd do without dear old Davenport. Raised fifty pounds for me only last week. Enough to keep the sharks away for a little while. Gone now, o' course,' he continued dully. 'Had to pay something to that slimy Rudd. Everything gets sucked out of me by that accursed snake. I tell you, Helena, he's grinding me down, pressing my face into the mire. Damn him to hell!'

'Richard. Please,' Helena interrupted. 'Calm yourself.'

'Calm myself?' he retorted, his eyes rolling alarmingly and he ran a thin hand through his already dishevelled hair.

'Impossible! Forgive me, I'm still a trifle bosky from last night. But curses on that monster, Rudd. If I had the chance I'd kill him with my bare hands and rid the world of a heartless, bloodsucking leech! Pass the brandy bottle, Helena.' And he reached out a pathetically shaking hand to slop some of the brandy into a dirty glass.

'No, Richard.' Helena touched his shoulder trying to dissuade him from gulping down the cheap spirit. 'Tell me how I may help you and then let's go home to Wintham.'

'Impossible, dear Sis'. I'm in hock to Jonah Rudd for my very life. He owns me body and soul and I'm in too deep now. All that's left to me is death in a debtors' prison,' he declared dramatically.

'Oh come, Richard. It can't be as bad as that. Who is this Rudd? We can surely free you from him and make a clean start.'

He gave a short laugh. 'Free me? I'll never be free of that bloodsucker, even if I had the money, and I haven't, Helena. It's all gone long ago.'

'But what about your allowance from Papa? Surely you could afford to live on the money he sends you every quarter?'

'It's always spoken for, Helena. I tell you, I'm hopelessly in debt to that damnable Rudd you see.'

'But I could pay your debts, Richard. I have full control over my inheritance now. Come, what do you say? I want you to be free and it would be a small price to pay for your peace of mind. You could take your rightful place again as Father's son and heir.'

He looked at her blankly for a moment, suddenly sober. Then he said slowly, 'Do you know how much I owe Rudd? It would take three thousand.'

'Whatever it is, I'll pay it all if only you'll come home, Richard, and be cared for properly. Papa longs to see you. We could forget the past. It would be a new start.'

'Of course, I'd pay you back, Helena,' he said slowly, beginning at last to sound hopeful. 'It would only be a loan.'

'Yes, yes, a loan,' she coaxed him, as though he were a child. 'But you'd have to agree to come home with me, Richard.'

'And if I did? What would there be for me back at the rectory in Wintham? I'd have to listen to Pa's sermons again and follow his rules.'

'Well, it's true, Father would want you to have done with cheap brandy and the likes of Percy Davenport.'

'But he's my friend,' her brother said, with his old childish obstinacy.

'No, Richard, he's no friend of yours and neither is this.' Helena stood up and removed the bottle firmly away from him. 'I can go and see Mr Stanley in Cheapside. He'll arrange for me to redeem your bills. What do you say, Brother?'

'What do I say?' he repeated, his expression lightening at the thought of being free. 'Oh, Helena. What can I say? You know it must be yes.'

In spite of his smile, his eyes filled with tears and he stood up weakly, staggering and holding the table for support. She put her arm round his thin shoulders to comfort him and they stood for a moment very close together.

'Oh how very affecting. What a very moving scene, indeed. The divine Siddons herself would have been proud of your performance, my dear.'

To her dismay, there standing in the doorway was Davenport, brushing away an imaginary speck from his immaculate unmentionables and sneering at them cynically.

'Yes, I intercepted your letter, dear Helena, and was told by my butler of your visit this morning. I knew you'd be here. So predictable, this devotion to your brother.'

There was a strained silence as they both continued to look at the intruder and Richard's shoulders drooped again as Davenport laughed softly and stepped into the room.

'So you're to be saved, are you, Richard?' he drawled. 'And by your beautiful sister, Helena? Your life is to take an about face, a return to the nursery and back on to leading strings, eh?' He laughed again.

'And what has it to do with you, sir?' Helena turned on him angrily, her eyes flashing fire. 'My brother's decision is his own.'

'Why nothing, my dear Miss Steer, except that until today, Richard was my friend and honoured me with his confidences about, shall we say, his financial difficulties? Isn't that so, dear boy?'

He stepped further into the room and laid an almost caressing hand on Richard's shoulder, at which the young man drooped more than ever and moved away almost imperceptibly.

'Yes,' he muttered. 'And what I haven't told you, you've managed to find out for yourself.' He reached again for the bottle, his hand trembling more violently this time and Davenport promptly pushed it towards him.

'Yes,' the Honourable Percy Davenport continued even more softly. 'You acknowledge I'm your friend, Richard, and you must never forget that. I suspect you never will.'

Helena saw her brother's expression turn to drab hopelessness again as he poured himself another brandy and she turned to Davenport indignantly.

'But not for very much longer, sir. My brother is returning to the family home shortly, when his affairs in London are settled.'

'So they're to be settled by your dear sister, what?' Davenport showed his small pointed teeth again in another cynical smile.

'As a loan,' protested Richard. 'Only a loan,

and I should be free of that scoundrel Rudd, for ever.'

At this, Davenport laughed again, but with suddenly narrowed eyes.

'My dear fellow,' he murmured, 'a change of master, is all it would signify. Not even master,' he continued mockingly. 'Petticoat government, don't yer know.'

'Ha,' he said. 'I hadn't thought of that. But I'd be starting a new life, Percy, away from that damnable Rudd. I'd have my self-respect,' he pleaded pathetically.

'But not in London, Richard,' murmured Davenport. 'You would have long hours to enjoy your self-respect, my dear old buck, in the quiet confines of the rectory, away from your friends. You would have all the time in the world. And country pursuits among the local peasantry would soon lose their savour. How long would it be before you started to crave your London pleasures again?' he continued silkily.

Helena put a restraining hand on the slopping glass which Richard was raising to his lips. 'Seeing that this is no concern of yours, sir, I would thank you to leave us. When his affairs are settled, my brother will return with me next Monday week.'

'No, damme, Helena. I haven't decided yet. Who are you to order my friends about? Let

116

me go, I'm not drunk. Think I've no pride? This is my place and I'll follow my own mind. I'm a man, aren't I?'

'Of course you are, my dear Dick. A regular Corinthian, an out and outer, who's not to be ruled by any spinster sister.'

Helena saw that there was nothing for it but to leave. She would return when Richard was in a more reasonable state and, more importantly, away from the direct influence of his so-called friend.

She turned away, taking care not to step near Davenport. Then she and the cab driver went down the dismal stairs to the street below, to the sounds of Richard's drunken ramblings and Percy Davenport's soft, mocking laughter.

5

Distracted though she was by Richard and his problems, Helena was confident that Mr Stanley would be able to offer sound advice and that when he was sober, her brother would see reason and agree to her terms. For appearance's sake, she stopped at the draper's and made a few small purchases on her way to back to the Villa Alba. She knew that she could trust to Rose's discretion and she offered no account of their activities to her friend, Sophie. Instead, she asked after Miss Malpass, who had already gone to lie down with some white poppy syrup in her wine and water. After her ordeal at the dentist, all Miss Malpass wanted was to sleep herself better. Left alone, the friends had a quiet dinner and settled down with some of the books Sophie had borrowed from her aunt's subscription library.

As she idly turned the pages of her book, Sophie mused aloud, 'I wonder if Aunt Maria will cancel the supper party? In view of the pain she has endured, I fully expect her to send a footman round to the other guests and cry off for tomorrow evening.'

Privately, Helena was not dismayed by the prospect of not having to appear in company. She told herself that she would be just as content to spend a quiet evening chatting, or reading a book. All Helena's concerns were still with her brother and underneath her calm exterior, she was still beside herself with anxiety about his drinking and the evil influence of the dastardly Davenport. While she answered politely and mechanically to Sophie's light chatter, her thoughts were preoccupied with various enterprising schemes for getting Richard to return home with her. Some of them, she had to acknowledge, were just unrealistic and she dismissed out of hand, but she toyed with the idea of confiding in George Arnold. Perhaps he could influence Richard. She didn't know. She gave a deep sigh as her thoughts turned to yet another possible solution.

'That's a heartfelt sigh,' Sophie laughed. 'Am I to take it that it signifies disappointment at the prospect of our supper party being cancelled?'

But Maria Malpass was made of sterner stuff. Far from being cancelled, by the following day, the soirée had swelled into a dinner party for sixteen, the numbers being added to by the recently appointed clergyman at St Mary's, where Sophie's aunt worshipped on Sundays, and his new young wife. At breakfast, she was almost her old self, even though she was still speaking in rather a muffled voice.

'And quite fortuitously,' she informed them, 'George is able to bring his old friend, Sir Thomas Capley, who is in Town for a few days on business. I expect you're already acquainted, my dears, coming as he does, from your own part of the country. Years ago, I knew his dear mother, dead now, poor lady, and I haven't seen my very old friend, Lavinia, these ten years and more. I understand he's received a legacy from a distant relative in the Indies.'

'Why yes,' Sophie said immediately. 'He has recently returned to live in Wintham and seems determined to work on the Capley estate. He has attended one or two social events in the past few weeks and has made himself very agreeable to Wintham society.'

The news that Sir Thomas was to attend the dinner party was yet another unpleasant surprise for Helena, but she hid her dismay at her inevitable embarrassment and merely murmured a polite response.

'My sisters and I are only recently acquainted with Sir Thomas, ma'am, now that he has returned to take up residence at the Hall, after being so many years in London and haven't met him often.'

'And what is your opinion of the young man?'

'Why, Aunt,' Sophie said, very amused, 'he is all that is personable and handsome and has already set many Wintham hearts a'flutter.'

She gave a sly glance at Helena. 'Am I not right, Helena?'

'Yes,' said Helena, colouring a little. 'Although I know very little of him, after such a brief acquaintance.'

'But Helena,' Sophie broke in laughingly, 'you must confess that he is all that is amiable and eligible in a young man. The mamas of marriageable girls for miles around Wintham, are all of a twitter about the young handsome bachelor who is in possession of such a comfortable fortune.'

Helena answered rather stiffly, 'Well, as to his amiability or otherwise, I'm unable to say. He certainly seems to have created a stir in village circles.'

Miss Malpass gave her a keen look out of experienced and intelligent eyes, but said nothing. Helena didn't expand on the nature of her feelings about Sir Thomas for after all, they were bound to meet when they moved in the same social circles, she supposed. She would just have to grit her teeth and be polite

121

to him. It was just a question of putting her feelings of antipathy to one side and observing the social niceties for a few hours. One thing she was determined on: she would look her very radiant best if she was to be in company with the hated Sir Thomas. Her demeanour would be of proud disdainful dignity. She would give no morsel of friendliness or tolerance to the man who had spoken to her so dismissively and kissed her with such rough cynicism.

Sophie suggested that they should spend an agreeable morning shopping and even though Helena didn't find the ideal bonnet for Eliza, she reflected that at least it was some distraction from her worries over Richard and she did manage to track down a copy of the *Pensées* for her father. Both young women admired some hand-embroidered shawls and Helena bought one each for Eliza and Charlotte. Sophie was to meet her husband at the end of the month, when he would return briefly from abroad, so Helena had to help her choose two new gowns from Madame Monte's Mantua-makers in Bond Street. Recognizing another potential customer in Mrs Malpass's beautiful young friend, Madame pulled out all her latest models to show them and was full of flattering affability as the gowns were displayed for their inspection with all the appropriate slippers, fans and shawls to match. Sophie finally settled on a dress of palest blue silk, very dashing with silver ribbons, ideal for formal occasions, and a more informal dress of buttermilk-coloured muslin, sprigged with tiny dots of pale lemon. They were promised for a fortnight, much to Sophie's satisfaction. She missed her husband and was looking forward to their reunion. She spoke very warmly of Jack Malpass in the coach on the way back and for the first time, Helena felt a pang of envy at her friend's obvious contentment with married life, even though she and the captain had to endure frequent separations. Helena realized, not for the first time, how supportive and comforting it must be to have a strong partner with whom to share life's burdens. Even an errant drunken brother could perhaps be coped with, if she had the right man, she supposed.

They finally returned to the Villa Alba to find lunch had been prepared in the breakfast parlour, the dining-room being an absolute hive of activity.

Their hostess was busy making preparations for the evening. She had a slight bulge in one cheek, which gave her the appearance of a rather lop-sided cherub, but seemed none the worse for her ordeal with the offending tooth. The butler was supervising the setting of the table and the unwrapping and washing of various precious items of china and Miss Malpass was personally arranging the flowers. She broke off when they arrived and joined them for lunch, exclaiming over the shawls and bonnets. Sophie's new gowns were described in great detail with much 'oohing' and 'ahing' from her beloved aunt, so that even Helena forgot her preoccupations with Richard's problems for a brief while and joined in the animated conversation.

There was a letter from young Eliza, couched very much in her ingenuous speaking style and very closely written with a set of lines written at right angles, making it quite difficult to decipher. However, the gist of the news from the rectory was that Papa continued to be well. The girls had got into a bit of a muddle with the way they wanted Monday's mutton prepared by the cook, but Mrs Chantry had rescued the situation. She ordered firmly that it was to be boiled to the master's liking and served up with thin gravy as the cook well knew.

'*And famous news, Helena,*' the letter went on, '*Mary's mama has invited us for luncheon on Thursday. Alfred, Frank and Fanny will be in attendance, so we may discuss plans for* the picnic, which is to be on Saturday. Charlotte thinks that she may wear her best chemise gown and blue silk bonnet. Papa says that he is very pleased for us to have such diversions while you are away in London, Helena, and that it is very civil of Mrs Carty to take such an interest in providing these pleasures for Charlotte and myself. Tomorrow, it is Charlotte who will write to you and perhaps she will have a more detailed plan of the picnic which is to be an excursion to Averthorpe-on-Sea. Fanny's mama reckons it will take a bare hour in the coach, and if the weather keeps fine, Frank and Alfred may ride with us on horseback. We are so looking forward to this and will write accordingly, dear Sister. Meanwhile express our kind regards and those of Papa to Miss Malpass and Sophie.'

★ ★ ★

Helena had a feeling of the warmth and security of the innocent rectory life, almost like a breath of the fresh Wintham air as she read the letter and smiled to herself as she put it in her writing case. She would reply tomorrow and be able to feel even more in touch with her father and sisters regardless of the miles which divided them.

In spite of her slight apprehension at the idea of meeting Sir Thomas Capley, she was prepared to enjoy the evening. After all there was no possibility of avoiding it without causing comment from others. They would be in formal company and Helena vowed to herself that she would be at her most polite and not give him any cause for criticism. Moreover, she felt easy in her mind that Mr Stanley, who had been the man of business to her guardians, Mr and Mrs Henry Steer, would execute her wishes speedily and efficiently and she would be able to return to her family. Once Richard was away from the evil influences that surrounded him, she was sure he would settle happily back into country life and become a member of the landed gentry. Who knows? she thought, Papa could even use his influence to get Richard a place in his own college, where he might study to take Holy Orders. She knew this would be the dearest wish of her father's heart. Perhaps one day, she sighed inwardly.

But, just for now, she was determined to look forward to an enjoyable party. She had several smart evening gowns with her and was going to look her best for the occasion and present a cool and dignified exterior. She went through her wardrobe of dresses one by one, rejecting this one as being too dowdy and that one for being too fussily trimmed, until she'd finally made her choice of the perfect evening dress and matching slippers.

Aunt Malpass insisted that the two young women should lie on their day beds and relax for the afternoon so that they should be fresh for the evening to come. She herself continued to whip up cream desserts, check the candle sconces and see to the thousand and one preparations that a conscientious London hostess must take care of. Sophie and Helena laughingly complied with her orders. The two of them were both in high humour at the thought of the dinner party and happily read and chatted the afternoon away. They both had their hair in curl papers and had glycerine and rose water rubbed into their hands to help achieve the desired soft whiteness of the fashionable lady, and they were comfortably relaxed in their loose day gowns and soft slippers.

Once their evening clothes had been laid out, the two friends dismissed the maids and went into Sophie's bedroom to dress each other's hair with much giggling and laughing as though they were both schoolgirls again.

'Will you do my hair slightly higher at the back, Miss Steer?' requested Sophie handing her the curling tongs and sitting down in front of the mahogany dressing-table striking a pose.

'And would you prefer it dressed with a ribbon or combs, madam?' Helena asked with pretended subservience, laughing as her eyes met those of her friend in the mirror.

'Both, please, and with two tiers of ringlets falling from the crown at the back.' Sophie's dark glossy hair was soon arranged and Helena fixed both combs and ribbon among the ringlets. She was well pleased with the result but realized with a moment of truly feminine insight, that Sophie's glowing looks owed as much to the news of Jack's impending visit, as any beauty treatment from a lady's maid.

Her own golden hair was a shining mass of curls, framing her face and tumbling down her back.

'Well,' she said, still laughing, 'now it's your turn to be the abigail. I'd like a Grecian arrangement, Mrs Malpass, with some smaller tendrils escaping from below my embroidered ribbons, which have been specially purchased in London to enhance my evening hairstyle. My front hair in smaller loose curls if you please.'

Neither of them wore the white, sashed dresses which were almost a fashionable uniform for young women. Sophie had chosen a sophisticated gown of lilac gauze as befitted a married woman, and Helena herself had decided on her newest dress which absolutely suited her blonde beauty. Her perfect shoulders were entirely bare and showed to advantage in an extremely elegant gown of palest green. The fitted bodice subtly emphasized her curved bosom and the tiny puffed sleeves flattered her graceful arms. The fashionably high waist made her look even taller than usual and she carried it off to perfection. Sophie had dressed her shining locks into a style that added even more height and drew attention to her already graceful carriage extremely effectively.

When they were satisfied that they were looking their best, both young women stood in front of the mirror and pinched their cheeks to give a flattering glow and make their eyes seem brighter. Then, buttoning up the regulation long white gloves, they curtsied to each other with mock politeness and turned laughing, to leave the room.

Dinner, which was planned to suit London hours was to be at seven o' clock and as they descended the carved dark-wood staircase, some guests were already in the drawing-room and more were being admitted as they entered the front hall. Sophie was a little behind her and Helena looked up at her as they continued to exchange banter on the way down. She was the first person Tom saw as he handed his driving gloves and hat to the maid and shrugged himself out of his greatcoat. Her face was turned slightly away from him, revealing the back of her slender neck and the small dainty ears, with delicate wisps of spun gold hair curling into her nape. She was wearing emerald and diamond ear-rings, which made her eyes look even bluer and her bare neck, with no necklace or adornment of any kind, served only to draw attention to the white perfection of her shapely bosom.

Tom had never seen a more lovely creature. At the sight of her, he felt emotion strengthen and burn deep inside him as though he'd been pierced with a knife. Unbelievably strong feelings gripped him and he gave an involuntary frown as he stepped forward to greet the woman who was beginning to fascinate him, in spite of his disapproval of her. Her face was still alight with laughter over the joke she was sharing with Sophie as she reached the foot of the staircase. Then her eyes met his. He heard her take a deep breath, saw her eyes widen a little before she acknowledged his polite bow with a low-voiced greeting.

Helena was struck again by his air of

unconscious elegance and quiet physical strength. Just the sort of man she'd hoped Richard would become, she thought regretfully. But the frown was not lost on her. She raised her chin slightly and made a supreme effort to control her breathing even though she could do nothing about the rapid beating of her heart.

'Good evening, Miss Steer,' he greeted her courteously, his eyes glowing with reluctant admiration.

His voice was as deep as she remembered, but still with the slightly cold edge it had the last time they'd met, as he kissed her hand with polite formality. Their eyes met for what seemed to Helena, a long moment and he appeared reluctant to relinquish the dainty gloved hand, seeming to make the contact last as long as good manners would allow. Then, everyone was swept along by Miss Malpass's determined organization and he moved on to greet Sophie.

Helena found herself placed next to the aged Captain Rickerby, and opposite to Sir Thomas. On her left at the end of the table was the rather intense young clergyman, who kept darting devoted glances at his gentle little wife, seated further down on the other side of the captain.

Helena was soon engaged in quiet conversation with the amiable old widower, who was clearly delighted to be at the side of the most beautiful young lady in the room. She responded politely to him while giving encouraging nods and smiles to the anxious bridegroom on her left. At the same time she tried to tame the turbulent feelings still raging inside her. She felt the familiar tension of being physically close to the man who disapproved of her so violently, and a fresh wave of resentment swept over her as she remembered the masterful pressure of his lips on hers when he'd kissed her and the comforting feel of his strong arms when they'd danced together. She recognized that if she were honest, in different circumstances, she would have found him attractive. Not just attractive either, but positively enjoyable, exciting, blissful. Determinedly, she dismissed this brief voluptuous daydream and concentrated on her neighbour. The elderly widower kept up a practised stream of polite and affable small talk and Helena made pleasant and mechanical responses.

The general conversation was as thin and mannered as was usual at the start of a rather formal dinner party, but gradually things thawed out and the wine helped to make their exchanges more lively. The soup bowls were removed and the fish course was brought in. She risked a glance at Sir Thomas and was startled to find him staring frankly at her and with a look of almost intimidating intensity. It was hard to read his expression, made up as it was of admiration and fascinated absorption, masked somewhat by his dark brooding eyes and the harsh line of his mouth. He was neglecting to speak to either of the guests nearest to him and Helena had a feeling of such disquiet that she looked away hastily. Turning to the dazzled captain, she gave him her most encouraging smile and listened with flattering attention as he commented enthusiastically to the guests at large on the performance of Mrs Jordan as Rosalind in *As You Like It*, at Covent Garden.

'You must definitely try to attend before you leave Town, ladies,' he concluded.

'Yes, indeed,' chimed in a rather faded friend of Miss Malpass. 'Nothing could be better. She's wonderful dressed as a boy in yellow knee breeches and a feathered hat. Her legs and feet are small but perfectly formed, I do assure you, my dear.'

Helena's eyes danced with mischief at this and she tried to catch Sophie's eye, but she was too far down the table and instead, she found herself once more caught in Tom's rather sardonic gaze. His expression instantly softened into an altogether more amused one and for the first time they exchanged looks of more relaxed and open enjoyment. Then Tom saw a conversational opening and took advantage of it.

'I'm sure, it's indeed well worth a visit, sir,' he said to the captain, and then he spoke directly to Helena for the first time.

'Mrs Jordan is reckoned to be a fine comic actress and excels in dressing as a boy. She is perhaps a little stout now, but still very convincing in breeches. She is so pleasant and natural, so full of spirit and has a very shapely leg. She has also been painted by Romney in the role of *The Country Girl*, you know.'

For the second time, Helena was intrigued at the different facets to his character, which were revealed in his conversation. Who would have guessed that the rustic land owner in leather breeches and stout country boots could also be intellectually interested in the finer points of Mrs Jordan's dramatic roles?

'I hadn't thought to meet you in Town, Miss Steer,' he continued. 'I was sure you were quite the 'country girl' yourself and never to be contaminated by wicked city ways.'

Helena gazed directly at him, prepared to give him one of her famous set downs, but as she raised her eyes to his, she encountered this time, his open youthful smile, the eyes still dark, but dancing with light, sparkling with the anticipation of her impending retort. She realized in that split second that he was deliberately enticing her to a spirited reaction and one that would afford him entertainment and amusement.

Before she could make a suitable reply, the nervous clergyman spoke for the first time, with much hum-humphing and wiping of his thin lips on his napkin.

'So what does bring you to London, Miss Steer? Is it business, or the usual fripperies which seem to delight you young ladies?' and he looked down the table at his little bride, with the utmost fondness. The look not only expressed his absolute devotion to his wife, but the comfortable certainty that 'fripperies' of any kind didn't interest her.

'Well, a mixture, Mr Glover,' she smiled. 'I have some 'fripperies' as you call them very much in mind for my sisters, and some commissions for various of my neighbours. I have to buy a stock of tea from Twinings in the Strand for the housekeeper. Most importantly, I have managed to make contact with my dear brother, Richard, who has been lost to us these past three years.'

She was aware of Tom's utter absorption in what she was saying to the young clergyman and feeling rather angry with herself for her earlier more friendly thoughts, on a sudden impulse, she decided to play him a little further.

'Yes, I hope our dear brother will be accompanying me back to Wintham next Monday week, if all goes well,' she remarked provocatively. 'Sophie and I will also try to visit the theatre while we are in town. We would certainly like to enjoy Mrs Jordan's performance. It is judged to be her finest role yet. I have also heard good reports about the opera at the Haymarket Theatre. *Le Nozze Di Figaro* is deemed to be quite a triumph.'

The Reverend Glover blushed and dabbed his lips again, feeling he'd done his conversational duty, but he was totally out of his depth in discussing the niceties of theatrical or operatic roles and merely contented himself with smiling adoringly at his little wife.

Tom, however, continued to keep his eyes very disconcertingly on Helena's face. She was determined to pretend not to notice his fixated gaze and turned to make conversation with the Captain. 'And you, sir, are you a devotee of the theatre, as most of London society appears to be?'

Before the good captain had an opportunity to reply, Tom spoke in a low voice, directly to Helena and Captain Rickerby turned tactfully instead to the clergyman's young bride and continued with his stock of small talk as though nothing had happened.

'And is your brother the Richard you intended to meet in Capley Woods, Miss Steer?'

'The same, sir,' she said coldly. 'And later, in Bentick barn. I had not thought on either of these occasions to cause any trespass, Sir Thomas.'

'Am I right in thinking that at each meeting, a third party kept the tryst?' he probed, his eyes still searching hers.

'Yes, that is so, the Honourable Percy Davenport,' she answered, not prepared to give any more details to this insufferable man.

But he was not to be deflected and continued pressing. 'And are you and your family then personally acquainted with this Davenport?'

'Slightly, through friends of my brother,' she said, dismissively, and turned very pointedly to resume her conversation with the young clergyman.

'I understand you are to be congratulated on your recent marriage as well as your appointment to St Mary's?' she said very affably to the Reverend Glover.

'Yes indeed,' he said. 'It's a very acceptable

living and dear Augusta is the best of wives.' Once more he gazed fondly down at his beloved who was shyly listening in to Sophie's lively chat with her brother George and several of their aunt's friends.

Far from being cast down by his latest rejection from Helena, George seemed to be in cracking form and was entertaining the group with an account of a first-class competition between some of the young bloods of his acquaintance who were to race against each other in a Gentlemen's Horse Racing Event at Bath next month. He himself intended to put money on Sir Marcus Tetley's horse, Bucephalus, as well as his own mount, Whirlwind. His Highness the Prince Regent himself, was to present the prize to the winner.

'I will take my oath,' he said enthusiastically, 'that Whirlwind has a good chance of being champion and Bucephalus not far behind and I'll warrant the prize money will not be contemptible, with H.R.H. in attendance.'

Once again, Helena was struck by the apparent detachment of the young man who had been professing to be dying of love for her and desperate for her hand in marriage, for the last few years. George seemed not to have a care in the world and certainly gave no impression of the unrequited passion for herself that he was always urging whenever they met.

Tom, meanwhile, was now politely but firmly excluded from Helena's conversational circle. She didn't even glance at him and resolutely refused to address any further remarks to him, so he had to content himself with listening to the conversation of his rather boring neighbours. He responded mechanically while gazing at the glowing beauty of the woman opposite. Her treatment of him merely served to add fuel to the fire of his passion and made him even more determined to find out the truth of her secret assignations in his woods. He desperately wished to find some innocuous explanation for her apparent involvement with the dastardly Davenport and chafed impatiently for another conversational opening.

The dessert covers were laid and afterwards, Miss Malpass led the ladies to the drawing-room to drink tea while the gentlemen remained in the dining-room to enjoy their port and claret.

When finally they emerged, Augusta Glover had agreed to sing and Sophie was pressed to accompany her. She turned out to have a surprisingly rich and melodious soprano voice for such a shy little mouse and chose as her first song, 'Porgi amor', from *The Marriage of Figaro*. Sophie's accompaniment was typically competent, straightforward and without sentimentality, as she sat down good-humouredly at the pianoforte in front of the assembled guests.

Tom made a point of sitting near to Helena and under cover of the music and in spite of her stiff response, tried to continue their conversation.

'I feel I must beg your forgiveness, Miss Steer,' he whispered, while the audience was applauding Augusta's first song. He leaned slightly forward towards her gazing so intently at her that she could see the golden flecks in his brown eyes.

'For what, sir?'

'Why, for my abominable behaviour and ignoble assumptions about your character.'

'A natural enough mistake I suppose, given the circumstances. I have no interest in either your assumptions or apologies, sir,' she hissed, under cover of the music.

Tom swallowed and began again. 'I beg you to accept my profound apologies for — '

'For what? For daring to think that I had an assignation in your barn? I am afraid the notes requesting meetings with my brother Richard, were just a ruse to get me to meet with his friend who's an unscrupulous rake and villain and has no real feelings for him.'

She was determined not to meet him halfway, but to keep up her cold politeness at all costs. Augusta's second song was another Mozartian piece, a simple arietta from *La Clemenza Di Tito*. She was in very good voice and when it came to an end there was further enthusiastic applause, to her young husband's obvious gratification, but she blushingly refused to try a third one. Some of the guests were preparing to play cards, but most of them were chatting politely to each other. Tom made no move to join another group. Instead he pursued their conversation where Helena had left it, asking questions about Richard's relationship with Percy Davenport.

'I know the gentleman, by reputation,' he volunteered, 'and indeed, met him on two occasions.' His eyes glittered a little as he remembered the bout of fisticuffs he'd had with Davenport. 'I'll wager that you're right in thinking he is no true friend of your brother. He's not the sort of young blood who is content to enjoy kicking up a lark; he is a well known and dangerous gambler who is frequently at the card tables all night.'

This confirmed Helena's own worst fears, and seduced in spite of herself by his unexpected warmth, was almost tempted to confide in him and then she became cross with herself. She gave herself a mental scolding at the idea of confiding in the man who had first seemed to do everything possible to alienate her and now was being unexpectedly conciliatory.

She said impatiently, 'I visited Richard at his squalid lodgings today and cannot bear to burden my father with the anxieties I feel about him. I wish I were a man and could move more freely in London. I'm sure I would be able to effect a proper rescue of my brother!'

She ended on a note of extreme agitation, her bosom heaving and her eyes bright with unshed tears. Tom looked at her, frowning with the intense stare that she found so utterly disagreeable.

'Miss Steer, please calm yourself,' he said. 'I have done you a grave injustice. Perhaps you would permit me to put it right and offer some support to your brother at the same time?'

Her eyes flashed and colour flooded her cheeks as she answered, 'No, I thank you, but I am not in need of assistance in this.'

She looked back at him defiantly and noticed a pulse begin to pound in his temple as he drew a deep breath.

'Miss Steer,' he said savagely, 'I would be

grateful if you will stop ripping up old scores and throwing your grievances in my face. I have apologized for my mistake and if I choose to go to your brother's aid, it is quite my own concern.'

This time Helena gave a scowl so ferocious, that she caught him in her angry blue glare like a fly in a spider's web. 'Oh, but it is not,' she hissed furiously, and she clasped her hands to her bosom, vibrant with repressed rage, her firm young arms tense with the strain and her eyes dark with passion. At that moment, Helena was in the mood to refuse him, even if he'd promised her the world in a Bond Street band box.

He said no more except, 'Perhaps we should make an opportunity to discuss this further.'

Before she had time to tell him that there was nothing to discuss, Helena became aware that George Arnold was approaching, determined to press Tom into a game of whist and she excused herself instead and went to congratulate Augusta on her singing. There was a general circulation as different individuals moved to other groups, gossip and news was exchanged and more tea was drunk by some of the elderly ladies, until it was time for the carriages.

Tom made a point of coming over to

Helena and Sophie to bid them farewell and issued a generous invitation to them which it would seem churlish of Helena to refuse while her friend was present.

Bowing over each of them in turn, he said, 'May I be permitted to escort you both to the theatre for *As You Like It* on Friday next? If your aunt is agreeable, Mrs Malpass, I have a private box at our disposal.'

Sophie's aunt was more than agreeable, she was positively encouraging, and before he took his leave, it was planned that he would send round his own carriage for them at six o'clock on Friday evening.

Both Helena and Sophie were quiet after the guests had departed, but before bedtime, Helena confided briefly in her friend about Richard's situation, although she didn't mention Tom's offer of help.

Sophie tactfully skated round the proposed theatre visit, merely saying, 'It should be a diverting evening, Helena, but nothing is as important as the problem of Richard. I pray God that it can be resolved so you can be easy in your mind.'

Miss Malpass said that she wouldn't go with them as she had already seen the play. 'But you two young things may chaperon each other,' she twinkled. 'And no doubt make some eyes green, back home in Wintham.'

6

As she sat up in bed luxuriously sipping her early morning chocolate, Helena had much to think about. She went over again the events of the supper party and Tom's offer to help her. She realized it was important to remain in charge of her emotions as far as Sir Thomas Capley was concerned, otherwise she might be in danger of giving way to a personality that was as determined and dominant as her own, one which was strong enough to engulf her. That would never do. No man had ever go the better of Helena Steer and she supposed that unless she were deeply smitten, no man ever would. She smiled to herself as she indulgently licked the last little bit of chocolate from the spoon. His apology had been more than handsome and the offer of help was delivered with patent sincerity. It was obviously provoking for him that she had refused, but she felt she owed him a little provocation in view of his prejudiced presumptions about her character and reputation. Then she was left wondering about the invitation to the theatre and where the evening would lead.

But her first duty this morning must be to visit Mr Stanley's offices in Cheapside and arrange for money to be available for her brother, so that his bills could be bought back. She had been obliged to confide in the other two women about her plan to rescue Richard and Miss Malpass had placed the carriage at her disposal. The three of them decided to make this visit to the lawyer their morning excursion. Miss Malpass and Sophie would accompany her in the carriage as far as Ludgate Hill and they would all meet in the Strand coffee house in the early afternoon. Miss Malpass and Sophie would then change their library books at the subscription library, while Helena completed her business with Mr Stanley and the coachman would wait for her. Taking leave of her friends, Helena proceeded to Cheapside and leaving Rose outside in the carriage, she climbed the steps to the lawyer's chambers and knocked at the door.

Josiah Stanley was surrounded by scrolls of paper and his desk was a mass of discarded pens and stubs of sealing wax. Both his face and fingers were a shiny pink colour as though polished with the same wax, and he seemed not to notice anything except the dusty documents which surrounded him. But he was as gentlemanlike and deferential as always, in his dingy black jacket and old-fashioned wig.

'And how may I be of service to you, Miss Steer?' he asked politely, once the pleasantries and greetings had been exchanged.

'Well, I have been able to contact my brother Richard, at last. As you know, he's been estranged from his family and friends these three years, much to our anxiety and regret. I have discovered that he has considerable debts, and would wish to acquire the bills for these and redeem him from his financial difficulties.'

Mr Stanley's expression was one of shock and horror at these confident words coming from the lips of a mere young lady. His smooth pink fingers trembled a little with agitation as he put on a pair of glasses. He gave her a severe look out of his watery old eyes and at first, didn't reply. Helena was aware that kind and avuncular though he was, Mr Stanley was disapproving of women taking any part in business. They should be gentle creatures, concerned with sewing, music and other domestic arts. The idea of a twenty something heiress of independent spirit, set free to engage in any kind of monetary arrangements was anathema to his old-fashioned soul. He looked down and shuffled his papers uneasily.

'My dear young lady, have you not

confided in your papa, asked for his advice, sought permission before pledging any part of your financial inheritance in discharging your brother's debts?'

'My father is not well, sir,' Helena said smoothly. 'It is his dearest wish to be reconciled with my brother before it is too late. Due to the generosity of my late uncle and aunt, I am an independent woman. The fortune my guardians left me is my own, to dispose of as I will. My hope is that I may pay Richard's debts and persuade him to return home.'

'But only think, my dear child, once having effected this redemption of your brother's bills, would it not be the case that further debts would be laid at your door and thus introduce a precedent from which you could not escape?'

'Certainly not,' she replied firmly. 'My expectation is that once Richard is free of his creditors and the bad influence of his unsuitable companions, he will return home and lead a more balanced life. As my man of business, Mr Stanley, I expect you to expedite this matter with the utmost urgency. It needs to be settled before I leave London on Monday week. My brother's health and happiness are involved, as is also the well-being of my dear papa.'

Mr Stanley sighed. Helena could see that he thought her much too forthright for a woman. She knew his own daughters were very conventional and biddable young women who would one day exchange their dependence on their papa to dependence on their respective husbands. No pretensions of financial independence for them and they would certainly not be unwed at four and twenty.

She waited for him to reply and he said, 'Very well, Miss Steer. I will, of course, execute your wishes and make available such monies as you require. I hope to arrange it before you return to Wintham.'

He pursed his lips and rearranged his papers once more. Then the old-fashioned gentleman in him came to the surface and he rose courteously to open the door for her, giving his kind regards to her father and sisters. So the pair parted amicably. Helena was content with the way the meeting had gone and on an impulse, directed the coach driver to call at 35 Pegasus Mansions. Leaving Rose and the groom to wait outside, she climbed the stairs to her brother's dingy room and tapped at the door. There was no reply and she pushed it open.

The room was as sordid as ever, but the difference was that it was eerily cold and quite deserted. There was no trace of the occupant, except for a few dusty bottles and empty glasses. The shabby clothes, bedding, chairs and cushions stood like bleak monuments to Richard's unhappy life, but the owner himself had disappeared. A solitary wax-encrusted bed candle remained in its sconce. There was an unhealthy chill in the room which contrasted oddly with the mild autumn day outside. Helena looked round helplessly, taking in the desolation of the untidy room, at a loss to know what to make of the empty silence.

There was a rustle behind her and she turned.

'Is that you, Richard?' The door opened fully and Helena saw a bent, wizened old man of indeterminate age and wearing a very long ragged overcoat. His head was bare and his gnarled hands held a shabby carpet-bag.

'Begin' pardon, ma'am,' he said softly. 'I ain't Mr Richard, ma'am. No. Name o' Snape, ma'am. Residing at number thirty-seven. Just going out to purchase a small loaf of bread. Mr R. ain't here, just now, on account he's gone orf with a very fine gent indeed.'

Helena was startled. 'And would that be the Honourable Percy Davenport?' she asked.

'The same, ma'am.'

Mr Snape shifted his carpet bag into the other hand uneasily and shuffled his feet.

'And do you know where my br — , Mr Richard is now?'

'No, but I opine that both gentlemen may be visiting Mr Jonah Rudd who is well known to the inhabitants of the Mansions, my lady.'

'And where may this gentleman, Jonah Rudd be found?'

'Chesterfield House, end of Chesterfield street, south of Mayfair, ma'am,' he said promptly. Then he sighed and looked at her dolefully.

'An evil man, lady. All of us in the Mansions are in thrall to Jonah Rudd. There's no escape. None can become freed men here. We're doomed, you see, ma'am,' he intoned hopelessly. 'Especially young Richard. I know for a fact he's being dunned by his boot maker and there's Mrs Bell needs paying. She comes Fridays' he explained, 'on account of her husband's the butcher and she tries to get summat out of him to pay off his account. I tell you we're doomed,' he said again.

'That remains to be seen, Mr Snape,' Helena said rather tartly. 'What time do you think he may return?'

'Why as to that, ma'am, it depends on how things goes with Jonah Rudd. Some of 'em is miserable after an encounter with him like,

151

and goes to lie down. Others' — he gestured, lifting a glass to his lips — 'is inclined to celebrate, ma'am. Has a few drinks like and gets merry. It all depends,' he said sadly.

He looked so mournful that Helena reached into her reticule and pressed a few coins into Mr Snape's hand.

'Please buy some bread and provisions, sir,' she said. 'I'll call another time to seek out my brother.'

Mr Snape almost snatched the money and muttering his thanks, melted away as fast as he'd appeared, so Helena went back to the carriage and made her way to the Strand to meet Sophie and Maria Malpass.

They'd had a successful morning and were both in good spirits. If Helena seemed slightly withdrawn, they appeared not to notice. All the talk was about the theatre visit and it was decided they would dine early. Aunt Malpass was adamant that Sir Thomas Capley should be invited to stay for a light supper after the performance. She herself was determined to stay up to join them.

'I shall rest for a while in the afternoon, for I'm going to wait on your return,' she said firmly. 'There are few pleasures left to a lady of my advanced years,' she twinkled. 'And I do so enjoy the company of a handsome young man.'

Helena felt a familiar sensation of both excitement and antagonism at the thought of meeting Tom again, but went to change into an evening dress of delicate white muslin, with layers of exquisite Bruges lace round the hem. She sat in front of her mirror and submitted patiently as her maid brushed and arranged every burnished gold curl of her shining hair, then scooped up one side and fixed it firmly with a silk rose.

'Oh, Miss Helena, you look so beautiful,' Rose told her, as they both studied her reflection in the glass.

Even Helena, used as she was to the great gift of her own beauty, was forced to agree. She wondered what her escort would think of her and her cheeks went suddenly pink at the thought that she would be with him so soon.

By the time he arrived in his carriage, both she and Sophie were keyed up at the prospect of the evening to come. Conversation was a little stilted to begin with, but Sophie's natural gaiety and friendliness soon set the mood of relaxed enjoyment and in no time at all Helena felt a little more at ease.

When they arrived at the theatre, they had to wait in a queue of carriages and there was already quite a crowd of theatregoers outside. At the corners of the nearest streets were posters on billboards and notices of the play advertising the names of the leading lady and the rest of the cast in *As You Like It*, by William Shakespeare. The evening was a mild one and people in the street seemed hot and perspiring. Men wiped damp foreheads with large handkerchiefs and now and then a soft breeze blew gently, disturbing ladies' curls and causing the edges of shop awnings to stir slightly.

As they left the coach, both Helena and Sophie felt the impact of this almost sultry heat and were glad to have their fans with them as they were escorted to Tom's private box. Helena's heart began to beat a little faster and she smiled with pleasure as they mounted the stairs to the reserved seats, while the rest of the crowd surged along the corridor to the stalls. Tom opened the tapestry doors at the rear of the box and as soon as they were seated, Helena leaned forward with undisguised delight and surveyed the scene below.

The theatre was beginning to fill, opera glasses were taken out of their cases and many of the ladies and gentlemen bowed smilingly when they caught sight of people they knew. Helena could see one or two shiny bald heads in the audience below her as the elderly gentlemen settled down quietly in their seats. There were, however, several dandies strutting about in the pit and showing off their exquisitely tied cravats and fashionable clothes, eager to see and be seen. She turned impulsively to Tom, surprised at the number of people who were paying close attention to their party.

'It seems we're under scrutiny from the *ton*, tonight,' she said. 'I wonder if our presence will be reported in the broadsheets?'

'Some part of the audience always comes to see the celebrities rather than the play,' Tom said, enchanted by her obvious excitement.

He and Helena noticed several couples who were making it clear by their stares and raised quizzing glasses how avid they were to know who were the two young ladies sharing a box with Sir Thomas Capley.

Then there was a hush as the curtain rose on the orchard scene and the play began in earnest. Helena felt herself transported to her youth when, as a young girl, she had been allowed unlimited access to her guardian's library and had spent many happy hours reading whatever she had a mind to. Now, of course, she was enjoying the visual impact of what before, she could only imagine. She leaned forward in her seat, feeling that she hadn't enough eyes to drink in every aspect of the play; the scenery, painted trees, the actors and costumes. Her remembrance of reading the play helped her to understand the action and she gave herself up to its magic as though totally unconscious of Tom's presence behind her.

Tom's own enjoyment was almost entirely in watching Helena. Her pleasure and absorption were more gratifying to him than a hundred performances by the famous Mrs Jordan. Helena's beauty and nearness entranced him and he forgot the play in his delight at being so close to her, so that it was almost a sorrow for him when the curtain came down on Act Three. The smell of the wax candles mingled with the breath of so many people on such a warm evening, made the air almost suffocating. Only the movement of the ladies' fans gave a little coolness and it was a relief to open the doors of the box. A few people were known by sight to the gregarious Sophie and during the interval, when Tom had ordered iced champagne punch, she discreetly excused herself to go and renew her acquaintance with them, leaving Tom and Helena alone.

The situation offered many opportunities for respectable intimacy. Although in full public view, they were at the same time, secure in the privacy of the theatre box. Helena leaned back in her seat sipping her champagne with a luxurious sigh and letting the cold liquid soothe her throat. She felt her senses slide as she gave herself up to the voluptuous pleasure of the moment and the enjoyment of the wine.

She reflected that, now that they were alone in the midst of a crowd of people, she felt strangely diffident in dealing with him. She was gradually beginning to relinquish her idea of him as a relentless critic bent on reading the worst possible motives into her every action but she did recognize him as a strong character, as self-reliant and enterprising as she was herself. She knew that he could be an implacable enemy and a formidable and dominant adversary, but she recognized that he had other facets to his personality.

As though reading her thoughts, he said softly, 'Have you been able to make contact with your brother?'

His concern was obvious and relaxed by the wine, she raised her head a little to look into his deep eyes and confided more than she intended. She told him of her last visit to Pegasus Mansions and her encounter with Mr Snape.

'And so you think your brother is impossibly entangled with the moneylenders?' he said at last.

'I don't doubt it, sir, and I'm sure he's in danger on that account.'

Tom, looking into her troubled eyes picked up her hand and stroked her fingertips with his lips as though trying to brush away her anxieties over her brother.

'My name is Tom,' he suggested quietly. 'Please allow me to support you in this. I would consider it an honour if you would let me visit Jonah Rudd on your behalf and help your brother out of this tangle. May I, Miss Steer?'

For the first time, Helena felt an awkward sense of self-doubt and indecision. One half of her wanted to retain the independence of spirit and action which had been hers for the past few years, but she also had to acknowledge that she was mad with worry about Richard and that it would be comforting to have such a capable supporter on her side. She drew back a little and gave him a questioning look.

Nothing like this had ever happened to her before. She had always prided herself on being so strong and self sufficient, never having to consider male assistance in any part of her life. This was yet another aspect of the insufferably determined Sir Thomas Capley and yet his deep voice was so soft and oddly enticing. She responded more gently than she intended.

'You're most kind, sir, but please don't press me on this. I prefer to act independently.'

His shapely lips tightened with disappointment and chagrin and he let go of her hand abruptly.

'It would be my greatest pleasure,' he said stiffly. 'And my name is Tom,' he reminded her again. People in the audience now began to take leave of their friends and stroll back to their seats and as Sophie stepped into the box, they moved further apart to watch the remainder of the play.

Aunt Malpass awaited them, all smiles of welcome when they returned to the Villa Alba and, as they entered the hall, said that three more of her friends were calling by for supper, so the dining table was set for six. The cook had prepared various cold collations as well as a whole salmon and braised pigeons with a tray of cheeses to follow. Aunt Malpass herself had seen to it that there were various light trifles and fresh fruits prepared. It promised to be a very enjoyable occasion as they all took their places in the dining-room.

Because there were only two gentlemen, Helena found herself opposite Tom and next to Sophie and in spite of her feelings of constraint towards him, the conversation seemed to flow effortlessly enough. The wine was full-bodied and mellow and the butler poured it freely because this evening, the gentlemen were not going to linger in the dining-room after supper.

Helena relaxed and forgot her problems over Richard. She discovered that Tom was quietly entertaining with a slightly ironic and oblique wit which kept the company laughing throughout the meal. Sophie, as always, was full of life and sparkle and her aunt listened appreciatively to her niece's wickedly amusing tales of her youth in Wintham. Aunt Malpass was obviously enjoying herself hugely. Although a maiden lady of mature years, she hadn't forgotten what it was like to have once been young herself. What she was enjoying most this evening, deep in the romantic soul of her, was the almost palpable tension between these two handsome young people. The fact that they seemed almost completely unaware of what was happening to them and continued to show almost open hostility while having to observe all the social conventions, gave an added edge to her pleasure. As for herself, Helena was content to eat her supper and sip her wine, while refusing to make any concessions to Tom's presence and his obvious admiration. With their healthy young appetites they did more than justice to the supper and both of them looked in such radiant good health, Maria Malpass was almost dazzled.

It seemed all too soon that the table was cleared and the elderly trio took their leave. Tom appeared to be in no mood to depart and moved with the ladies to the drawing-room, where he and Helena lingered over a folio of prints that Miss Malpass had produced for him to look at.

Absorbed in the pictures, Helena didn't notice Sophie's departure upstairs and then later, Miss Malpass said, 'Excuse me my dears, I must go to the kitchen and speak with Cook.'

Suddenly they were left alone. Tom was showing her the delicate hand-coloured etchings of 'Early American Cities'. He had regaled the company with stories of some of great Uncle Silas's more respectable exploits in Jamaica and later in America, and Miss Malpass had remembered these pictures which she'd had from a dealer.

Helena looked up at him as he returned a view of 'Philadelphia from Belmont Hill', to its folder and turned towards her. It seemed perfectly natural to lift her face towards his at the exact moment that his mouth moved to cover hers.

At the first contact, Helena felt such an

exquisite pleasure that it was almost painful. It was a kiss that was so passionate and demanding and yet so deep and loving, quite different from the last one he had given her in Bentick barn. Her pulse was racing and her throat was dry as her lips parted softly under his own. He clasped her firm young body so tightly that she could feel her heart pounding against his as she let her head fall backwards and pressed herself even closer against him. Her arms slid upwards round his neck as though they had a life of their own. At first his lips had felt cool and firm, almost like a young boy's, but they swelled and softened as they roamed around her mouth. She felt the warm masculinity of his body as he pulled her to him and held her for a long moment before stroking her lips gently once more and letting her go. Both of them struggled to control their hurried breathing, as they heard a warning cough and the sound of Miss Malpass's feet on the hall floor before she re-entered the drawing-room.

They sprang apart and Helena retreated to the sofa table to replace the print collection in its folder with slightly trembling hands. Tom stood where he was as if turned to stone, his hands by his sides.

Glancing from one to the other, Miss Malpass said calmly, 'There, that's settled, my dears, and what a very fine evening we've had. Such gracious friends and kindly companions,' she went on, as though she'd noticed nothing.

She seemed to be in an unaccountably good mood and was worldly wise enough to recognize what had happened while she was out of the room. There was a distinct air of tension between Tom and Helena. Throughout the evening, every movement, every glance, had seemed to spell out the attraction that they felt for each other. Lavinia Capley was one of her oldest friends. She was delighted to think that Tom might have found love at last. She had grown fond of Helena in the last few days and was sure that this particular love match was bound to succeed.

Tom had now collected himself together. He bowed over the older woman's hand.

'I think I must now take my leave, Miss Malpass,' he said pleasantly. 'Many thanks for your kind hospitality.'

He was so obviously unwilling to leave Helena, that Miss Malpass smiled with satisfaction at his reluctance to go. It did seem hard to say goodnight when they were such soul mates, she thought.

But aloud she said, 'Why, goodnight, Tom. Let us hope we may meet again soon.'

As the door closed behind him, Helena was

already making her way slowly up to bed, feeling suddenly drained by the evening's events and the strong emotions he had raised in her and Rose made a silent note of her mistress's weary movements and the unaccountable heat of the beautiful bent head as she gently brushed out Helena's hair.

As for Helena, she was perceptive enough to recognize in Tom a strength of will which was equal, if not stronger than her own. Before drifting off into sleep, Helena finally acknowledged to herself that the unthinkable had happened: for the first time in her life, the independent and spirited Miss Helena Steer seemed to be falling in love.

7

Even Helena didn't appreciate just how single minded and determined Tom could be. As a first step he was eager to apply himself to the task of interviewing Mr Jonah Rudd and the following day ordered the horses to be ready promptly for his visit to Chesterfield Street. Travelling in his phaeton through the early morning streets of London his thoughts were all of Helena and he reflected on a poem he had read recently by Mr William Wordsworth. The lines:

'This City now doth like a garment wear
The beauty of the morning: silent, bare,'

came unbidden into his mind and exactly suited his feelings of quiet joy at the way Helena had responded to his kisses at the Villa Alba. His heart still pounded at the memory of holding her in his arms, at the sweetness of her lips under his own and the trembling of her mouth and body as she'd artlessly pressed herself against him. At last, he dared hope that she might like him, and at this thought he was suddenly elated. He was convinced that on a beautiful September morning like this, with the sun making everything look so clean and new, even in the grimy City, a man could hope for anything. He was sure that he would be forgiven for going against Helena's express wishes in the matter of her brother, as soon as he had settled the problem of Jonah Rudd once for all.

Leaving the groom to mind his horses, he strode up to the imposing front door of Chesterfield House.

Not for Jonah Rudd the sordid squalor of Pegasus Mansions or the dusty Cheapside offices of Mr Stanley. Chesterfield House was a pleasant Georgian mansion, part of a well ordered scheme in a distinguished part of town. The elegant stone façade with its classical lines and sash windows proclaimed the immense wealth, influence and power of its evil owner and bore silent testimony to his lucrative trade in human servitude.

Tom rapped firmly on the panelled front door and, having presented his card, was almost immediately admitted by a clerk and taken along the rather gloomy hall and up the staircase. The small landing was dominated by a large ornate clock, whose gilded face shone in the dim light and whose harsh metallic tick seemed to echo through the whole building. In spite of his elegant and luxurious surroundings, he was aware of an almost indefinable atmosphere of misery and degradation, quite at odds with the elegance of the house. The clerk ushered him into a small outer office, bowed stiffly and then disappeared.

Left to wait for Rudd, Tom walked towards the imposing fireplace and stared down into the empty grate, listening to the inexorable ticking of the landing clock. He wondered what Helena was doing. Was she awake? Writing letters? Sewing? Out taking the air with her friend and Miss Malpass? Apart from his grandmother, Tom had little experience of what ladies did in their daily lives. His joy would be to find out at first hand. If Helena would only accept him as a husband, he thought, it would be a delight to share all her waking hours for the rest of their lives. As he stood with his elbow resting on the mantelpiece lost in his thoughts, he gradually became aware of something disturbing the dignified quiet of the money-lender's chambers. The sound of dreadful wrenching sobs, of a grown man weeping uncontrollably. On an impulse, he stepped into the room beyond and took in the scene in the clerk's office.

A common workman in dust-stained

clothes, crouched on a wooden bench, his head buried in his hands while Mr Rudd's assistant lolled behind a desk, picking at his nails with the end of a quill pen. As Tom opened the door, the clerk turned to glare at him but the despairing client never even glanced up.

'Sir,' said the clerk. 'This is a private office. You are intruding I'm afraid, sir.'

Although his tone was soft, almost servile, he stood up from behind the desk in a very threatening manner.

Tom ignored him and addressed the wretched man whose head was still bowed in utter desolation.

'Tell me your trouble,' he said to him simply, but before the man could reply, the clerk intervened once more.

'My client's problems are his own, sir,' he said suavely. 'And this is a private office. Please give us some privacy if you wouldn't mind.'

'First,' said Tom, 'is your name Jonah Rudd?'

'No, it is not, but I'm employed by Mr Rudd.'

'In that case, please sit down again while I find out what is troubling this poor fellow here.'

Looking into those pale, pitiless eyes, Tom

was suddenly overwhelmed with cold fury and taking hold of the clerk's immaculate cravat, he pressed him forcibly into the chair. Red-faced, the clerk opened his mouth as though to speak, but then immediately closed it again.

Tom turned to the unfortunate workman once more and said quietly, 'Please tell me, what is your trouble?'

The man wiped the back of his hand across his eyes. 'Oh sir,' he said wearily, 'it's my poor wife. She's been ill this year and more and now she's dying. I borrowed thirty pounds to buy medicines for her and to pay a woman to mind the children. I scraped and slaved and worked day and night to pay the money back with the interest, but now they tell me it must be another three pounds. And my wife dying. Dying. I can't do no more, sir.' He covered his eyes again.

Even as Tom stood, appalled by the man's abject misery, a tall, slender figure appeared silently in the doorway.

'What is it? What's happening here?' he asked, in an icy voice.

Tom saw a man with a curiously mask-like face, dressed in smart but sombre clothes with a large solitary diamond on one of his long fingers. His silver hair was thin but beautifully cut and arranged, his slender hands white and perfectly manicured.

'Are you Jonah Rudd?' Tom asked him.

'The same, sir. And you are?'

'Sir Thomas Capley.'

'Please step this way, Sir Thomas. We may conduct your business in private.'

'But first,' said Tom politely, 'I need you to sign this gentleman's papers,' and he opened his purse. 'I would like to settle his debt.'

'Oh, I see,' said Rudd after a pause. 'Certainly, Sir Thomas. Although, my clerk usually attends to that quality of person,' he said, with a twist of his thin lips.

He saw the thunderous expression on Tom's face and continued smoothly, 'I'll sign the receipt personally, sir.'

Tom gave the precious paper into the workman's eager hand. 'Hurry home to your wife,' he said, brushing away the man's incoherent thanks. 'And here, buy something for your family. Go, man,' he said, and turned back to Jonah Rudd.

'So nice to meet with open gratitude,' murmured Mr Rudd silkily, as the man rushed from the room still gasping out his thanks. 'And now, step this way and tell me what I can do for you.'

Tom followed him into his private office and Jonah Rudd seated himself behind the mahogany desk, his sensitive white fingers playing with a long silver paper-knife whose gleaming, pointed blade shone in the sunlight casting rainbow reflections around the room.

'I'm here on behalf of a gentleman whose debts I have undertaken to liquidate.'

'Indeed?' said Rudd, his fingers suddenly stilled. 'And may I know the name of this gentleman?'

'His name is Richard Steer,' Tom replied. 'Acting on behalf of his family, I desire to pay whatever he owes in both principal and interest accrued, immediately.'

'This isn't possible,' Rudd answered softly.

Tom pressed on, 'I understand that his liabilities are in the region of three thousand pounds, but if you tell me the exact amount I will make up whatever is owing.'

'Impossible, sir. I make it a rule never to discuss my clients' debts with a third party.'

'Then you refuse to say how much he owes?'

'It is quite impossible.'

They stared at each other for some moments, then Tom said, 'Suppose I were to offer twice that sum? Suppose I were to double it to six thousand pounds?'

There was another silence as Jonah Rudd once more fidgeted with the knife. 'Impossible. I cannot,' he said at last.

'Very well,' said Tom. 'I'll treble it. Nine

thousand pounds.'

Jonah Rudd gazed straight ahead. His face was ashen. Sweat beaded his brow and he let out his breath in a long sigh. He shook his head.

'Impossible,' he again intoned, hopelessly.

Tom's anger now surfaced almost out of control. 'I came here to redeem those bills,' he growled. 'If my offer isn't enough, name your price, Mr Rudd.'

But Jonah Rudd remained silent, almost deathly in his stillness, while the two men stared at each other.

Tom was aroused by the clerk's hand on his elbow.

'Don't you see, sir?' he said, indicating the still silent Rudd. 'You've made him an offer no man could refuse. And he's refused you. He can't redeem them: they're not his!'

'What? Then whose are they?' demanded Tom harshly. 'Tell me in God's name,' he appealed to Rudd.

But Jonah Rudd merely closed his eyes and then covered them with one twitching white hand and the clerk led Tom, stunned and unprotesting, to the door.

The next day was Sunday and Tom knew that Helena and Sophie would be at church with Miss Malpass in the morning. He hesitated about going back to Helena when he had nothing of any note to report about her brother, but he guessed that Maria Malpass would be receiving visitors as was her usual habit in the afternoon and decided to call anyway.

Still in a black mood after his interview with the moneylender, he felt the need to see Helena again, to drink in her beauty and enjoy the bitter-sweet pleasure of being so close to her and yet so far. Last night he had found it almost impossible to draw back and bring their kisses to an end. Before his inheritance from Uncle Silas, he had of necessity, been obliged to stifle such urges. Eligible young ladies of the *ton* had been denied him because of his circumstances. The occasional London cyprian or bit of muslin had only ever satisfied him on a shallow level, but now all his hopes and dreams of a happy future were embodied in this one woman, Helena. Could there be a more beautiful or perfect creature in all the world? he asked himself, but he recognized that she would never say 'yes' to anything until her brother's difficulties were resolved and this could take time. He would have to work hard at procuring her happiness and contentment, before he could even begin to consider his own feelings. It was paramount to find out Richard's real creditor and rid him of the loan sharks and get him to return home. Only then would he have any chance of marrying her. He frowned as he entered his carriage. One thing was certain, he was going to do his utmost to woo and win Helena Steer.

His mood lifted gradually at the thought of seeing her again, even though they'd be in company and it would not be possible for them to be alone.

The Villa Alba was positively buzzing with guests by the time Tom arrived and presented his card. As he relinquished his greatcoat and cane to the butler, he heard at least one voice he recognized. George Arnold had called to see his sister and aunt and was enjoying a joke with Captain Rickerby whom Tom had met at the dinner party.

'And how are your sisters, Miss Steer?' the captain was asking Helena.

'Well, sir. I thank you. And my father also,' she replied. 'I received a letter from Charlotte today and both the girls are housekeeping at the rectory as to the manner born. Nor are they forgetting their social obligations. They have issued an invitation to our good friends, the Radfords, and have planned a supper party with entertainment.'

Helena smiled fondly at the activities of her young sisters and expressed with her eyes, the love and affection she felt for them as she told him how much she missed them already. In fact, Helena was looking forward impatiently to being back at the rectory again.

Entering the drawing-room, Tom's eyes immediately sought hers. She was listening smilingly to George and Captain Rickerby. Tom thought she seemed even more beautiful than he remembered her, in a soft turquoise muslin gown which clung to her upper body and fell in subtle folds from below the fashionably high waist. Her smile brought on a yearning in him that was so deep and strong, he was almost glad that he couldn't immediately greet her. He gave her a smile and a bow as Miss Malpass took his arm and led him to a small group by the window.

'Sir Thomas, I don't think you have met Mrs Chamberlain and her daughter, Emma.'

Mrs Chamberlain was an imposing lady whose stately appearance was much enhanced by a rich silk turban, which added even more height to her rather bulky figure. Tom bowed politely and was introduced to Miss Emma Chamberlain, a young slip of a girl who looked considerably younger than her nineteen years. She gave him a pleasant shy smile, revealing small perfect pearly teeth and looked down modestly while her mama went into a rather involved explanation about Emma's delayed coming out. It seemed mainly to have been caused by the late Mr Chamberlain's utter lack of consideration in dying so suddenly and causing every arrangement to be cancelled.

He was obliged by etiquette to exchange pleasantries with these two ladies while at the same time remaining uncomfortably aware of the lighthearted chat between George and Helena, concerning the trip to Bath and the forthcoming horse race.

'It won't be until towards the end of the month, you understand,' George confided to Captain Rickerby, 'but I'd be deuced put about if I missed it. I'm wagering a few guineas on my own mount of course, and a few of the bucks from the Furnace Club are backing us to the hilt.'

'Furnace Club?' Helena smiled, raising a shapely eyebrow.

'The Devil's Furnace is a deuced dangerous place,' he grinned. 'A small, very select group of us sets up a hazardous task every year. Very exclusive club, you know. Only twenty members. None of us fortunate enough to belong to the Hell Fire Club, you understand, but we're all game for any challenge and that suits me down to the ground.'

'Is the race a challenge, then?'

'Oh yes. And too much of a lark for any of

us to hedge off now. Lord John Dexter is entering and Davenport, naturally. Sir Marcus Tetley also. Prinny is presenting the purse to the winner. None of us can cry off now and risk being blackballed.'

'Did you say Davenport?' Helena asked, giving George a serious look.

'Why, yes. The Honourable Percy Davenport,' George said carelessly. 'A deuced fine rider and ten to one he'll be up with the leaders all the way.'

At this moment, several of the groups dissolved and reformed and Tom was at last standing before Helena and George.

'Tom, old fellow. It's uncommon good to see you in Town. I'm persuaded the bustle of London suits you. You're looking devilish handsome, you dog. You must take supper with me this evening. I insist. How is your grandmother?'

'She's well, I thank you, George, and many thanks for your invitation, which I am pleased to accept. Very civil of you.'

He gave his old friend a smile and a nod and then his glance was drawn again to Helena.

Looking up at his tall, graceful figure, she drew a deep breath, fighting against the now familiar tightness in her chest, as she said with deliberate lightness, 'We all seem agreed,

Sir Thomas, that the play last evening was exceedingly enjoyable and that Shakespeare must be our most famous playwright.'

'Indeed so,' he replied gravely. 'Yes to both those observations.' And the complicit smile he gave her sent a pleasurable shiver leaping down her spine as she remembered the evening before. The recollection of their passionate kiss and his deep eyes, gleaming with desire, swam through her mind. She made a conscious effort to stand straighter and shake these thoughts away as George moved on smilingly to chat to Miss Malpass and at last, they were alone.

'I have visited Mr Jonah Rudd, today,' he said in a low voice. 'I fear I was unsuccessful in completing any financial business, but I have discovered that he is not your brother's principal creditor. The bills have obviously been sold on, but I intend to persevere until I find out more.'

His confident assumption that she would approve of his interference in her affairs for some reason angered Helena and she didn't allow him to recount what had happened before saying, 'You have exceeded your duties, sir. My lawyer has everything in hand and you had no need to intrude.'

He tried in vain to recount what had happened, but they were interrupted. Mrs and Miss Chamberlain who were departing had come to say goodbye very prettily to the most important guest in the room. Miss Chamberlain said all that was civil and made a graceful exit with her stately mama. Their moment of privacy was over with no opportunity for him to justify his actions. He scowled with frustration as she walked away from him, her expression displeased and her colour high. Etiquette decreed that Helena should circulate among the guests until it was time to go and he was powerless to do anything about it.

When he came up to make his farewells, Miss Malpass made a point of chatting to them both. She'd noticed the little cameo played out between them, Helena's annoyance and Tom's scowl, and she was enjoying the feeling of romantic friction between the two of them.

'Good news,' she said. 'Your dear grandmama is going to honour me with a visit next Wednesday, Thomas. It is now a good few years since she and I met, so I hope she will not find me too much changed.' Here, Miss Malpass gave them both a smile. 'Heigh ho, we must all grow old, my dears so, 'Gather ye rosebuds while ye may'!'

She gave a smile of such knowing mischief that Helena was now convinced that she must have seen their embraces in the drawing-room. She glared at Tom, only to find he was looking at her with such angry, open desire, that she had to look away.

As he took his leave of her he said mulishly, 'With or without your permission, I am going to seek out your brother and persuade him to return with me. It will be a point of honour for me to be successful in this, Helena.'

It was the first time he'd called her by her first name. How strong he is, she thought resentfully. She had to acknowledge that there was no way that she could control the actions of her self-appointed knight errant and although it went against the grain, on this occasion she might have to give in gracefully.

Resisting the urge to crush her in his arms and cover her with kisses, Tom left the Villa Alba and made his way next to Pegasus Mansions.

It was as dingy and squalid as when Helena had visited. Entering the dark hall and climbing up the even darker stairs, to number thirty-five, Tom encountered Mr Snape lurking about with the ubiquitous carpet-bag. The sounds of low life echoed miserably on every landing and the desolate wail of a crying baby came from behind one of the scratched and worn old doors. He was hardly aware of Mr Snape quietly dogging his footsteps until he reached Richard's room.

Tom tapped on the door and receiving no reply, hesitated for a second and then walked in. Carefully closing the door behind him, he paused for a moment and took stock of the bare room with its threadbare furnishings and grimy windows. There was no sound in here except the regular deep breathing of the slight, still figure on the *chaise-longue* near the wall. Holding his breath so as not to disturb the sleeper, Tom stepped nearer and looked down at the young man who was laid out in the oblivion of deep sleep.

His heart missed a beat as he gazed at the young vulnerable face, so like Helena's, and yet with an unhappy petulant expression, even in repose. The sad weariness overrode all the beauty and pride of his handsome features, but the dark lashes fanning out on the pale cheeks, caused Tom's breath to catch in his throat with the remembrance of Helena as he had first seen her in Capley woods.

There was a soft tap on the door, which opened to reveal Mr Snape.'

''Scuse me, gents,' he said blinking apologetically at Tom. 'Snape 'ere. And how is young Mr Richard today?' he asked. 'Rather the worse for wear, sir, if last night was anything to go by. Yes, a trifle foxed was our young man when he came home at last. Was you in his company, Sir? I didn't quite catch your name.'

'That's because I haven't offered it,' Tom said. 'But no, I was not in his company. I am Sir Thomas Capley, a friend of this young man and his family.'

'Pleased to meet you then,' Mr Snape said, holding out a friendly hand. 'Sidney Snape, at your service, Sir. You must be a new friend because I've never seen you afore today.'

'And does Mr Richard Steer have many . . . friends?'

'No, sir, with the exception of yours truly and the Honourable Percy, none, sir. And talking of Mr Richard, you may find him a trifle . . . difficult when he wakes up.' He raised an imaginary glass to his lips. 'Definitely a little foxed last night.' Once again Mr Snape tossed back an imaginary glass of brandy.

'And does he do that sort of thing very frequently?'

'Yes indeed,' replied Mr Snape. 'Like many as lives in Pegasus Mansions, sir, he drinks to forget. And my friend Richard has quite a lot to forget, Sir Thomas.'

'Yes to be sure,' sighed Tom. 'Poor fellow.'

'Poor fellow indeed, sir. But even so, my friend Mr Richard Steer can do without any man's pity. I just wish sometimes that his friend, the honourable, wouldn't be quite so openhanded with the juice, sir, the gargle, Sir Thomas. The flowing bowl don't need to be quite so flowing, if you gets my drift.'

'So, the Honourable Percy Davenport is a friend of his then.'

'Yes indeed,' said Mr Snape again. 'One of the few who, like yours truly, has not deserted him in his hour of need. The hon. gent is quite a bit taken with Mr Dick's sister, Miss Helena. But for my part, I'm just a friend, sir; one who has learned to cope with creditors who are constantly pressing us. One who understands the devilish grip suffered by all those in hock to that evil fiend Jonah Rudd.'

'Who in particular is pressing at the moment?'

'Why, Mrs Bell, the butcher's wife, sir. Comes regularly of a Friday, to try and get a little bit on account.'

Tom fumbled in his pocket and pressed some sovereigns into Mr Snape's hand. 'I'd be obliged if you could see to it for him,' he murmured.

Mr Snape blushed and stammered, 'I'm honoured at the trust you put in me, sir, and Sidney Snape shall never betray that trust.'

At this moment the sleeper stirred and stretched out his cramped legs, cursing as he woke.

'Ah Siddy, is that you?' he muttered weakly, and sat up, pushing his thick blond hair away from his bleary eyes. 'Must have fallen asleep. Been at the brandy again, Siddy. Shot the cat last night, I'm afraid.'

'This is Sir Thomas Capley,' Sidney Snape explained, as Richard Steer struggled to rise.

'How d'you do, sir?' Richard staggered a little as he drew his tattered dressing-gown around him and attempted a bow. 'We're a little crowded here, sir, as you can see. Siddy, old fellow, clear a space for Sir Thomas, if you please. Pass the brandy, Siddy, there's a good man.'

But before Mr Snape could do this, Tom laid a gentle hand on Richard's shoulder. 'Call me Tom,' he said softly. 'Please, no brandy for me,' and he removed the bottle carefully from the young man's unsteady grasp. 'I have recently returned to live at Wintham and have promised your sister that I would assist you in any way I can. Your father is quite frail and wants nothing more than a reconciliation and lasting peace with his only son. I would be honoured if you would let me help you to return safely to the rectory.'

Richard Steer began to weep drunkenly at this and threw himself dramatically into the broken-down old chair, burying his head in his hands. 'But it's too late,' he sobbed. 'Too late by far. I'm in too deep with Jonah Rudd. There's no escape, no escape but death itself. Oh how I hate that grasping villain. Someone should kill him,' he raved on, while Mr Snape and Tom got him to his feet and helped him to dress.

Gradually his ranting subsided and he sat sullenly in his chair while Tom explained that all would be taken care of if only he would agree to return to his family. Once Richard was calm, they agreed that Tom would call for him with his own carriage, and promised they would travel together back to Wintham.

Meanwhile, he wrote a quick message to Helena telling her that Richard seemed much improved and was willing to go home. He shook hands with the meek Mr Snape who promised to see that it reached her and then he made his way back to his own modest Town house. He must change his clothes in readiness for supper with George Arnold.

Although the problem of Richard's debts had yet to be resolved, at least he had an agreement with the young man that he would return home and be reunited with his family. Tom decided to leave the problem of Rudd for another day and just concentrate for the present on making sure that he fulfilled his solemn promise to Helena and delivered Richard back to the rectory.

George had a small but elegant establishment and proved to be a hospitable and generous host. The two men were dining alone and the table was set at one end only.

'No point in sitting so deuced far apart,' George said cheerfully. 'Easier to pass the port, if we're cheek by jowl. Easier for Bates as well,' he added, giving his rather frosty butler a grin.

'Just so, Mr Arnold, sir,' said Bates, and removed the lid of the tureen with a flourish. 'Soup, gentlemen?' As soon as they were served, he withdrew tactfully, closing the door behind him.

Tom felt somewhat constrained with his old friend for a time because he had made up his mind to confide in George about his determination to marry Helena. Remembering the Radfords' garden party and his grandmother's opinion that the Arnolds' wished for a match with Parson Steer's daughter, he cast around in his mind for some way of broaching the subject with his host but none presented itself. He needn't have worried.

George, giving a sly smile, said casually, 'Must say, old fellow, I'm quite glad to be dining under my own roof at last. Been burning the candle somewhat, just recently. Truth is, Tom, I've fallen for a sweet little ladybird and mean to make an offer for her.'

'If you're alluding to Miss Helena Steer,' Tom said stiffly, 'perhaps I should warn you that I intend to marry her myself.'

George threw back his head at this and laughed with such open enjoyment and gay abandon that Tom glowered at him thunderously.

When he was able to control his mirth, he said, 'No, Tom. I have pleased the old pa these five years and more and offered for the beautiful Helena on a regular basis. She has turned me down equally regularly, old fellow. Fact is, whatever Pa may think, we ain't really suited. She is so devilish high and proud, Tom.'

'That is exactly how I would have her,' Tom said.

'And she is so deucedly hard to please.'

'I know,' Tom agreed, sighing.

'She is an heiress, you know, Tom. Inherited great wealth from her guardians. Very much sought after by every fortune-hunter this side of the Channel.'

'No matter,' said Tom. 'I have no need of her money.'

'I tell you this, Tom, she is full of missish fads and fancies. Always has to be queen bee, in control of all around her. The man who marries Helena Steer will have to be richer, stronger, handsomer and more pleasing than all the rest of the finest London bucks put together.'

'Or more determined,' said Tom with his open smile. 'That is why I know that I will marry her one fine day.'

'Yes, significantly more determined than all the others,' George said seriously. 'I wish you all the luck in the world, Tom. Hard truth is, I cannot feel disappointed. Dashed fine girl, but a will like iron. There is no man born yet who could tame her wayward spirit. I am quite out of her league. My heart is just not in it, Tom. Just obeying the aged pa's orders as it were. Now, I have met the real love of my life and she has accepted me. Intend to inform Pa and be done with proposing to Helena.'

It was now Tom's turn to laugh. 'My dear George,' he said, 'congratulations. My very best wishes for your future happiness. May I know the name of your intended?'

'Yes,' smiled George. 'Met the little girl this afternoon as it turns out.'

'Who . . . ?' Tom asked, frantically searching his memory as to who 'the little ladybird' might be.

'Why, Emma. Miss Chamberlain, of course,' said George, proudly, as Bates came in to supervise the clearing of the soup course. 'She's the only one for me, Tom, and her mama seems to be in agreement. She has no papa to consider,' he said succinctly. 'Dead, Tom, over a year ago. Now that they are out of mourning, her mama has given me permission to get engaged Emma, Miss Chamberlain, is agreeable. She is such an amenable little puss, Tom. I tell you there is no happier man in London than I.'

Bates set out the main meat and game courses impassively as Tom leaned forward and pumped his friend's hand.

'Congratulations,' he said again. 'You are a lucky man, George. May you both be very happy.'

'Only problem is she don't take kindly to the idea of the race, Tom. Highly strung like all young fillies. Worries her little head about me all the time. Tried to dissuade me you know. Too curst timid by half,' he said fondly.

It was obvious that Miss Chamberlain's nervous concern for him was very gratifying to her beloved.

He went on to talk of the horses and riders and urged Tom to attend as a spectator.

'Could wager a few guineas yourself, old fellow. Chance to meet Prinny you know. Charming interlude, a few days in Bath away from the petticoat brigade. Come, what do you say?'

'I will give it some thought,' Tom promised cautiously. 'If I can conclude my business in London, that is.'

With that, Bates brought in the port and the two men drank a toast to George's future happiness and the hope of an equally happy betrothal for Tom.

8

The next day at the Villa Alba passed in a whirl of activity as Miss Malpass prepared for the visit of Lady Lavinia, and Sophie made ready for Jack's return from abroad. She was to travel to Rugby where she and James would meet at his school and then go on together to Portsmouth to join her husband.

Helena received a letter from Mr Stanley by special messenger, to the effect that the papers were in order and awaiting her signature, to make £3,000 readily available to her whenever she wished. Tom's note came a little later, mid-morning and delivered personally by Sidney Snape, who was able to reassure her that all was well with Richard, before disappearing as silently as ever.

Miss Malpass was personally supervising the airing of the bed linen in Lady Lavinia's room and so for the first time on her London visit, Helena was without the usual distractions of company. Sophie seemed to be staying in her room and sorting clothes and toiletries with her maid, and at first, Helena concentrated on her sewing, embroidering a very fine lawn petticoat for Charlotte, but sitting alone sewing in the long narrow library soon palled and Helena finally folded up her work and determined to do something else. She decided to seize the opportunity to see for herself whether Richard had indeed stopped drinking and whether or not he was determined to settle his affairs and mend his ways before returning home to his family. Miss Malpass readily put her carriage at Helena's disposal and she and Rose set off together to visit her brother.

The area was as dismal as she remembered it and on a rather dull day, seemed almost deserted. She stepped down slowly from the carriage and approached Pegasus Mansions, hoping that at least Richard would be out of bed and fully dressed when she arrived.

He looked pale and drawn, but at least he was washed and dressed and as far as she could tell, he was sober. Mr Snape materialized silently and was despatched to fetch fresh bread for Richard's luncheon. She noticed a meagre slice of meat on the dresser, so it was clear that Mrs Bell had been paid something on account. Richard even made a joke about Mrs Bell calling and himself answering with the ringing of some coins. She was in an almost lighthearted mood as she and her brother set off for Cheapside.

Although he still looked pathetically emaciated, Richard was eager to talk about home and his future. 'I expect Father is busy with the harvest at Glebe Farm,' he remarked wistfully.

'Yes, of course, but more and more he is using the bailiff as his land-steward to manage things for him. It will be such a great comfort to him when you are at home, my dear Richard.'

'And what of Charlotte and Eliza?' he asked next. 'They must be quite grand young ladies after my three years' absence.'

'They are indeed,' Helena answered warmly. She hesitated and then volunteered laughingly, 'I think there is already a fondness between Charlotte and our neighbour, young Alfred Carty. Shh,' she said, putting a finger to her lips. 'Eliza writes of picnics and suppers and a closeness which seems to be encouraged by his mama, but Father knows nothing of this at present and nor does he need to unless things develop somewhat.'

They exchanged conspiratorial glances and grinned at each other, much as they'd done long ago as children.

'And am I to understand, dear sister, that you have a particular interest yourself?'

'What do you mean, dear Brother?'

'Why, the handsome Sir Thomas Capley, of

course. You would not be throwing your bonnet strings in his direction by any chance, would you?'

Helena blushed and laughed again. 'That is for the future; who knows what fate may hold for a humble country parson's daughter? Do not be so wicked, questioning a lady so indiscreetly.'

'Then I think I know the answer,' he said more seriously. 'In truth, my dear Helena, he seems a fine fellow, a true blue Corinthian. If he is your choice, I wish you both very happy.'

When they met Mr Stanley, he was obviously reassured by Richard's sober demeanour and when the business was completed, they returned to Richard's lodgings to find Sidney Snape waiting for them with some light luncheon prepared.

He coughed, nervously. 'Had a visitor while you was away, Mr Dick.'

'Oh yes. Who was that then?' Richard asked lightheartedly.

'The Hon. Davenport,' he said even more nervously.

Richard frowned a little, but said carelessly enough, 'Did he say what he wanted?'

'No, but he mentioned the race and seemed to think he would see you before the end of the week. Left a note for you on the dresser.'

Richard's face fell immediately and he approached the note as though it were a poisonous snake, picking it up gingerly and glancing round desperately as though to look for an escape route. There was none. The brandy bottle, long since empty, had been discreetly removed by Mr Snape and, as Helena looked at him, slightly askance, Richard of necessity, had to open the note and read its contents in front of her.

'What is it, Richard? Not bad news I hope?'

A muscle in his face began to pulse and he laughed a little wildly. 'No. It is of no moment, Helena. Siddy, old chap, I must forgo luncheon for the moment. Need to go out for a while, but I shall return later this afternoon. Business, my dear Helena. We shall be meeting again soon. Until then, *adieu.*'

He saw the bemused look on his sister's face and kissed her cheek reassuringly before striding out of the room with the sort of false bravado which tore at Helena's heartstrings. She and Mr Snape looked at each other helplessly. 'Do you think he will be all right?' she asked him. 'Is there some appointment he has to keep? Will he be safe like that, alone and on foot in the streets of London, Mr Snape?'

Mr Snape gazed at her mournfully. 'Who

knows, ma'am? But Sidney Snape will be looking out for him and will stay near if danger threatens.'

He gathered together the provisions he'd brought and shovelled them into his carpet bag. Giving her a watery smile and a weak salute, he shuffled away.

Helena was obliged to return to the Villa Alba and help to entertain Lady Lavinia who was due to arrive for supper with Tom in attendance. She was able to confide briefly in her friend Sophie, who proved very comforting even though she was so distracted with her own plans.

'You may count upon it, my dear Helena,' she murmured reassuringly. 'Richard will soon be back in Wintham and you will be able to receive him into the bosom of your family once more. Now, dear friend, forget your troubles awhile and just see what glorious gowns Madame Monte has sent me.'

She opened a long box which lay on the bed. Parting the layers of delicate tissue paper, she drew out the first of the dresses, the sprigged muslin, which seemed to epitomize the warmth and light of a sunny day. The two tones of yellow and the delicate pattern suited Sophie's colouring perfectly and Helena almost, but not quite, forgot her own worries in the pleasure of seeing her friend's delight. The evening dress was quite breathtaking and both young women agreed that Madame Monte had excelled herself. The pale-blue silk shimmered like moonlight and the silver ribbons seemed to have a life of their own. Once again, Helena was a little envious of her friend's obvious enjoyment and satisfaction with life, but she stifled this thought as quickly as it had appeared. They went downstairs together with their arms around each other's waists and prepared to greet the guests. Helena was excited at the prospect of seeing Tom and hoped for a few moments alone with him so that she could hear at first hand what had been arranged with Richard.

Lady Lavinia entered the hall in a cascade of luggage. Hat boxes, trunks, and valises seemed to swamp the porch and hall in a welter of parcels and presents and wicker baskets. The old lady herself looked as robust and roguish as ever in her pale-grey travelling dress and matching bonnet. Above the excited greetings and kisses from the elderly ladies, Helena and Tom exchanged glances and polite greetings before Lady Lavinia and Miss Gill were swept upstairs to change their clothes and prepare for supper.

It was a happy meal with the two senior

ladies talking of old times and Sophie dreaming of the reunion with her husband and son, while Helena and Tom were able to exchange information and plans for their return to Wintham.

'Although I am only able to stay for three days and will be obliged to depart on Monday, myself, it is such a great pleasure and comfort to be with you once more, my dear Maria,' Lady Lavinia said, as the candles were lit and the butler poured the wine. 'The recent upturn in the fortunes of my grandson has enabled me to visit old friends and to entertain new ones and I hope we may be even closer in the future. You will be more than welcome to share the chaise with Gill and me, Miss Steer, and we could travel back together on Monday. The Queen's Head is always a reliable and safe place to put up overnight, if you're agreeable.'

'Why, yes, ma'am,' Helena said softly. 'That's very obliging of you, Lady Lavinia. It will help to make the journey shorter if I have such congenial company.'

'Flatterer,' Lavinia laughed. 'Go to, you young people. I'm sure you can find amusement in cards or music in the drawing-room while we two old ladies recall times long gone and drink to absent friends. Gill has orders not to prepare for bed too early this evening, for Maria and I have a lot to talk over.'

She gave them a very knowing glance out of her bright dark eyes and, as the butler poured her some more red wine, prepared for a long intimate chat with her old friend. The dessert dishes were cleared and Helena, Tom and Sophie moved to the drawing-room to drink tea and listen to Sophie playing the piano.

They sat together on a small sofa under the window and Helena immediately spoke glowingly of the improvement in Richard. 'He's so much more serious now in his intention to take up his life again in Wintham, Sir Thomas. Tomorrow I shall write and break the good news to my father and sisters.'

He pressed the hand which lay next to his on the sofa. 'I'm delighted that your brother is in such good heart,' he smiled. 'And my name is Tom, Helena. May I hope that when we're finally returned home you would like me to continue to be a friend to your brother?'

Helena glowed. 'Why, yes, Tom.' It was the first time she'd tried using his name and she felt deliciously bold and at the same time rather shy with him.

'I'd like us to pursue our own friendship as well,' he murmured, stroking her hand softly.

'Oh Helena, I know Lady Lavinia admires you very much and I would like to know your father and sisters better. In a small place like Wintham, there's no need for any reticence between our two families.'

He was squeezing her hand quite mercilessly now and Helena said laughingly, 'Shh, Sophie will hear you. You must be more decorous, Tom, and not compromise me in this way. Let go of my hand,' she whispered. 'You're hurting.'

He let her go immediately, but then raised the hand to his lips just as Miss Malpass and Lady Lavinia came into the drawing-room.

'What, no tea yet?' Miss Malpass said gaily, taking in the scene of the pianist with her back firmly turned towards the lovers and the absence of any pretence at drinks.

Flustered, Helena rose. 'I do beg your pardon, dear Miss Malpass. The music is so captivating, I quite forgot. Very remiss of me. Please let me offer a cup to both of you.'

'No matter,' trilled Aunt Malpass, and she reached for the bell rope to summon the servant to pour it out for all of them.

Helena noticed Lady Lavinia giving her a shrewd glance over her teacup. 'So, are you longing to be back with your sisters now, Miss Steer, after your time in the big city?'

'Why, as to that, ma'am, the answer must be yes and no. I miss them and have had only letters to keep up with the news of home, but once back in Wintham, I shall be away from the kind hospitality of Miss Malpass and the sights and sounds of London.'

'Very prettily said,' Lady Lavinia smiled. 'And you, Thomas, are we to think that you too are pining for the country life? Wanting to be back at the Hall?'

She unfurled her tiny fan and began to tap it gently on the arm of her chair. 'It's my opinion,' she teased him, 'that you have managed to see more of our neighbour, the beautiful Miss Steer, in the teeming crowds of London, than you would have done in the quiet of Wintham society. Am I not right, Miss Steer?'

Knowing that Lady Lavinia was being slightly mocking, Helena did her best to answer evenly. 'Why indeed, Lady Lavinia. Sir Thomas has been most civil to Miss Malpass and myself during our stay in London.' Her eyes were drawn irresistibly to Tom's and Lady Lavinia smiled with satisfaction at the glance they exchanged.

Tom went to take Lady Lavinia's cup and passed it to the servant to be refilled.

'Dear Grandmama,' he smiled and kissed her on the cheek. 'I'm delighted to tell you that I have indeed been able to see more of Miss Steer and her friend, through the kind offices of Miss Malpass.'

As Helena went to the pianoforte to choose some more music, Lady Lavinia and Miss Malpass exchanged beaming smiles and sipped their tea with evident satisfaction.

Helena was now persuaded to sing with Sophie accompanying her and chose to sing Cherubino's song, 'Tell me Fair Ladies', a very popular tune which the friends performed with some panache and fire and which was much admired by the others. Tom had never heard Helena sing or play on the pianoforte and gazed at her intently, throughout. For her part, his grandmother kept her wise old eyes on her grandson with some amusement, taking in every nuance of his expression, as Helena sang the part of the young page. Her voice was a very light soprano but pure and with a true pitch.

'And now, my dear Lavinia,' Miss Malpass exclaimed, as the applause came to an end, 'you must positively make a point of seeing the wondrous gowns chosen by my niece from Madame Monte's in Bond Street. Sophie, my dear, Lady Lavinia must be allowed to view them before they're packed away for Portsmouth, or she will be deeply disappointed.'

'Of course,' Sophie laughed. 'It would be a pleasure, ma'am.'

They went upstairs and the maid went to take the tea things away to the kitchen. Helena and Tom were left alone for the first time that evening. Helena stood by the piano closing up and tidying the loose sheets of music that they'd been using. She turned round not knowing that Tom had made several swift strides across the room and was now just behind her.

'Helena,' he said, and as he spoke, his arms went round her and he drew her close to him. His kiss was so possessive, so demanding, that Helena was forced to surrender to her own passion for him. He was sabotaging her careful social defences as she lay in his arms dazed and melting with her desire for him. As he possessed her lips endlessly, her breathing became harsh and rapid. Then a still small voice of conscience recalled her to sanity and she struggled to break free.

'Tom, Oh please, let me go, I . . . Oh . . . I can't breathe. Let me go, please, before someone comes in!'

As he released her reluctantly, the two elderly ladies entered the drawing-room. Miss Malpass and Lady Lavinia looked on the flushed faces of the young lovers with tolerant and rather misty eyes, but Miss Malpass merely said, 'Sophie sends her kind regards for a good evening to everyone. She is tired and weary and has decided to retire early in preparation for tomorrow.'

'But what exquisite dresses she has chosen,' sighed Lady Lavinia. 'If only we were young again, Gill. What a dash we could cut in those gowns.'

Even little Miss Gill added her admiration and approval of Sophie's choice and begged leave to hope that Captain Malpass would also appreciate them.

While the ladies were still exclaiming and commenting, Tom came to take his leave of her, and Helena said quietly, 'Tomorrow I will try to get Jonah Rudd to give me the name of my brother's creditor so that the debts may be settled once for all. My lawyer has made the money ready for me to discharge his bills and then I shall be able to return home with a quiet mind.'

'And dare I hope that we two may take up our own lives once Richard's troubles are at an end?' Tom smiled at her. Although laughter gleamed in the depths of his dark eyes, they glowed with seriousness and the intensity of his love for her.

She raised her eyes to his and returned his smile. 'Yes. I sincerely hope so, too,' she answered.

It was as though at that moment, they were the only two people in the world. They gazed with such longing at each other that Miss Malpass and Lady Lavinia exchanged the sort of glances that meant they would be discussing this particular phenomenon exhaustively at the first opportunity.

The next morning, Helena went early to Chesterfield House with an envelope of money fastened safely in one of Mr Stanley's canvas bags.

The dignified building seemed strangely silent and, as she raised her hand to knock on the elegant front door, a very dashing curricle rounded the corner of Chesterfield Street and drew up alongside the Malpass carriage. It was Sir Thomas Capley, looking most elegant as he stepped down, brushing away an imaginary speck of dust from his immaculate jacket and striding up quickly to open the front door for her.

'Allow me,' he said, and Helena spun round so quickly that she almost staggered and fell off the well-swept smooth step and was caught immediately in Tom's strong arms.

'Oh, you quite startled me,' she gasped, her heart beginning to flutter wildly as he smiled down at her.

He seemed to be in no hurry to release her

and she instinctively put up a hand to push him away and disengage herself but he caught her wrist and bent to kiss her hand. In spite of the dismal day, his hands were warm and strong and she knew he was smiling at her, although she couldn't raise her eyes to meet his. She knew that if she did, she would forget her sense of purpose and just give herself up to the pleasure of his nearness. She drew a deep breath and stepped back a little.

'I came to interview your brother's creditor,' was all he said by way of explanation. 'Shall we go up together?'

Helena was conscious of Rose watching the proceedings from the carriage window and nodded agreement. Surprisingly, the door opened immediately when he turned the huge brass knob. This time, there was no clerk to meet them or usher them up to the main office. The whole place seemed deserted. Puzzled, Tom led the way up the stairs to the well-remembered gloomy landing. The clock ticked as loudly and brassily as ever, but that was all. There was an uncanny silence over the whole building which they both found unnerving. Instinctively, Helena took Tom's arm as he opened the door of Jonah Rudd's private office and they walked in. The whole place was in darkness and Helena realized that this was because the thick heavy curtains were drawn tightly across the window. They stood listening in the gloom. There was the sound of the ticking clock which Tom remembered from his previous visit but that was all. Gently removing Helena's hand from his arm, he walked across the room with forced calm and drew back one of the curtains. He stood hesitating for a moment only and then turned to look at the ornate heavy desk.

Helena's eyes were now accustomed to the gloom and following the direction of Tom's gaze, she saw an upturned chair and the scattered papers on the floor, but more horrifically, the man himself, lolling almost indolently behind the desk. Something in his attitude and most of all, his uncanny stillness made her freeze and almost swoon with terror. His neck was at a strange and broken angle. His head drooped sideways onto his shoulder, his throat pierced by a glittering paper knife, hideously bloodied and dappled. On the expensive blue fabric of his coat was an ominously dark bloodstain, already congealed and beginning to dry. Over all, was the sickly smell of death.

Helena staggered back to lean against the wall feeling suddenly sick and faint and Tom moved swiftly to hold her close to him, shielding her from the sight of the ghastly

Jonah Rudd. He was unable to take his eyes off the lolling figure and now he realized for the first time the significance of the strange sickly smell. It was Jonah Rudd's life blood, which had oozed from the gaping neck wound.

He noticed that the loan shark was clutching something in his right hand. The pale slender fingers were clenched even tighter in death than they would have been in life. Taking a deep breath and fixing his eyes firmly on a corner of the polished desk, Tom clenched his teeth and, sweating and shuddering with loathing, he carefully prised open the dead fingers. He drew out of the rigid white hand a bit of paper which he read out loud through pale compressed lips.

Dear Mr Steer
In reply to your letter regarding the interest on your loan and requesting more time to pay, I would point out that I am no longer your creditor, merely his agent. I am obliged to demand payment within the next twenty-eight days, otherwise steps will be taken to enforce the original agreement.
Your obedient servant,
Jonah Rudd

Tom folded the crumpled note neatly and put it into his pocket. Neither of them spoke a word, but still with Tom's arm around her, they backed out of the room trying not to look at the dreadful figure behind the desk. Helena's legs felt weak and trembling and she clung onto both the banister and Tom as they went quickly down the stairs to the front hall feeling for the door handle in the gloom. As they left in haste, the last memories Helena had were the sound of the ticking clock and the sight of the hideous stain on Jonah Rudd's coat.

Tom gave instructions to his groom and then he and Helena got into the Malpass carriage. The driver whipped up the horses and they drove with as much speed as possible to Pegasus Mansions.

Still shaken and speechless with the horror of what they had just witnessed, Helena could only be glad of his supporting arm and the gentle explanation that he gave to the curious Rose.

'We must make all speed to find Mr Steer,' he said to the bemused maid. 'Your mistress needs to see him urgently.'

Helena opened her mouth to try and reassure her maid, but no sound came. She could only hope that Richard was at home. There was no answer to Tom's knock, but Mr Snape materialized silently and said, 'Mr Steer is still lyin' down, ma'am, sir. He was late in last night you see and he's lyin' down.'

'Yes, yes, thank you, Mr Snape,' Tom said. 'But now we have to see him urgently.'

As she entered Richard's miserable room, Helena became aware of a muffled wailing noise which kept rising and was accompanied by thumping from hands and feet on the poor worn-out *chaise-longue*. Richard was lying face down and was beating and wailing to a rhythm of his own. She went up to her brother and touched him gently. The grovelling figure raised himself up on one elbow.

'Wha' . . . ? What is it? Wha' do you want? Please leave me. Leave me alone. Do you hear? Go away?'

'No,' Tom said calmly. 'It's you who must go away, Richard. Your sister and I are waiting for you and we're going to leave here now, this very moment.'

'Is that you, Tom, old fellow?'

'Yes. And Helena. Come, Richard, put on your coat and we'll be away.'

Richard slowly reared up onto his hands and knees. 'I can't, Helena,' he whispered. His lips were as white as his face and he groped towards the end of the *chaise-longue* and tried to stand up. 'I can't, Tom, old chap.'

For a moment, the three stared at each other, Tom bending over him strong and adamant that they should now be going, Richard, struggling to rise and trying desperately to speak, Mr Snape and Helena intervening here and offering a supporting hand under each of Richard's elbows, to get him to his feet.

'Let's just get your coat, Dick, and then we can get you into the carriage,' Tom said soothingly. 'There. That's just it. Good chap. Steady now.'

By coaxing and manipulating him, they manoeuvred Richard out of the room and down the stairs to the waiting carriage and then on to Tom's own place in Green Square.

During the short journey, Richard continued to twitch and jerk convulsively and to ramble about Jonah Rudd. Helena settled a cushion under his head and tried to be as soothing as Mr Snape, in spite of the terrible images that crowded her mind. By the time they were at Tom's modest town house, Richard was considerably calmer and was persuaded to lie down and try to sleep in a darkened bedroom, but far from being able to sleep, he sat bolt upright on the pillows, and stared straight ahead while his nervous fingers convulsively twisted the edges of the coverlet. Helena took his hand and stroked it, trying to calm him, while Tom strode to the window and said with a cheerfulness that he didn't feel, 'Well, my dear Richard, I hope you may be able to sleep and then be ready to take a little refreshment and a drop of wine to sustain us before we journey back to Wintham.'

He kept his voice deliberately calm as he drew the curtains across the window and then walked towards the bed. Richard Steer turned his feverish gaze towards his sister and his fingers twisted the creased coverlet even more nervously as he said desperately, 'No, Helena. I c-can't return to Wintham yet. I . . . I've . . . I've left something behind at m-my lodgings.'

'And what is that, Dick, old fellow? Tom asked. 'Is it something valuable? Could I return to Pegasus Mansions and retrieve it for you?'

Seeing the concern and compassion in Tom's face, Richard's mouth trembled weakly and tears started in his eyes. A look of utter exhaustion and defeat appeared on his young face.

'N-No, it's nothing valuable. When Mama died, on a P-Palm Sunday, you know, my father gave us all a P-Palm Sunday cross for our Prayer books. You remember, don't you, Helena? To . . . to mark the place of the psalm, do you see? I c-can't go home without my Prayer book. I can't, I can't. Father would never forgive me if I parted from it, don't you see, Helena?'

He pushed his thick blond hair out of his eyes with an impatient febrile hand and clutched at her wrist. 'It's in m-my room. In the dresser. I must g-get it. I must. I w-won't go home to my father without it.'

'Very well,' said Tom, gently. 'Don't get into a taking about it, Richard. No need to fret. I'll go back to your lodgings and you, meanwhile, must try and get some rest. We shall be on our way this evening.'

Richard gave a sigh and leaned back weakly on his pillow, closing his eyes while Helena gratefully agreed to Tom's suggestion, that she and Rose should return to the Villa Alba while he set off once more for Pegasus Mansions.

Entering the now familiar room, he found the shabby leather-bound little Prayer book easily, the place of the thirty-third psalm marked with a palm cross as Richard had said. He turned with some relief, to leave the sordid room for the last time.

'Good evening, sir. And how is young master Dick feeling now? More like his old self, I hope.'

As always, Sidney Snape had materialized silently in the doorway, startling him for a moment by his sudden approach. 'Oh, good

213

evening, Mr Snape,' he said, and shook his hand warmly. 'Yes, Richard is much improved and will be returning home this evening. I have merely returned for a personal item belonging to him that he particularly wanted.'

'That's good news indeed,' said Mr Snape quietly. 'In fact, I'd hazard that it might be dangerous for our young gentleman to remain in the Mansions. Come over here for a moment, if you please. I'd beg to draw your attention to Pegasus Court, Sir Thomas. Look down from the window, sir. There's a couple of 'Robin Redbreasts,' if Sidney Snape is not mistaken.'

Tom looked down through the small grimy window into the cheerless courtyard below. Leaning against the patched and balding stuccoed wall were two stoutish men wearing distinctive red waistcoats and leather stocks, looking deceptively relaxed, as they lounged smoking their pipes and conversing with each other. They were not apparently taking much note of what was happening around them, but Tom observed how often they both surveyed the courtyard and how keenly they squinted up to examine the windows above them.

'Yes. Sidney Snape stands to be corrected, but I'll lay a shilling to a guinea that them's Bow Street Runners, sir. They're after somebody, that's for certain. There's a rumour that Jonah Rudd has been foully done to death.' Mr Snape shivered slightly and looked even more dejected than usual. 'It's expedient of Master Dick to return home just now and as there's no place for a loyal friend like Sidney Snape any more, he's going to disappear forthwith, sir.'

Tom had a feeling of extreme disquiet that the news of Rudd's death was out, and he gazed into Mr Snape's mournful face with some concern. 'My dear Mr Snape, you have indeed been a good and loyal friend to Mr Richard. What are your plans, sir? Where will you go?'

'I have a sister in Norwich. I'm determined to make my way there and perhaps find employment along the way. Whatever the outcome I shall finally land among friends.'

'I sincerely hope so,' Tom said. 'And here, take this card to the Bank in Threadneedle Street and ask for Mr Moore. He is my man at the bank and will see to it that fifty guineas will be made available to you, so you needn't return to your dear sister empty handed and relying on her charity.'

Sidney Snape's incredulity caused him to gasp and then he pumped Tom's hand with uncharacteristic energy as he thanked him for his generosity.

'I can never repay you, but I'll remain true to my friend Richard Steer as long as I live. Make sure you're not seen as you leave here, sir,' he went on in a low voice. 'The Runners are waiting and they'll want to get their man. Let me go first, if you please, and divert them, while you slip away.'

Taking his leave quickly, Tom moved silently to his waiting coach and Sidney Snape sauntered out of the back way, across the courtyard where the Bow Street Runners were waiting.

Richard was ready, still rather pale but much more composed as Tom returned to Green Square and within half an hour they were ready to depart and leave the house-keeper to manage the Town establishment. Before he left, Tom had time to scribble a hasty note to Helena and the footman was ordered to deliver it personally.

9

Sophie Malpass departed in a flurry of farewells and many promises of an eventual reunion when she returned to Wintham, but Helena knew by her friend's radiant face that the reunion Sophie was aching for just at that moment was with Jack Malpass and her young son.

'In all truth my dear Sophie, I shall miss you sorely,' said the usually restrained Miss Malpass rather sadly, as they embraced at the front door amid a welter of luggage and boxes. 'It has been such a pleasure to have your company these last weeks. The only good thing is I am persuaded that you may be able to repeat your visit now that James is settled at Rugby.'

'That is indeed true, Aunt,' Sophie smiled at her, but it was clear to the observers even if they'd had their eyes tightly closed, that Sophie's mind was at this moment far away from the Villa Alba and she was already with her beloved family in spirit, if not in fact. Helena felt a pang of envy at the uncomplicated happiness of her friend's married life and stifled a sigh as Sophie kissed her goodbye.

The two older ladies waved lace handkerchiefs as the carriage rolled down the quiet street and then settled down in the library for some sewing and a chat. The weather was still mild for September but the library was on the north side of the house and had quite a sombre aspect. This was Maria Malpass's justification for having a cosy fire and steaming hot chocolate prepared for her guests and when the carriage was finally out of sight, she bustled off to organize the servants.

Helena had brought some sewing of her own into the library. She was still working on the dainty edging for the petticoat which was to be Charlotte's Christmas present. It was painstaking work as the embroidery was so fine, but she was determined to have the design finished in time. She wondered if Charlotte would be inclined to keep it for her trousseau and then almost immediately her mind flashed back to the ghastly scene in Jonah Rudd's office. She shuddered and unconsciously shook her head to try and dispel her troubled thoughts. She wondered where Tom and Richard were at this moment. Did Richard know who had done such a terrible deed? Whatever Jonah Rudd's sins, he had paid dearly for his wicked ways. Perhaps now they would never find the true identity of the one who held Richard's promissory notes. Who knew what the future might hold?

She made a determined effort to concentrate on her sewing and to think of something else. Perhaps Charlotte would be the first of them to get married. The artless letters from Eliza seemed to confirm that Alfred Carty was paying his attentions quite seriously to her sister. Did Charlotte really return his interest? She hoped with all her heart that it wouldn't be so. Charlotte seemed so young and had so far seen nothing of life. And yet, she thought of her own situation. It was very difficult for a young woman in such a small community and with such social constraints on her activities as were imposed by the conventions. She sighed and took up a length of peach silk thread for one of the embroidered rose-buds.

'Heigh ho!' said the bright-eyed Lady Lavinia, noticing the slight droop of Helena's mouth as she concentrated on threading her needle. 'Whatever can be the cause of such deep thought and heaving sighs, my dear?'

Helena blushed and stammered a little. 'Why, nothing of any moment, ma'am,' she said at last. 'My thoughts were dwelling on my sisters back home in Wintham. This morning I received a letter from Eliza about a very pleasant outing to the seaside at Averthorpe-on-Sea. They had a picnic organized by the mama of one of her friends. They set off early in the morning with the young ladies in two carriages. Both Mrs Carty and Mrs Radford were in attendance. The young men rode on horseback. It is only an hour's journey to the seaside, you know. It was so kind of these ladies to organize the outing for them. Mrs Radford provided an abundant picnic and the young people fished for shrimp and played catch-as-catch can. They seem to have had such a carefree day. Eliza writes that she found some very interesting wild flowers for her scrap book. They finished with a supper at the Radfords' and singing and cards until late evening. My sisters had a splendid time and were treated with such care and courtesy, being taken home in Mrs Carty's carriage. Eliza's letter made me feel so nostalgic that I long to see them again.'

'Such pretty behaved young girls,' remarked Lady Lavinia placidly. 'So agreeable that they are being entertained in your absence, my dear. And Charlotte is becoming quite a beauty, is she not? I warrant she will be turning a few heads at the Assembly balls this season.'

'Yes, you are right, ma'am. And yet she seems so pitiably young to confront all the difficulties and temptations that lie in wait for young girls.'

Again, she was thinking of herself as she said this. In her coming-out year, rakes, fortune hunters and flirts had laid siege to her own eighteen-year-old heart, in particular the odious Davenport and she'd been grateful for the guidance and protection offered by Sophie Malpass and her good common sense and experience of the world. Percy Davenport, she realized now, had planned her seduction with the cunning of a military general. Every ploy that he could command had been used to try and win over the inexperienced country parson's daughter. He'd appeared so considerate and kind, utterly trustworthy and never by word or deed revealing his true intentions. Where other young men had offered smooth or stumbling words of adoration and desire, his own demeanour had been one of respectful admiration. He'd lulled her into a false sense of security at a time when her mind was whirling with the novel and testing experience of being a society success. It had never crossed Helena's young mind that her inherited wealth could be the lure which had made Percy Davenport so determined to marry her. Because he was Richard's trusted friend, it hadn't occurred to her until the very last minute that she herself should be wary of trusting him. She still remembered with the utmost chagrin the bitterness of his final betrayal when he'd finally inveigled her into Lord Thursglove's London home and she'd realized the full enormity of what was about to happen to her.

First, he'd brought a note from Richard asking her to honour them with her presence at his friend's house for dinner and a visit to Vauxhall Gardens. He even offered to put his own carriage at the disposal of Helena and another respectable female who was among the guests. Lulled into a false sense of security by this, Helena had accepted the invitation without thought. Sophie and Jack Malpass knew the lady slightly and felt that Helena would be adequately chaperoned for an evening with her brother and some friends.

As for the respectable widow, Mrs Fawthorpe, she was indeed in the carriage when it drew up at the door, but before they'd reached Lord Thursglove's home, the coachman had declared a crack in the front axle and advised that they must call at the nearest hostelry to get it fixed. Mrs Fawthorpe went to seek refreshment while Helena waited, but quite suddenly, the driver leapt onto his seat and they set off at an alarming rate not stopping until they reached Thursglove's town house. Even then, she fully expected the whole thing to be some aberration on the part of the coach driver. It was only when she was ushered into the hall and saw Davenport's triumphant leering face that she had realized the true situation.

She snipped off a piece of thread and said aloud to Lady Lavinia, 'Life can be hazardous for unprotected females and that is why I watch over my two young sisters so carefully, ma'am.'

Lady Lavinia smiled at her solemn expression. 'Of course, it was different in my day. My dear parents chose carefully the man I should marry, but nowadays parents are reluctant to do this unless there is some love and affection involved. I admit, my dear, that this can be a difficult path for a young girl to tread, especially if she is attracted to a particular young man at the outset, but your sister has all the benefit of your support and a loving family to keep her from any foolishness.'

Helena answered ruefully, 'Yes, I think there is indeed someone, but she must not be seen to be running after him or husband-hunting, which would bring her into contempt in such a small community as Wintham. I just hope that it is not merely a flirtation on the part of the young man, or a youthful passion which he grows out of. Then I feel Charlotte would be quite laid low and I would not be capable of advising her.'

'Why ever not? You seem more than capable in your own management of the opposite sex, Miss Steer.'

The old lady smiled again at the recollection of all the young men at the Radfords' garden party who were fondly carrying red roses around for the whole afternoon.

She gave Helena a very shrewd look and continued, 'Flirting is an agreeable game enjoyed by women as well as men and as long as they both know the rules, it can be very diverting, my dear.'

Helena thought of the evening at the theatre with Tom and her feeling of excitement and pleasure at their tête-à-tête, which was in full view of the rest of the audience and perfectly proper, but at the same time, thrilling in its intimacy. It seemed such a long time ago now although in reality it was only a few days. She was missing him so much that the whole episode had about it an almost unreal quality.

'But the rules are different for men,' she said at last, rather sombrely. 'A man can go as far as the woman will let him, while she must be careful all the time not to allow any liberties that could be misconstrued.'

Her mind dwelt on her own youthful inexperience and the inept way that she'd handled the evil man who was determined to have her at any cost.

'Why, yes, that is very true,' Lady Lavinia agreed. 'For if she herself puts no value on her virtue, no one else will. And society is always eager to condemn the woman and excuse the man in this situation.'

'And if she changes her mind,' said Helena, rather bitterly, 'she will be judged a common flirt or a frigid ice maiden who attracts men merely to reject them.'

'Frigid ice maiden', was in effect what Davenport had contemptuously called her all those years ago when it had become obvious that she hated and despised him. She thought again of his unspeakable baseness and bit her lip.

'I admit that young women who set out to attract every man they meet, or flirt as a matter of habit, can be cruel and heartless and are to be deplored. Yet if Charlotte's feelings are truly engaged, how is she to treat a young man who wants to accompany her on picnics, dance with her, pay her every attention and even visits her with his mama in attendance? Until he has made some kind of serious declaration she is quite unable to confess her true feelings for him.'

'It is certainly difficult for a well-brought-up young female to gauge the depth of a man's commitment to her, but if there is a genuine degree of attachment on both sides, a girl usually knows how to give encouragement without cheapening her own self worth.'

'But how is she to know the strength of his feelings, or indeed, whether his intentions are honourable or totally disreputable? Charlotte has been brought up never to do anything improper, so she must wait upon his time and inclination, not knowing whether he is serious or not.'

Lady Lavinia pressed her hand sympathetically. 'You speak with such passion, my dear Helena,' she said softly. 'Am I to infer that you have been in this predicament yourself?'

'Long ago,' Helena answered. 'Fortunately I discovered my mistake in time.'

She thought back to her first meeting with Percy Davenport. Her friend Sophie and her husband had given a party in honour of her coming out and several young men were present who declared themselves to be in love with the 'divine Helena' including George Arnold. The most suave and polished of the group of admirers was, without doubt,

Davenport. His handsome face, immaculate clothes and apparent sophistication coupled with his extremely good breeding were obvious enough. What set him apart from the rest was an indefinable air of maturity and experience which was so much above her mainly young and aspiring group of admirers that Helena had been totally misled.

'Yes,' she said again, remembering the scene at Thursglove Park. 'I thank God, I discovered it in time.' And now Percy Davenport had come back into her life, with his attempts to ruin her only brother, she thought with bitterness.

'My dear, I am conscious of the honour you do me by confiding in me like this. And what about your present situation? You seem to have put my beloved grandson into quite a taking. Heaven knows what he is about, making such haste back to Wintham with your brother Richard.'

Although she spoke smilingly, it was obvious that she was probing for some explanation and somewhat lamely Helena said, 'That is true, ma'am. I am exceedingly grateful for Sir Thomas's kind offer to accompany my brother back to the rectory. He . . . he . . . has not been at all well lately, you know, and I know my father will be relieved to have him safely home.'

She faltered to a halt feeling confused and not knowing how to continue without revealing the whole of the situation.

'We are, of course, all indebted to Sir Thomas's kindness,' she said more firmly, very conscious of the old lady's perceptive gaze.

'Pooh! Fiddle faddle!' said Lady Lavinia, but she said it very softly and gently and with such an understanding smile that Helena was tempted to tell her everything.

The truth was she had barely got over the shock of her aunt and uncle dying so close to each other, when the death of her mother and the consequent withdrawal from life of her father, had compelled her to return to the rectory to look after them all, just as Richard departed for London. All this time, she had been quite resigned to being a single woman, helping her father to bring up the two young girls and doing good works in the parish. Falling in love with Tom seemed almost like a mirage, an unreal wonderful dream unexpectedly come true.

She couldn't explain all this to his lively grandmother who was waiting with rapt attention, hanging on her every word.

Instead she repeated, 'He has been extremely kind to us though, and in particular, offering to escort Richard home to

Wintham has been very helpful.'

'I think it is more to do with Tom's own affections being engaged, my dear, rather than any noble or altruistic notions of returning a lost sheep to the rectory fold. He has been so far away from genteel life and female company since his father died, he seems quite bowled over by the beautiful Miss Steer.'

Her bright eyes were dancing with mischief as she waited for Helena's reply, but at that moment Miss Malpass entered smilingly and summoned the maid to make up the fire and serve the hot chocolate and oat cakes and the conversation immediately turned to other things, much to Helena's relief.

After lunch, Miss Malpass had her at home afternoon as usual and the three women were pleased and intrigued by the number of former acquaintances who sent in their visiting cards and declared themselves to be desirous of renewing old friendships while Lady Lavinia was in Town. The most exciting of these was an embossed missive from the Most Honourable the Marquis of Atherton, requesting the presence of the three of them at a ball on Saturday in honour of the betrothal of his daughter, Amelia to Mr Frederick Morley. It was delivered by a liveried footman no less, who appeared in a very dignified outfit which included a pale-pink satin waistcoat and white stockings. Lady Lavinia said cynically that this was all of a piece with Atherton's fashion of doing things. 'Always the fellow for the grand gesture, the extravagant style,' was how she described him.

'Why, when dear Tom's father was alive, Atherton used to give the most tremendous parties,' she declared. Some of the gentlemen would think nothing of staying up all night carding and drinking three or four bottles of claret each. 'Until his wife died, he was always a leader of the fashionable set, you know, and entertained like a real out and outer. Many's the time that Atherton's friends slept dead drunk all night on the drawing-room floor and were got up by the footman and helped through the front door before breakfast. Well I never thought to see the day, my dear Maria, when I would be invited again to Atherton House, especially for the betrothal of that faded little dab Amelia. I am persuaded her dear papa must have dangled the carrot in front of this Frederick Morley, whoever he is.'

Maria Malpass smiled and said comfortably, 'Well, my dear Lavinia, the good Lord makes 'em and He matches 'em. In His own good time, of course, He despatches 'em. No doubt, Mr Frederick Morley is to be congratulated on his engagement and my best wishes go to the bride-to-be. I remember her from the schoolroom. An undistinguished little thing as you say, but every bride is beautiful on her wedding day. She's not the first and she won't be the last to have her papa's riches dangled in front of her marriage partner. I wish her joy of him, Lavinia. And remember that Atherton has two more dowdy little misses to be launched into the marriage stakes. Not an easy task for a lone papa.'

Both women were intrigued and flattered by the invitation, which was of such short notice that they wondered whether in fact, all the guests would be able to attend. They entered into prolonged speculation about the date and venue for the marriage, suitable choices for a wedding gift and what would be the probable guest list on that occasion. Once they'd exhausted all these conversational possibilities, they both got into a flutter about their dresses and hair and whether to have an early supper before setting out to the ball, or whether it would be more dignified to appear a little later when most of the guests were assembled. This dilemma was presently resolved by Lady Lavinia who read His Lordship's scrawled message on the gilt edged card more carefully and noticed the words 'for dinner at six o'clock, before the ball', and that they should come to the house a little before the appointed hour, as several persons who were clearly of the *ton* were to be present. The house in question was a grand one in Grosvenor Square and for the rest of the afternoon and evening, Lady Lavinia regaled them with tales of the marquis and his misspent youth and some of the more flamboyant episodes that she had personally witnessed at Atherton House. As for Helena, she tried to enjoy the slightly malicious remarks of the two old women, but her mind was still troubled by the murder of Jonah Rudd and her fears for her brother. Later on in the afternoon, she received Tom's note, delivered punctiliously by his servant. She made her excuses and retired to the privacy of her room to read it.

My own darling Helena,
We departed London last evening as planned and will be almost to Wintham by the time you read this and yet, already I am missing you so much. Richard sends all his love and we are speeding with what haste we can to the rectory. On the matter of Jonah Rudd, there is conflicting news. The Bow Street Runners are investigating his hideous death. There is a whisper that he

has been killed by one of his clients. The
only consolation is that Richard is now out
of his reach once and for all.

Oh Helena, I am longing to see you once
more. Please let it be soon.

Tom.

Helena read and reread the note several times. She still had a terrible sense of doom about Rudd's death and was unable to shake off her gloomy thoughts, but finally, she persuaded herself that Richard was now safe and that she would see him at home very shortly. She was now longing just to be there.

On the night of the ball, she left Rose to choose her evening gown and slippers unaided, along with the organizing of such hair decoration, reticule and fan as her maid considered suitable. She lay on the day bed in her own room reading, and occasionally laying aside her book to day-dream about Tom. What was he doing now? She longed to be with him, feel his eager mouth against her own and his strong arms holding her. He seemed intent on making an offer for her and she knew Papa would be delighted for her happiness. She had never discussed her ideas of marriage with her father. If it was ever mentioned in his presence he would merely give his vague sweet smile and murmur gently, that of course his eldest chick must one day fly the nest, but they were so happy as they were. Helena was indispensable to his parish work now that her dear mama was no longer here. He recognized that one fine day, Helena would choose a suitor who would take his darling away from him, but there was plenty of time for that in the future. His other- worldly attitude would become more positive, she knew, if she were to discuss a betrothal, but until then, Francis Steer would avoid all mention of a change in their situation. He would miss her terribly if she became a married woman with her own home to run.

Lost in a reverie of home, she was still aware of Lady Lavinia's excitement and the intensity of anticipation on the part of Miss Malpass. They were busily preparing themselves for the evening to come and curling irons were being heated, dresses laid out, and jewellery chosen as carefully as though they were young misses on their way to their first ball. As far as Helena was concerned, she was content to go along with the evening that had been planned and to which Miss Malpass and Lady Lavinia were looking forward so avidly. For them it would be a golden opportunity to observe the wear and tear and state of decay of some of their contemporaries, as well as taking note of some of the fast young things who were now in the ascendancy in London society. For Helena, it would be a pleasant interlude of distraction, which would pass the time on until Monday and her journey home.

She was sufficiently experienced at *ton* parties to realize that in inviting the elderly ladies and herself to dine at Atherton House before the ball, the marquis was conferring a most special honour on them. He obviously wished to present them to his own motherless daughters and several people who might he thought, wish to renew acquaintance with them. Looked at cynically, it might be supposed that his lordship was very aware of Lady Lavinia's singularly happy change of fortune and that he and many of his friends were extending the arm of friendship because of it. Lady Lavinia and Miss Malpass didn't see anything untoward in this, on the contrary, it seemed as though he were paving the way for their return to polite society and their full acceptance by the highest in the land.

They therefore prepared themselves for the evening with pleasure, fully expecting to enjoy an exceptional experience. Helena was quieter. She knew she was looking her best but attached little importance to it, being prepared merely to be polite and well mannered in the company of aristocratic and well connected people.

She was not to know that the marquis had, in fact, arranged a guest list which included some fine young blades such as Sir Marcus Tetley and Lord John Dexter, who were top notch as far as the racing stakes went and were serious contenders in the forthcoming Furnace Club race. The Honourable Percy Davenport was also among the guests.

10

Helena, in happy ignorance of Davenport's presence at the party, dressed with care, determined to do credit to Lady Lavinia and Miss Malpass by looking her best on the evening of the ball. The carriage was brought round and the three ladies took their places cheerfully and with much lively chatter about the evening to come. A soft drizzle of rain had fallen during the afternoon and Miss Malpass was careful to urge them not to let their skirts brush against the step of the carriage in case of mud. Rose and Miss Gill were given permission to have the library to themselves and Rose planned an evening of sewing while Gill had volunteered to read aloud from her latest subscription library novel. They were agreed that the time would pass pleasantly enough for both of them until supper, which they would take in unaccustomed comfort in front of the fire. Both of them were proud and happy at the turn out from the Villa Alba and were sincere in their hopes that the three ladies would thoroughly enjoy the evening.

Once settled in the carriage, Lady Lavinia smoothed her rather stiff skirts and once more declared herself intrigued by the unexpected nature of the invitation from a member of the highest *ton*.

She said rather briskly, 'It's probably all of a piece with Atherton's desire to see his other daughters well settled, and now that dear Tom has come into his inheritance, he may be thinking of an alliance with the Capleys. But we shall never really know what that old fox's game is. Always plays his cards close to his chest you know, Maria. Why, I mind when he and old Lord John Dexter fell down drunk on their way home from Whites, when old Lord John struggled to rise from the mud, Atherton told him not to waste his strength exerting himself because the night watch would be along shortly and pick them both up from the mire, with no effort to themselves.'

Maria Malpass tut-tutted and supposed cynically that the marquis's distant family connections with Lady Lavinia and the sudden good fortune of that lady's grandson must have occasioned the summons to Atherton House, coming as it did the moment his lordship heard she was in Town. Lady Lavinia was avidly looking forward to meeting old acquaintances and observed wickedly that she expected to find some of them much changed. It was obvious that she considered her own appearance very well preserved. Both ladies seemed content with the thought that they would be obliged to sit with the chaperons at the ball.

As for Helena, she fully expected to find the party enjoyable and knew from past experience that her dance card would be full. She was in high bloom and aware that her new-found happiness and peace of mind were directly attributable to the love of her life, Sir Thomas Capley. Moreover, she had found the time to return to Madam Monet's and had bought an impeccable dress of blue sarsenet over a petticoat which was of shimmering satin, such a pale blue that at first glance it was difficult to say whether it was blue or white. The slender three-quarters dress was delicately frogged all down the front with tiny white roses, a seed pearl buried in the heart of each.

Rose, having being given *carte blanche* in the choice of Helena's costume had laid out the newest gown on the bed and had arranged Helena's shining ringlets with identical satin and pearl rosebuds pinned carefully among her golden curls. Her final flourish was the little satin roses which she'd fastened to the toes of Helena's kid slippers. In her own way, Rose was just as competitive as Lady Lavinia, and was aware in inviting the three ladies to dine at Atherton House, the marquis was doing them an honour which was quite exceptional. She was determined that Helena should do herself justice and at the same time proclaim the competence and skill of her faithful abigail. Who knew what exalted guests her mistress might meet, or what comments would be occasioned among the other ladies' maids by Helena's stunning appearance?

Rose needn't have speculated. His lordship being for the past three years the lone parent of three marriageable daughters, only one of whom was spoken for as it were, had thought it prudent to renew his acquaintance with the Lady Lavinia, who had a significant influence in the life of one of England's most wealthy bachelors. In the back of his mind was the thought of a return invitation and the opportunity for one of his other girls to catch Sir Thomas Capley's eye. Not that either of his two remaining daughters was very eye-catching, he admitted to himself. Still, their dowries were attractive, even to a wealthy man like Capley and although plain, both were of childbearing age and would be able to produce an heir. Atherton had been in the world long enough to know that these considerations counted for more in a prospective wife than looks. After all, husbands could always get their pleasures elsewhere once the male line was secured.

This planned self interest on his part was entirely lost on Helena as she and her two companions arrived at Atherton House a little before the appointed hour. As the ball was not to start until seven-thirty, there was no queue of carriages to negotiate at the massive front door and they were shown every courtesy as they were introduced to Atherton and his daughters, a dowdy aunt who was overseeing their care, since the death of their mama, the marquis' sister, Lady Beaverstone, and various ladies and gentlemen who were unknown to them.

Except that is, for one. When she caught sight of him, Helena gave a start of surprise and revulsion, which she quickly stifled. It wasn't, it couldn't be the odious Davenport, could it? She almost fainted when he bent slimily over her hand murmuring what a pleasure it was to meet her again. With a tremendous effort of will, she deliberately let her hand remain passively in his as he prolonged the greeting quite unnecessarily. She held herself proudly upright, determined that he was not going to disturb her confidence or spoil her evening and summoning up all her courage, she made an appropriate response without betraying the slightest trace of the fear and disgust that she felt.

After a gracious nod to Davenport and a murmured, 'Good evening, sir', turned with her usual grace to greet the next guest who was waiting to be introduced to her and tried not to notice the glances that Davenport was giving her.

As far as the marquis was concerned, two elderly ladies and an unwed female of four and twenty, constituted a prime group for the ranks of the dowagers, so he was both surprised and gratified at the beauty of the unknown Miss Steer from some little known rectory in East Anglia. He even fancied that perhaps the beautiful heiress would see himself as an eligible marriage partner. This was a role he'd enjoyed performing with varying degrees of success since he had decided that it was proper for himself and the girls to come out of black gloves, after the period of mourning for his late lady wife.

After all, he reasoned, as he smoothed his rather sparse greying locks and pulled in his somewhat spreading stomach, he was still a fine man not yet sixty, in the prime of his life. If the beautiful Miss Steer played the cards that fate had dealt her to advantage, he might even consider a second marriage. She was seemingly respectable and unattached. Yes, she might be the lucky object of his amorous attentions, he decided.

Consequently, Helena was placed near the marquis and the betrothed couple, while the Honourable Percy Davenport was left to entertain the younger daughters at the lower end of the table. Lady Lavinia was seated at the marquis's right hand and he was able to renew their long-standing friendship while at the same time, commending his eldest daughter Amelia and Mr Frederick Morley to her ladyship's attention.

As for Lady Lavinia, she accepted all the compliments and invitations for her grandson to enjoy Atherton's hospitality with gracious smiles and answered all of his questions with, 'Yes, My Lord, my grandson is indeed well. Unfortunately he is out of London but I'm sure Your Lordship's invitation will be well received when he returns from the country.'

'And what, pray can be keeping him rusticating in Wintham?' his lordship asked languidly.

'Country affairs and estate business,' Lady Lavinia replied swiftly. She exchanged the merest lightest glance with Helena as she said these words, and Atherton immediately said, 'And as that is your own place of residence also, Miss Steer, perhaps one may hope for a country visit before too long?'

Helena made a polite but non-committal reply to this and the talk turned to the forthcoming horse race in Bath. Sir Marcus gave it as his considered opinion that George Arnold on Whirlwind, must be favourite, while the Honourable Percy Davenport drawled to the youngest Atherton daughter that Lord John Dexter was such a noted whip that even mounted on any parson's old hack, he would acquit himself very creditably. The two young girls were too shy to venture much conversation, but listened wide eyed to all this manly talk of bets and wagers, and the famous exploits of some of the more notorious members of the Furnace Club.

No such reticence for Lady Beaverstone, however. She was a tall, hawk-nosed lady made even taller by an imposing arrangement of her thick grey hair. She had every bit as commanding a presence as her lordly brother and gave it out that in her opinion, young men nowadays were unutterably foolhardy in taking such risks and needed the discipline of marriage to make them calmer. These pronouncements made no impression at all on the dashing young blades around the table, who continued to brag and pose as though she hadn't spoken. Although she listened politely to the talk generally, Helena confined her own remarks to polite felicitations for the happy couple, who blushingly accepted them as they exchanged bashful glances.

When dinner was over, the marquis gallantly insisted on escorting Helena into the ballroom where the musicians were busy setting up and some guests were already assembled. After they had been announced, Lady Lavinia and Miss Malpass soon had their heads together, nodding to people they thought they recognized and posing polite enquiries to those who were introduced to them. In between times, they stored up quite a few caustic observations of the assembled company which they would bring out the next day when they were alone.

Mr Morley led his bride-to-be onto the floor to start the ball off and Helena granted the first dance to the marquis. Her hand was soon claimed for almost every dance. A couple of latecomers, who, judging by their dress were two fashionable young bucks, were disappointed almost to the point of rudeness because they were denied the pleasure of waltzing with her. She refused to stand up with the same partner twice, but allowed the now quite skittish marquis to escort her in to supper, much to the chagrin of Lady Beaverstone who felt that as his eldest sister, the honour should have been conferred on herself.

Helena was soon very favourably impressed by Mr Frederick Morley. He was young and lacked the lively sporting conversation of some of the other gentlemen present, but nevertheless had an air of quiet sense and good breeding which did him credit. They were soon chatting like old friends and by the end of supper, he was earnestly pressing Helena to attend his forthcoming wedding in October. Amelia laughingly joined in his entreaties and Helena thought she had never met such a pleasant and unaffected young couple. Poor little dab she might be, but Helena discovered a vein of extremely infectious good humour and personality in Amelia which was just as attractive as good looks. She began to like the young couple extremely but all the time she was enjoying their company, she was aware of the odious Davenport's presence. During the evening, she took pains to stay near to Amelia and Frederick or Lady Lavinia and Miss Malpass, if he came within five yards of her. She gave him no smile or friendly gesture of any kind, but even so the inevitable happened.

As the master of ceremonies announced the first dance after supper, he sauntered up with the lazy grace which she remembered so well and stood slightly to Frederick Morley's right, where she was forced to notice him. He gave her his usual sneering scrutiny from under his heavy lids, the sensual lips parting in an arrogant smile which disclosed his sharp white teeth. With languid insolence he asked her for the next dance.

'May I renew our acquaintance, Miss Steer, and beg the pleasure of partnering you? The next dance is the quadrille, I understand.'

Helena felt the revulson and dislike that Davenport always engendered in her, but she was not going to reveal herself to him in any way. Rather, she would meet guile with guile, in any hateful encounter with this man. Without flinching, she summoned up her most charming smile and even pretended to consult her card. Then she took Frederick Morley's arm.

'I am so sorry, sir,' she said sweetly. 'This gentleman has just engaged me for the quadrille. Such a pity, it was the only space left on my card.' She gave a very slight pressure on Frederick's arm.

The young man who had momentarily looked stunned by this untruth, immediately rallied and bowed to Davenport. 'Your loss, my gain, old fellow,' he said politely.

Then he led her gracefully to join a set at the top of the room, leaving Davenport with a face like thunder. The surprise on Frederick's face when he was informed that he was bespoke for the dance with Helena had been noticed by Davenport, but he had no redress against Helena's cunning wit. He stood for a moment frowning blackly and then abruptly turned on his heel and, composing his face into a more pleasant expression, he asked the youngest of the Atherton girls to dance.

As they formed the set with the other couples, Frederick Morley remarked quietly, 'I take it you had a particular reason for wanting to avoid Percy Davenport as a partner?'

'Yes, I had,' said Helena. 'I trust I haven't presumed too much on my new-found friendship with you and Miss Atherton, by getting you to stand up with me?'

'Certainly not,' he replied. 'It is a pleasure, Miss Steer. But I'll wager Davenport would make a formidable enemy if crossed.'

Helena offered no explanation, but as he took her hand for the start of the dance, she shivered slightly.

She didn't speak to Davenport again for the rest of the evening, but remained wary and acutely conscious of his watchful presence. He danced only twice more and then sauntered off to play cards. Helena didn't see him again before she and her two companions made their farewells. The marquis had made himself more than agreeable and had hinted several times that their paths would cross again, but Helena answered politely and rather mechanically and was pleased when their coach arrived to take them back to the Villa Alba.

It was quite a relief for her to prepare for the return home to Wintham. After church, the three friends were in a quiet and reflective mood and on Sunday evening, now that all the discussion of marquis's ball had finally been exhausted were able to make their final preparations. Both Helena and Lady Lavinia were looking forward to an early night as they would be setting off at five-thirty the next morning. Rose and Miss Gill were busy packing and preparing for their departure, while Miss Malpass supervised the food and refreshments which she considered necessary for the journey.

Later, while the two old friends chatted together quietly, Helena wrapped the presents she had bought in prettily coloured paper, tied with narrow bright ribbons. Her father's book, she merely enclosed in a piece of linen to protect it at the bottom of her portmanteau and then finally, all her tasks completed, she leaned back in her chair and took a deep breath.

'Oh my goodness gracious me, what a deep sigh,' observed Miss Malpass. 'What may have occasioned it, I wonder? Is it thoughts of home which are troubling you, or are you sighing with longing for an absent friend?'

Helena laughed and disclaimed, 'Well, of course, I am thinking of home. Your welcome has been so warm and your hospitality most generous, ma'am, but I must confess that now the moment is almost upon us, I am eager to see my papa and sisters again. Added to which, my dear brother will be awaiting me, God willing.'

'Well, naturally,' smiled Miss Malpass. 'But you are more than welcome to my home, my dear. I only hope Wintham will not prove too quiet for you after the hustle and bustle of London.'

Helena once again had a flashback of memory at the thought of Jonah Rudd's dead body and said, 'No, I think not. I have enjoyed the social scene very much and, of course, the shops and the theatre. But that is not to despise all that is dear and familiar in Wintham. The fact that we are now all to be united for the first time in three years, concentrates my thoughts and feelings in a very singular way.'

'Yes, I'm persuaded you will take up the threads of your life very quickly, once you are home,' Miss Malpass agreed. 'But please do not forget Maria Malpass entirely. It is so pleasurable for a childless old woman to be in the company of lively young people and you and Sophie have made my life delightful these last two weeks. I hope, my dear Helena, that whatever the future holds for you and your brother, you will return again to my modest home.'

'Most assuredly, ma'am. It has been a great pleasure and one that will retain so many happy memories for Sophie and myself.'

With that, the three women retired to bed in order to rise early in the morning.

Helena was already wakeful when Rose brought her morning chocolate and the hot water for her bath. The night had been a restless one with jumbled dreams of Percy Davenport's hateful face, the hideously murdered Rudd and once, of the sensation of Tom's strong arms encircling her again. She was pleased and relieved to see the misty September light over the London garden as Rose drew back the curtains and it was time to get up.

Lady Lavinia, as always, displayed the energy and liveliness of a woman half her age as she bullied and nagged poor Gill until everything was packed into the carriage and every check had been made to make sure nothing had been forgotten. Then suddenly, it seemed, after all the preparation and anticipation, it was time to depart. Gill minded all the hand boxes and Rose had the food hamper between her feet. After fond kisses to Miss Malpass, the ladies were in their places and the coachman whipped up the horses. They were off. The early morning still had the faint mystery of dawn and as they left the quiet London square, Helena couldn't help noticing two men loitering in the deserted street. Both wore the distinctive red waistcoats and dark-blue coats with yellow buttons, which identified them as Bow Street Runners. One smoked a pipe and both of them lounged apparently casually towards the Malpass residence where the one with the pipe carefully knocked out the ash against the heel of his sturdy boot before rapping a smart rat-a-tat-tat on the solid front door. They were bent on finding out in a most polite fashion of course, the destination of the ladies in the carriage and, satisfied, walked purposefully away and went about their business.

The carriage meanwhile, rolled on its way with the quiet occupants oblivious to any enquiries being made about them. Helena was sleepy at first but by the time they were in Holborn, the City had sprung to life and she was fully awake. She now began to really believe that she would shortly be with a united happy family and felt a sudden surge of happiness. Lady Lavinia and Miss Gill had settled back in their seats and closed their eyes. As the coach proceeded through Shoreditch and towards Hackney, they gradually left the City centre behind and joined the coach road to Wintham. The scenery imperceptibly began to change and after a few more hours they were able to stop for refreshments. Lady Lavinia woke up and Gill and Rose spread the snowy cloth on top of the wicker hamper and laid out plates and glasses.

'Dear Maria has prepared a royal repast as always,' murmured Lady Lavinia. 'Gill, hand up a plate of pie and some of the cold chicken to the coachman. Helena, my dear, shall you try some of the stuffed quail and a little wine? I doubt whether we'll be at the White Hart before seven this evening, so we must all take some refreshment while we may.'

Helena was surprisingly hungry and all four of them did more than justice to the picnic hamper. Refreshed and rested, they set off on the second leg of their journey and entered the yard of the White Hart at precisely seven o'clock. Miss Gill and Rose began to collect the small pieces of baggage together and a servant came to open the carriage door and usher the ladies into a private parlour, while the ostlers unhitched the horses and led them to the stables for the night. An attentive parlour maid waited to conduct them to their rooms. Already, Helena felt nearer to home, on the last stage of her journey to Wintham. The privacy and comfort of her room and the opportunity to wash and change her clothes was at the same time, stimulating and relaxing and Helena emerged for supper an hour later, feeling in very good form.

'Well, my dear Helena, you look as fresh and unspoiled as though we were just embarking on our journey,' exclaimed Lady Lavinia.

'And you the same, ma'am,' Helena replied.

And indeed the old lady was as bright and lively as ever. Her travelling dress had been changed for an old-fashioned gown of pale-grey silk and a pretty little cap trimmed with a dainty lace edging. Her young eyes were sparkling with anticipation as she made her way to the parlour.

They began their dinner very cheerfully and had started on the mallard with oranges when there was a slight commotion beneath the window. A very dashing curricle came swinging into the inn yard at top speed, drawn by four steaming horses which came to a shivering halt on the cobble stones in a high lather. The driver was a handsome gentleman in a dark-blue cut-away coat of fine super-cloth, with the highly polished top boots of a true aristocrat. Looking out, Helena observed with dismay, the Honourable Percy Davenport, leaping down from the curricle with his usual air of commanding assurance, the tall hat tipped over his arrogant profile, the patrician gaze surveying the scene with characteristic disdain.

The inn servant was at his side in a trice. 'Why, Mr Percy, sir. What can I do for you?'

'Well, see to the horses first. Then get me some home brewed, I've the devil of a thirst, man.'

He broke off to give instructions to his own groom and then sauntered into the inn, disappearing from view as he went into one of the public rooms.

Helena's face showed the anxiety and turmoil she felt at the sight of him and Lady Lavinia immediately noticed her altered expression.

'What is it my dear?' she said, pressing Helena's hand with some concern. 'Is something upsetting you? What can be the matter?'

'Why, it is nothing, Lady Lavinia. Nothing

at all. I merely thought I saw someone I knew. I was mistaken. That is all.'

But that was not all. As she tossed and turned in her bed that night, Helena knew that there must be a vile and sinister reason for his presence at the White Hart. She guessed it must be something to do with Richard and the death of the abominable Jonah Rudd. She could hardly wait for morning and hoped that they would be on their way very early without encountering Davenport again.

11

As it turned out, they were away promptly and made excellent time to Kesthorpe without seeing Percy Davenport again. There, Francis Steer's own carriage awaited Helena and Rose and they took their leave of Lady Lavinia and Miss Gill with many promises to meet again soon.

Helena entered the rectory with a sense of peace and gratitude. In spite of all the pleasure she'd taken in her trip to London, it was so wonderful to be home. Her father was as always in his study and as obviously pleased as Helena at her return.

'We have been able to put ourselves about to manage while you were away, my dear, and to run things in your absence,' he said smilingly. 'But you know, the girls and I are but novices in the art of household management, while you, my darling Helena, are an expert. We could not reasonably be expected to go on without you for very much longer. The very fabric of life at the Rectory was falling apart without your presence: windows have not been washed; jam has not been made; even the Sunday School has languished without your personal supervision. Only one positive ray in all the gloom of your absence is the return of your dear brother Richard.'

'And how is he?' she asked quickly. 'I do hope that he is well and able to take up his life again. He looked so hagged when he was in London, Papa. I hope he's showing some improvement now he's home.'

'Well, somewhat,' he answered. 'Somewhat. But he is not yet fully well and so you shall judge for yourself. He's at present out for a walk with Charlotte and Eliza and no doubt will be delighted, as they will be, at your safe return.'

That evening was one of the happiest of Francis Steer's life. It was obvious how much it meant to him to have his son at home with him at last and although Richard still looked extremely pale and thin, he was able to enjoy the company of his family and the supper was an occasion for celebration.

Helena noticed that the only sad note was struck by Charlotte, who had returned from the walk with rather red eyes and was in an unaccountably subdued mood during the whole of the meal. Eliza, too, was quiet but seemingly quite agitated. Her usual open teasing had disappeared and she spoke only when spoken to, meanwhile darting rather anxious looks at the subdued Charlotte. Helena took note of this and was resolved to tackle Charlotte's problem, whatever it was, at the first available opportunity. Now though, she was determined to make the meal a festive one and even produced the presents for her father and sisters while the cheese was being served.

She watched fondly while they unwrapped their gifts, meanwhile keeping an observant eye on Richard. He still looked tense, and occasionally a nerve twitched in his cheek as though his teeth were tightly clenched, but he was cheerful enough and chatted about the walks he'd had with Charlotte and Eliza and his tour of the Glebe Farm with the estate manager.

Even Francis Steer stayed at the table after the meal instead of disappearing to his study and drank a toast to the safe return of his only son and his eldest daughter. The presents from London were much admired and Eliza gradually relaxed and entertained them all with tales of the domestic catastrophes which they'd endured in Helena's absence, with much hilarity and a great deal of embroidering. Charlotte, although still rather silent, gave a few smiles and the evening went well so that Helena was almost content by bedtime. Still, the gnawing feeling of anxiety wouldn't quite go away and she longed for Tom's quiet strength and reassurance.

Oh Tom, she thought, as Rose unpinned her hair and brushed it through. When will I see you again? This longing made every delay almost unendurable. She felt she was being foolish giving way to her romantic thoughts and tried to shake them away and concentrate on the present. First, Charlotte's unhappiness, second, the as yet unknowable threat posed by the death of the hateful Jonah Rudd. She must make time and opportunity to address both these problems in the next few days. In trying to make her own happiness take a decidedly third place, she let out an involuntary sigh.

'Oh, Miss Helena,' said Rose. 'What a deep sigh that was. Enough to summon the archangels from Heaven to assist you in your hour of need.'

Her eyes met Helena's in the mirror and reflected the affection and concern that she felt for her young mistress.

'It is of no moment, Rose,' Helena replied with false cheerfulness. 'They say each sigh a woman gives, like each kiss, can shorten one's life by a few seconds. So, what are a few seconds in a happy lifetime?' She got into bed and sighed again as Rose extinguished the candle.

It was the next morning when Helena finally found Charlotte alone in the breakfast parlour. The discomfiture of the younger girl was plain and wasn't made easier by the direct way that Helena tackled her.

'You seem to have been seeing quite a lot of Alfred Carty while I've been away in London,' she said, trying to make her voice neutral and not sound censorious.

Charlotte coloured up at this but said somewhat spiritedly, 'Why, yes, Helena. His mama has been very welcoming and hospitable to Eliza and myself and Alfred . . . Mr Carty . . . has been present on quite a number of social occasions that we've attended.'

Helena suppressing a desire to grasp Charlotte's shoulders and shake them, but said instead, 'How fortunate then, that I should have returned from London in time to provide the supervision that you need to conduct this friendship, Charlotte. In the absence of your own mama and elder sister, you must surely know that it is not quite the thing for you to be so friendly with this young man. Indeed it is quite improper and has imposed a responsibility on Eliza which she must have found very difficult.'

Charlotte blushed again and began to tremble visibly, tears once more dewing her eyelashes. 'Papa was agreeable and Alfred . . . Mr Carty's mama was always present on every occasion. Oh. How can you be so unkind, Helena? Just because I have found his company agreeable doesn't signify anything at all improper. Oh, it is impossible to talk to someone with no understanding at all!'

She ran from the room, the tears now overflowing down her cheeks and took refuge in her bedroom, leaving Helena feeling uncomfortable and sad. At the same time, she felt so exasperated that she resisted the temptation to go after her sister and point out the pitfalls that confronted a young woman who was so foolish as to go against convention in the matter of love and courtship. It was certain to make Charlotte start crying again and it was such a pity that the silly girl had fallen violently in love with a puppy still wet behind the ears. Alfred himself was so young, she wondered if any serious thought of matrimony had even entered his head. However, since Charlotte had apparently developed a lasting passion for him and seemed likely to fade and die if her hopes were thwarted, perhaps she should have a word with Alfred's mama and nip the affair in the bud. She knew that her father would be a weak straw in this matter and would sit back and benignly allow Charlotte to ruin her life before it had properly begun. She resolved to approach Charlotte later and advise her about her romance when she was calmer. She sought out Eliza, who, although overcome with loyalty to Charlotte and guilt at her own unwitting role in furthering her romance, was soon made to see that it wasn't her fault.

'Indeed, I did tell Charlotte that we shouldn't impose so much on Mrs Carty's hospitality, Helena,' she faltered. 'But Alfred's mama was so insistent and Charlotte thought there was no harm. Oh Helena, I'm so glad you're back from London. I confess I could not know how to go on with so many pressing invitations. Not to accept seemed so uncivil, but at the same time I felt it was not quite the thing, you know, to be so much in the Cartys' debt.'

'There is no harm done, Eliza. I am sure Mrs Carty meant only kindness to you both and I shall take it upon myself to thank her at the first opportunity.'

She spoke so reassuringly that Eliza's small face visibly relaxed with relief as she almost skipped off to have a walk with Richard who had acquired a new puppy and until the novelty wore off, was determined to exercise it every day.

Helena was hourly expecting some sort of message or note from Tom, but nothing came. It was a shock therefore, when Rose opened the door to a gentleman caller and ushered him into the drawing-room.

When she tapped on Helena's door and announced, 'Gentleman to see you, madam,' Helena fully expected the curate or one of the church wardens, come to consult her about the Sunday School, or charitable gifts to poor parishioners.

She knew that while she'd been away, Mrs Foster at Redmile Cottages had given birth to her sixth baby and there was a pile of hand-me-down baby clothes from wealthier families, waiting to be delivered to the latest little Foster, who was a strong and lusty girl.

She was therefore horrified when she entered the drawing-room, to see the Honourable Percy Davenport turn to greet her with an ironic bow and a cynical smile.

Helena's face drained completely of colour and she looked round helplessly to see what had happened to Rose. Where was Charlotte? Her father? How had the footman let him in? How dared this wretch impose his presence on the calm rectory and intrude into her life like this, unasked and unwelcome?

While she gazed at him in dismay and disbelief, he nonchalantly drew out an exquisitely enamelled snuffbox and posed with his finger and thumb raised in an exaggerated gesture of sensuality and pleasure.

'Oh, my dear Miss Helena,' he drawled, as though noticing her presence for the first time. 'I do hope this is not an inconvenient moment to call. Your servant let me in do you see, so I assumed you would be at home to visitors.'

Helena recovered herself slightly. 'What do you want?' she asked repressively. 'I am sure that you and I have nothing to say to each other, or any business to conduct together. I would ask you, sir to be so kind as to leave this house, forthwith.'

'Oh, indeed?' he said with his hateful mocking stare. 'And this is before you have even heard what my business is. How do you know that we have none to conduct?'

'There is none I would care to discuss with you, sir. I shall send for the servant to show you out,' she said with dignity.

She reached for the bell pull.

'Not so fast, madam,' he said smoothly, but his eyes glinted dangerously and the hand that grasped her wrist was like steel. 'First, hear me out if you please.'

Helena decided to await her opportunity instead of meeting him head on, so she merely turned her face away from him, without struggling. He let her go and replaced his snuff box. Then he smoothed a finger across his full sensual lips and she could see that he was enjoying the tension of their encounter.

'You know, of course,' he said softly, 'that Jonah Rudd is dead. Murdered by an unknown hand. The Bow Street Runners are after a suspect who was well known to the dead man.' He paused and inhaled deeply while she waited in silence.

'None other than your dear brother Richard, in fact,' he said spitefully.

Helena didn't answer, but looked towards the bell rope desperately, weighing up her chances of reaching it before Davenport could stop her.

'No, my dear Helena,' he said again in his softly threatening voice. 'Before you look for an escape, think about the danger your brother is in. He was the last person to see Rudd alive. He was deeply in debt and drinking very heavily. All this is known to the authorities who have put out a description of him in the *Quarterly Pursuit*. He is high on their list of suspects.'

'Yes, drinking cheap brandy supplied by

yourself! And Jonah Rudd had sold on the promissory notes,' she exclaimed passionately. 'Richard could never have been responsible for murdering him. It is not in his nature.'

'Yes, my dear. Rudd sold them to me,' Davenport said silkily. 'They are in safe hands, never fear. But still, your brother is the main suspect. Enquiries have been made and all the evidence points to him. Only think, my dear girl. At best he faces transportation and disgrace; at the worst, a public hanging on the gallows usually reserved for vagabonds and thieves. Is this what you want for him?'

When she didn't reply, he allowed the silence to lengthen and then went on, 'There is a way out of this quagmire, Helena. It could easily be resolved if you proved sensible.'

Now she turned to look at him for the first time, still without answering.

'Only marry me and Richard's future will be safe. Come. What do you say? We could deal extremely well together, Helena. I've always admired you and you are no longer the romantic girl you once were. You are a mature woman now, able to see where your true interest lies.'

He didn't wait for her answer but came and stood very close to her, gazing at her so intently that she immediately averted her face again, her shoulders drooping and her expression blank and hopeless.

'And what if I refuse?' she asked tonelessly, but she already knew the answer.

'Why then the Robin Redbreasts will get to know of this quiet country rectory. Richard will be apprehended. Your father's safe world will fall apart. Your whole family disgraced. Come, Helena, make a decision. Our life together could be very comfortable. Richard would be safe, your sisters respectable, your father content, just for the sake of one small word. It needs only 'yes' from you, Helena, and everything is solved. Come,' he said again, 'is it yes, or no?'

Her thoughts flew to Tom and the hopes which would now never be fulfilled. So many people depended on her decision to ally herself with this contemptible man. If she had to make this dreadful choice, she might as well be dead. She thought briefly about flight or even suicide, but then calmer, more logical emotions took over. If she appeared to acquiesce, she might even be able to think of a way out.

After a bitter struggle with herself, Helena finally whispered, 'Yes'.

'What? I didn't hear you.'

'Yes,' she finally said again, and this time he

let her reach for the bell pull and summon the servant to let him out. She neither looked at him or acknowledged him as he pressed his lips to her hand in a lingering kiss and took his farewell.

'I shall be away in London for a few days on business,' he murmured. 'When I return, it will be my intention to speak to your father and set in motion the plans for our wedding. Until then, my dear, I shall look forward to our union with ill-concealed impatience.'

Smiling and triumphant, he was shown out, leaving Helena on her own.

She sat by the empty grate with her head in her hands. Charlotte was nowhere to be seen. Richard and Eliza were not back from their walk and her father was visiting a sick parishioner. Richard had achieved a kind of precarious mental balance in the last few weeks, but she knew that it would be totally destroyed if he were to find out about her interview with the Honourable Percy Davenport. As for Francis Steer, it would kill him if he discovered that his son was a murder suspect. She felt a sense of complete unreality. Even the rectory seemed to have a deathly silent quality, just as she remembered it after Mama had died. She stood suspended, overcome by her jumbled thoughts, casting this way and that in an effort to make some sense of her situation. Her thoughts turned to Tom. How would she tell him? There was still no message from him and now the full enormity of her wretchedness overcame her and at last the scalding tears began to run down her cheeks. She sat in the window seat and rested her head on the small sofa table as she sobbed her heart out. But it was only for a few moments. Helena never cried. In all the terrible moments of her life — the parting from her parents when she went to live with her aunt and uncle, and, of course, the death of her mother, she had found some relief in tears, but she rarely gave way nowadays, she was too strong and self-controlled. Years ago, when the awful Davenport had inveigled her into the Thursglove house, and she'd first realized she was trapped, her weeping had been from fear and anxiety. Her tears had seemed to please her tormentor and afford him some extra frisson of pleasure, so she had raised her chin proudly to deny him his triumph. Now, she cried in hatred of him. She made a determined effort to stop weeping and went into the small breakfast parlour, where sandwiches and lemonade had been prepared for her.

She wasn't hungry but the cold liquid soothed her burning throat and she was able to give some more rational thought to the situation. First, Tom. She must write to him with a plausible explanation of why she didn't wish to see him. If only she could talk to him, but no, a letter would be best. It would be a great relief to be able to tell him everything, but she rejected the temptation to unburden herself and shift responsibility on to him when the solution lay in her own hands.

She fetched her polished wood writing case and began her note.

My dear Tom

The first time she'd ever written his name. She paused for a moment and looked at her words. Dearest name, she thought, and the tears started to her eyes again, but dashing them away, she tried to press on, wondering how to express in writing that she was no longer in the same frame of mind and in fact was about to commit the ultimate betrayal and be married to someone else.

Suddenly, she heard voices in the hall and Rose entered the room to announce the arrival of Sir Thomas Capley. Helena's already overstretched nerves made her start up in alarm, but at least she had the presence of mind to sprinkle some sand on her letter and close the writing case before rising to greet him.

He was dressed to advantage in a close-fitting coat and flowered waistcoat, his collar fashionably high and his cravat arranged with the lower folds absolutely perfect in their symmetry. For all that, his dark glossy hair was ruffled and he brought with him into the room the atmosphere of the confident energetic male who spent long hours in the open. As Helena turned, he strode across the room and stood smiling before her, his lively dark eyes sparkling with pleasure in his eagerness to see her again. Her heart gave a great leap as all her feelings of love and longing now came rushing back and she realized that her letter would now be impossible to write.

She forced herself to be calm as she said, 'Sir Thomas, this is most unexpected.'

'But I knew you were back from London and I felt I should pay my respects.'

He didn't at first approach her closely, but stood near the empty grate, resting one highly polished Hessian on the iron fender.

'Not only that. I have something to say to you that is of a very personal nature. I'm sure you can guess what it is.'

Now he moved swiftly across the room to stand in front of her. He was smiling directly into her eyes with such open adoration Helena could hardly bear to look at him. She glanced away and lowered her eyes.

Deliberately making her voice flat and non-committal she said, 'No, as it happens, I cannot.'

'Well,' he said, the eager smile never leaving his eyes and not entirely recognizing the frigidity of her response. 'My darling Helena, you must know that I want to ask you to marry me.'

'I can only say that I didn't guess it and this is a most inopportune moment to mention such a thing,' she replied coldly. For an instant she could hardly breathe as she saw his expression change.

His eyes were still on her but were now puzzled and clouded. 'My dearest love, surely we had an understanding that once you were back in Wintham, I would ask you to marry me and gain your approval before speaking to your father?'

Helena bit her lip but answered calmly, 'Perhaps it was a case of my mistaking your intentions, Sir Thomas. I do assure you, there was no commitment on my own part to any romantic attachment with yourself.'

They stared at each other for a moment. She was cold and rejectful. His smile had completely vanished and he looked first bewildered and then rigid with anger. He moved slowly away from her, his face reflecting his feelings of disappointment and disbelief. At the door he turned for a parting shot.

'You mentioned to me once that girls who led men on and then refused them were common jilts. So what are you, Miss Helena Steer, to refuse a genuine offer of love and marriage as though it were an unlooked for nuisance? I suppose I should apologize for any inconvenience caused and regret that I have humiliated myself by so openly declaring my feelings for you.'

Helena made no reply but stood with her head bowed as he strode out of the room without another glance at her.

She went up to her room where in the privacy of the bedchamber, she sat on the bed staring into space. She shivered as she thought of what he would do when he discovered she had agreed to marry Davenport. He could hardly be blamed for thinking her a heartless jilt. She must take care never to be alone with him again, never let him know how much she cared.

Wearily, she let herself fall sideways onto the pillow and once more allowed the tears to pour unheeding down her cheeks. Even when her weeping came mercifully to an end at last, but there was no peace. She closed her eyes, tortured by the memory of Tom's voice, the pain in his eyes, as he'd last looked at her. She sat up trembling several times, trying to compose herself and think calmly, but each time, all she could think about was the hateful memory of her promise to Davenport.

12

It was fortunate that the family weren't together again until evening and Helena had had time to get her emotions into some semblance of order. She felt eerily calm after the passionate feelings of the morning and bathed her face carefully, concealing her weeping from the sharp-eyed Rose. As they sat down together, even her unusual air of detachment wasn't noticed because of her father's expansive mood. As Francis Steer took his place at the head of the table, he was more convivial than she had ever seen him before.

'Helena dear,' he said, 'do you think that a little dinner party would be within our capabilities now that Richard is restored to us once more?'

He beamed round at his family, just as unassuming as always, but Helena's spirits sank even further. A celebration was something dear to his heart and it was natural, she supposed for him to want to share his satisfaction with his friends and neighbours. Whatever her private feelings, any request from the undemanding and modest Francis

Steer was so infrequent as to make her want to please him and it might even allay any suspicions of Richard's involvement in murder.

She replied cautiously, 'Why, yes, I think so. Whom had you in mind to invite, Papa?'

'Well,' he answered diffidently, 'Squire and Mrs Arnold of course, and the Cartys. Mr and Mrs Radford have been most kind and hospitable to the girls while you were in London. I feel we should also include Sir Thomas and Lady Lavinia.'

His thin cheeks flushed a little. 'What do you think, Helena? It would be some small recompense for the generosity of our good neighbours.'

Helena forced herself to remain calm, her mind racing. If Tom and his grandmother were to accept, it would be impossible to carry off such a difficult situation. If they refused it would be a snub for her father. It would be even more devastating if, in the meantime, Davenport lived up to his threat of speaking to her father about marrying her as the price of his silence. She would have to cross that particular bridge when she came to it she decided. Just for now it would be better to concentrate on the matter in hand and hope for the best. If she had to succumb to a hateful marriage with the enemy, then at least she was determined she would carry it off with some dignity and courage. Somewhere deep in her innermost being, Helena still hoped rather wildly, that the whole thing would turn out to be a horrible dream.

Aloud, she said, 'Very well, Papa, I shall instruct Mrs Chantry that we will have the dinner party on Saturday. I can plan the menu this evening. We have flowers ready in the garden and plenty of produce from Glebe Farm.'

She saw that he was looking anxious and apologetic.

'I hope it is not going to put you about my dear.'

'Not at all,' Helena reassured him. 'It is a great pleasure to indulge in some entertaining on our own account. All the more enjoyable since you have not been eager to do so since Mama died. We shall make a real success of it, Papa and a fitting celebration of our dear prodigal's return.'

She spoke with a false heartiness that had a hollow ring even to her own ears, but saw his visible sigh of relief that the suggestion hadn't caused any disruption. She went to him and kissed him gently on the forehead.

'Leave it to me and everything will be attended to,' she reassured him gently, but she could see problems, not only with Tom's presence, but the numbers. Her father had also agreed to invite George Arnold's fiancée as well as Alfred and Mary Carty and all the Radfords. Even with the extra leaves in the dining-table it would be a struggle for the servants to wait on a family of five and so many guests. But still, Helena was determined to put aside her own private feelings and make the evening a success, as much for her own self-esteem and pride as for Francis Steer's wish to re-establish his son in Wintham.

The invitations were despatched the next day before noon and as soon as luncheon was over, she went to see Mrs Chantry and organize a menu which would be sophisticated enough to satisfy her guests, while at the same time, be within the capabilities of the rectory cook. Helena helped out by preparing lemon flummery and a compote of seasonal fruits to be placed on the cold slab of the larder ready for Saturday.

Mrs Chantry checked the best dinner service, silver and glass and saw to it that the napkins were properly starched and ironed, while Helena ordered the gardener to produce late summer pot plants and huge bowls of Michaelmas daisies, glowing chrysanthemums and graceful Japanese anemones to fill vases and jardinières in the drawing-room. She decided that the flowers for the table would be incorporated into the dishes of luscious fruit from the hot house at Glebe Farm. This would save space on the table as well as having visual appeal.

After a great deal of inner struggle she put her own problems and anxieties about Percy Davenport firmly to the back of her mind and immersed herself almost frantically in the preparations for the party. Charlotte and Eliza were only too pleased to leave Helena to her arrangements. They'd both had enough of housekeeping duties and were happy to be relieved of any responsibilities now that their older sister was back. Eliza in particular, was happy and carefree, walking with Richard and playing with the new puppy. Helena had hoped in vain for some co-operation from Charlotte, but none was forthcoming. She was able to give Charlotte the good news that her beloved Alfred had been invited, but Charlotte proved absolutely useless as far as helping was concerned, preferring to spend her time moping in her room or whispering with Eliza. Her eyes seemed permanently red-rimmed with the tears she was obviously shedding in the privacy of her bedroom and Helena began to feel a touch impatient with the situation. As

Charlotte left the dining-room, after dinner, pointedly avoiding any looks or speech with her, Helena followed her and made a last attempt to shake her sister out of the destructive depression which threatened to engulf her.

'Charlotte. One moment,' she said gently. 'As your elder sister and one who loves you, I feel I must talk to you about — '

Charlotte blushed and trembled and then stammered, 'There is nothing to discuss, surely. Alfred and I are friends merely. His mama — '

'That is not quite true, Charlotte. Whatever his mama does or does not think, the fact remains, you do not seem to have conducted the friendship with any discretion. You have relied on Eliza's lack of experience and involved her in this, so that she has been quite worried about the whole situation. Why should we not start again, now that I am here to help you and be the chaperon? You are old enough to know how to conduct a friendship with a young man without occasioning any gossip.'

Charlotte laughed rather hysterically. 'It is just not like that, Helena.'

'No, of course not,' Helena answered soberly. 'It never is until it is too late and a girl has ruined her reputation.'

'Oh, you just do not understand,' Charlotte exclaimed, and her eyes began once more to brim up with the ready tears.

'Oh, but I do,' Helena replied more gently. 'I do understand, my dear Charlotte. But it will not do, you know. You are both so young, my darling. And yet you have acted as though you were already affianced.'

Charlotte tried to protest then, overcome with sobs, ran back to her bedroom.

Helena found it so exasperating that she thought the sooner she had the chance of a private word with Mrs Carty the sooner this foolish affair could be ended. At the same time, Charlotte's inarticulate appeal for understanding touched a chord in her because of her own situation. She thought with great longing of Tom and, sighing deeply, carried on determinedly with the preparations for her father's celebration.

The guests would be invited for six-thirty and after dinner, it was planned that they should take the various carriages to the Assembly Rooms at Kesthorpe. Helena thought that this would not only reintroduce Richard to the wider social community, but would also encourage her father to take up the social life he had lately neglected. She was still deeply worried by the invitation to Tom, longing at one moment for him to know her situation, vis-à-vis Davenport, the next moment determined he shouldn't know anything at all of the appalling sacrifice she was about to make to protect her brother.

She was still in a state of hopeless confusion when a polite but rather cold note was delivered from Capley Hall to the effect that Sir Thomas and Lady Lavinia would be unable to accept the invitation as they had a prior engagement. This resolved Helena's difficulty somewhat and she gave a sigh of relief. In view of their last meeting, she knew intellectually, that the less she saw of Tom the better, but emotionally, she wanted to be near him at whatever cost. Now the decision was made for her, she consoled herself. She would devote herself for the time being to organizing the dinner party and would put off thinking of Davenport until he actually declared himself to her father. She had a few days she supposed and would make the most of them.

The rest of the guests were delighted to accept the invitation to dinner and George Arnold, as expected, was to bring his young bride-to-be. Their engagement had now been formally announced and after a period of readjustment, Squire and Mrs Arnold were delighted with his choice. Helena had never seen her father so animated as Saturday drew nearer. He checked and rechecked his wine cellar, brought up claret and dusted off cobwebbed bottles of old port and placed them ready in the dining-room. He gazed admiringly at Helena's flowers and got in Mrs Chantry's way several times a day. Helena had never known him so happy and even Charlotte seemed to cheer up a little now that Helena was back in control of the household and she realized that no further recriminations were to be offered at her friendship with Alfred. Helena was confident that everything would go well and was hopeful of having a quiet word with Mrs Carty at some point during the evening.

The guests were all true to time and in very good mood and so, notwithstanding the rather crowded dining-table, everyone was enthusiastic in praise of Helena's artistic skill. The flowers and fruit glowed almost waxily in the candlelight and the food was, as always, of the highest quality. Helena allowed herself a deep breath as she looked round at the results of her handiwork. The table was magnificent and all the arrangements successful. The brutal interruption of her life by the hateful Davenport seemed almost to be fading like a bad dream, except she knew it wasn't a dream. At the memory of her last meeting with Tom, Helena's spirits were utterly crushed and she felt herself unequal to the task of confronting marriage with the monstrous Davenport and denying forever the only man she had ever loved. It didn't bear thinking about and instead, she forced herself to concentrate on pleasing her father and his guests. Her own pressing problems would have to take second place. She could do no more than work towards the enjoyment of the rest of the company. The women glowed with the effort they'd put on with their fine jewels and attractive gowns. The more senior members took obvious pleasure in Francis Steer's delight in his united family. Everywhere she looked, Helena saw only smiling faces and good wishes.

She dared not even think about the fact of Richard's innocence or guilt in Rudd's death. One part of her refused to believe that her beloved brother, who had all his life been brought up to observe the strictest Christian principles, could be so wicked as to murder another human being, but inside her head, a nagging little voice whispered that Richard had always been weak, that he was desperate and, when drunk, was capable of anything.

She looked in anguish at the smiling happy face of her father and then to her brother Richard, in whose honour the dinner was being held. He was quiet at first but then after the wine had been poured, he drank several glasses rather quickly and began to exchange some banter with George Arnold about the Furnace Club Race in Bath.

'Well you must know, George old fellow, I shall be wagering a few pounds myself on your Whirlwind. That's not to say that Sir Marcus and Lord John are not in with a chance. I own that it will be one of the most cracking meetings of the season. Well worth a visit. I might even try to persuade my dear old pa to travel down for the occasion.'

Francis Steer smiled fondly at him but shook his head gently. 'No, my dear boy. The race is truly to the swift and I shall not be venturing a decision on the winner. I leave that to you younger men. I only hope that everything will be safe.'

At these words, Miss Emma Chamberlain, George's intended, turned rather pale and gave George an agonized look at the thought of how unsafe the whole proceedings could turn out to be.

'Safe as the Bank of England,' George reassured everyone in a very bluff and masculine manner. 'By the way, Richard, a friend of yours is in Bath for the race. Percy Davenport. Rumour has it he is backing his own mount, Desert Fox, very heavily for a win. He will never overtake my Whirlwind though.' He smiled confidently at Emma and she returned his smile a trifle tremulously.

Squire Arnold joined in at this point to observe that the day after tomorrow would surely see the end of all speculation.

'No doubt there will be many who will wager successfully on the winner, but after the dust subsides it will be a case of who would have thought so, among winners and losers alike. I own I'm looking forward to the race meeting myself, particularly as His Royal Highness will be involved. But we old ones do well to keep away from the action and just watch you young dandies,' he said, beaming at George.

'The problem is that there will be many who are utterly rolled up and ruined by the betting books,' Mr Radford said quietly. 'My own inclination is to back George's Whirlwind, but Viscount Kingston's Slipper seems to be much fancied in the London Clubs as does Davenport's Desert Fox.'

'But no match for Whirlwind. He is bound to leave the field nowhere and will absolutely run away with all of them.'

George gave a mischievous smile round the table. 'And what about you, Richard? Have you a mind to risk a few guineas elsewhere than my Whirlwind? For my part, I am prepared to stake a few guineas on Regency

Buck. He is an outsider, but who knows? He may be in with a chance. The unexpected often happens and an outsider may win. The race is certainly going to attract the elite of the sporting world. Dash it, the entry requirements of the Furnace Club are so deucedly stringent, it should be a memorable occasion.'

Richard made a very non-committal reply to this and said very little afterwards. When dinner was over and the carriages were at the door for the Kesthorpe Assembly ball, he seemed almost subdued. Helena was quite distracted from her covert observation of Alfred Carty and Charlotte, who, so far this evening, had been models of decorum and discretion. Mr Carty was as quiet as always, but Alfred's mama seemed to be going out of her way to make encouraging and pleasant remarks to the young people, and beaming round the table at them as though they were on stage as star-crossed lovers. It seemed that she was intent on orchestrating a fine romance between the two of them and Helena was more convinced than ever that some plain speaking was needed. As soon as they entered the darkened atmosphere of the carriage, however, Alfred's mother broached the subject herself. She cordially but rather defiantly brought up the subject of

Averthorp-on-Sea.

'It was such a lovely day for the outing,' she said gushingly to Helena. 'And the young people get on together quite famously, you know. We are all so excessively fond of Charlotte. And dear Eliza, of course,' she added as an afterthought.

Helena who had hoped while she was in London that it was just a youthful friendship, between Alfred and her sister, had long since put that comfortable notion aside. There could be no doubt that Charlotte thought herself head over heels in love. She was dismayed to realize how far Mrs Carty had aided and abetted the romance.

When Eliza had so naively let fall in her letters, tales of the kindness of their neighbours, Helena had been rather amused, but listening to Mrs Carty caused her some disquiet. She herself had often been rebellious and impatient of social conventions when she was a girl, but her aunt and uncle had brought her up very carefully and she had been reared far more strictly than her younger sisters. It came as something of a shock, therefore, to hear Alfred's mother's open approval of Charlotte's behaviour.

'I am pleased and delighted that the young people had an enjoyable day, ma'am,' she replied to that lady at last. 'But with respect, I cannot encourage my sister in too particular a friendship with Alfred. She is only recently out of the schoolroom you know and has not yet had her come out. Alfred has to finish his term at Oxford. They are both too young for me to wish for their affections to be seriously engaged.'

'Well, of course, that is so,' conceded Mrs Carty in an indulgent tone. 'But if she has a *tendre* for Alfred.'

'In that case, ma'am, the correct course is for Alfred to speak to my father before paying his addresses to Charlotte.'

Helena delivered these words calmly but rather frostily and in the dim interior of the carriage, noticed that Mrs Carty had the grace to blush. She and her family had been established in the neighbourhood for many years, but still, she must be careful not to offend anyone. In spite of their wealth and privilege, Alfred Carty's attentions towards Charlotte may not be welcomed by the Steers. It was true, they *were* both very young.

'Yes, yes, you are right, Miss Steer,' Mrs Carty said. 'And Alfred is too well brought up to cause dear Charlotte any embarrassment on that score. He will always do what is proper.'

She patted her tight curls with a satisfied

smile. Helena realized that Mrs Carty considered her son to be a prize that any girl with such modest expectations as Charlotte must be pleased to land. At the same time, for her precious Alfred to marry into such a prestigious family would be an advantage for him.

The only thing that prevented Helena from laying the whole thing before her father was the thought that this might put Charlotte on the defensive and make her believe herself to be more in love with Alfred than ever. No useful purpose would be served by quarrelling with Mrs Carty, or making Francis Steer anxious. After all, Alfred would be back at Oxford soon and it might be possible to give Charlotte an enjoyable holiday somewhere and help to forget him. She smiled pleasantly at Mrs Carty and let the matter rest.

In spite of her various distractions, Helena felt the party was going well. She noticed with approval that Charlotte seemed to have taken at least some of her advice to heart and was being punctilious about behaving correctly, only dancing twice with Alfred in the country dances. Even Richard seemed to be doing his duty by standing up with various of his sisters' friends and although she lost sight of him in the crush for supper, he seemed to be enjoying the occasion. It was only at the end of the evening when the guests departed to their own carriages, that she realized that she hadn't in fact seen Richard for some time.

'Depend upon it, Helena, the Arnolds will have taken him up in their carriage. He will be sitting up waiting for us in the drawing-room when we get home,' said her father. 'He is no doubt still discussing the race meeting.'

Helena herself spoke reassuringly in front of the younger girls and they went bed thinking nothing was wrong but she knew with sickening certainty that Richard was somehow more deeply involved than she'd realized. If he was implicated in Rudd's death, her own fate was sealed. There would be no escape from marriage with Davenport now.

She stayed up with her father hoping against hope that they would soon hear the sound of the carriage bringing him home, before going slowly upstairs, but Richard was still not home when Francis Steer reluctantly went to bed himself in the early hours of the morning, his face grey with fatigue and worry.

13

The next day when there was still no sign of Richard, Francis Steer sent the footman to Squire Arnold's to see if by chance he had stayed the night with them. There was no trace of him and no one could recall which carriage he'd been in at the end of the evening, or even remembered taking their leave of him. Francis Steer was now frantic with worry and Helena herself was quite unable to keep her own anxieties from surfacing. The two younger girls were acutely aware of the atmosphere of unease and strain and went about very subdued and talking quietly among themselves. It was Fanny Radford who finally recalled that Richard had been set down by the Cartys at the end of the Rectory Lane and she sent a message with one of the servants to let them know. Then, at ten o'clock, Stubbs requested a word with Helena and she approached the stable yard to find him strangely diffident and twisting his cap round and round in his hands in an agony of embarrassment.

'Why, what is it, Stubbs?' she said directly.
'Well ma'am. It's Blueboy,' he muttered.

'Yes? What of him?'

'He's gone, Miss Helena. I went to his stall this morning and . . . '

'Gone?' she echoed disbelievingly. 'What do you mean, gone?'

'Well, he weren't there when I checked on 'im and there was this note, Miss Helena.'

He proffered a crumpled piece of paper which she snatched eagerly and opened out to scan impatiently.

Helena

Sorry to borrow your favourite mount, but I can't let the race pass unchallenged, so am going down to Bath and try my luck with dear old Blueboy. I hope at least I shall be placed with the front runners.

Wish me good fortune!

Richard.

Helena felt at once relief that Richard was safe, but at the same time that he was out of his depth in an undertaking where so many more skilled and sophisticated riders would be competing. She wondered what had possessed him to take this course of action. A whim? A wager? What was he letting himself in for now and what was Davenport's role in all this? Perhaps he was exerting the squeeze of blackmail on her brother as he had on herself.

As she brooded silently in the stable yard, Stubbs came up once more to murmur softly, 'There has been a couple of Bow Street Runners, Miss Helena. Two chaps putting up at Kesthorpe. Been hangin' around like, but I've had no words with 'em, ma'am. They won't state what they want. Just general enquiries is what they say if asked. But they're lookin' for someone. You may be sure of that. God help the poor wretch whoever he is.'

In spite of the mild air, Helena shuddered but maintained a calm air as she replied, 'Very well, Stubbs. I am sure there is no reason why you should speak to such people. I know Mr Richard will bring Blueboy safely back after the race. It was thoughtless of him to act like this, but he's young, Stubbs. He will learn sense as he gets older. I expect it is just one of his pranks. I shall tell my father that all is well.'

She smiled with more confidence than she felt.

The groom scowled his disapproval, but Helena ignored his dark frowns and went indoors to reassure her father that everything was fine and that Richard was merely on a lark to race with the other young bucks of his acquaintance, so there was nothing to worry about.

Her father appeared to be satisfied by her reassurances but the worried frown didn't leave his face.

'I own, Helena, I wish he could have been more open in his intentions and not put us in such a coil like this. He is still but a lad, I suppose, and I pray he will come to no harm with this adventure.'

Privately, Helena doubted that Richard could come out of any of his adventures unscathed and was still in a state of worry and indecision. She now wished she'd not been quite so precipitate in her rejection of the man she loved, particularly since she'd now discovered that Davenport was not in fact in London on business but was with his cronies in Bath. If only she'd confided in Tom and let him help her instead of trying to manage the whole sorry business on her own. She stood staring out of the window thinking about Stubbs's latest bulletin, in a state of sick anxiety. If what Davenport had said was true and Richard was the last person to see Jonah Rudd alive, there could be no mistaking the reason for the presence of the Bow Street Runners at the White Hart.

She gave a start as she felt her father's hand on her arm. He had entered quietly and said softly, 'I am busy with my sermon for Sunday, my dear. I shall be in my study if you need me.' Smiling fondly, he disappeared into his study, leaving Helena to think about what was to be done now.

There must be something, she thought wildly. Should I let matters take their course and see what happens? No . . . no . . . What am I thinking of? She forced herself to think calmly and assess the situation quietly. After a few minutes of reflection, Helena was sure of her most sensible course of action. If anyone could help her it must be Tom. In spite of her churlish treatment of him, he was the only person with the strength and good sense that was needed in the present situation. She hurried over to the writing-desk and sat down, dragging a sheet of writing paper towards her and dipping her pen in the ink. I shall write to him, she thought and the very decision seemed to bring her comfort. She signed her name quickly to the very brief note she had written and rang for Rose.

'I want this delivered to Sir Thomas Capley immediately, Rose,' she said, as she sealed it. 'Make sure Stubbs takes it at once to Capley Hall. It is not yet twelve o'clock, so Sir Thomas will not have left the house. And Rose, be sure to tell Stubbs that it must be delivered into Sir Thomas's hand and not left with the servant. Go quickly.'

After one glance at her mistress's distraught expression, Rose merely said, 'Very good, Miss Helena. I shall see to it straight away.'

When she returned it was to announce a visit from Mrs Radford and Fanny who entered the drawing-room to find Helena with rather an unusually high colour and seeming very distracted, even though she received her two guests cordially and with her usual civility. If they noticed her agitation, they put it down to the panic that had ensued at Richard staying out all night and made no comment about it. Under the calming influence of Mrs Radford's bland social chit chat and Fanny's polite remarks, Helena was able to regain her composure and concentrate her attention on what the two ladies said to her. They stayed for some twenty minutes and relieved her mind of at least one of her cares. Charlotte's affection for Alfred Carty seemed not to have been noticed by their other neighbours and in fact, graceful compliments were paid to the way that Eliza and Charlotte had fulfilled their social obligations in Helena's absence.

'I am persuaded that young Eliza did very well with the Sunday School class, Helena,' Mrs Radford smiled. 'And dear Charlotte has been most conscientious in her parish visiting. Several aged relatives of our servants have remarked on the quality of the food and gifts that the girls have delivered while you were in London.'

They went away with Mrs Radford recommending Helena not to fidget herself about Richard as young men were ever thus and that any time she was of a mind to visit the big City, the Radfords would be honoured to keep an eye on things at the rectory.

Meanwhile, Stubbs, with his habitual grim taciturnity of manner had delivered Helena's note into Tom's hand as instructed, displaying his usual dogged determination to follow madam's orders to the letter and refusing to part with it to the rather stately footman who had opened the door to him.

Tom had been on the point of setting out with Lady Lavinia to visit Squire and Mrs Arnold but opening Helena's note and reading it in one rapid glance, he gave the faithful Stubbs a shilling and nodded dismissal.

'What is it, Tom dear?' asked Lady Lavinia. 'Not the Arnolds crying off?'

'No,' he said, and handed her Helena's note. 'But it must be something serious. You must excuse me from accompanying you, Grandmama. Pray offer my apologies.'

'Try not to be such a muttonhead,

Thomas. I shall offer both our apologies. I am coming with you. Something dreadful must have happened. Poor Helena, she is plainly beside herself with anxiety.'

'Yes, so we must go without delay, then,' he answered quickly.

They reached the rectory just as Helena had settled down in the drawing-room in a vain attempt to get on with some sewing and calm her jangled nerves. Tom mounted the stairs two at a time, unannounced and leaving Lady Lavinia to follow him. Helena looked up eagerly when he appeared in the doorway and threw aside her sewing as she rose to her feet.

'Oh Tom, I knew you would come,' she said gratefully. 'I am sorry it was such a hasty note but Stubbs said there were Runners hanging around and Richard has gone to Bath and . . . '

'Never mind that, Helena. What is the matter? What has happened?'

He took both her hands in his warm firm grasp and held them steady. 'Now just draw a breath and tell me about it.'

Lady Lavinia arrived on the threshold of the drawing-room in time to see the proud and beautiful Miss Steer break down completely and begin to sob loudly into the front of her grandson's immaculate jacket.

She stood blinking disbelievingly as Tom produced an extremely large and very white handkerchief which the heiress accepted with a loud unladylike sniff and then he gently stroked the shining golden head as he waited for Helena to tell him all about it.

'Thank you,' Helena said at last. She tried to give a weak smile and said, 'Oh, I am so sorry to have bothered you like this. I don't know why I asked you to come . . . No one can help me. It is all so useless.'

'Try me,' Tom said gently.

'It is all so dreadful. I can hardly bring myself to speak to you of it. Oh, Lady Lavinia — ' she broke off. 'I beg your pardon I did not see . . . '

'That is of no great consequence my dear. If you prefer to speak to Tom in private, I can wait in the library.'

'Oh no. You are very kind. I hoped to keep it a secret, to go through with it on my own. But it is impossible. Too much has happened and of course Papa will have to find out.'

Tom remained calm but he held her closer still. 'Find out what, Helena?'

'Why, that Richard was the last person to see that vile money-lender, Jonah Rudd, and the Bow Street Runners are at the White Hart in Kesthorpe, asking questions. It will only be a matter of time. And Percy Davenport knows

301

all about everything and he . . . he . . . ' Here she shuddered and sobbed again. 'And he says . . . he says . . . that I must marry him or . . . or . . . he will turn Richard over to them.'

Quite distraught, she moved away from him and mopped her eyes. Lady Lavinia gasped and drew Helena to the sofa saying, 'My dear, you must surely be mistaken. You cannot mean that you believe the evil wretch could force you into matrimony? How wicked,' she murmured.

'What else can I think?' Helena sniffed dolefully. 'He is quite adamant that he will pay his respects to Papa when he returns to Wintham and I shall have to marry him in return for his silence about Richard.'

Lady Lavinia patted Helena's hand once more, but Tom was staring into the empty firegrate, one polished toe on the black metal fender, his eyes hard and angry.

'Then you can stop thinking it!' he ordered abruptly. He continued to frown into the fireplace for a few more moments then he began to pace the room as though his rage had to find an outlet in movement.

'And this was the reason for your quite exceptional behaviour towards me last time we met, was it, Helena?'

'Yes . . . well . . . you see, I thought you would not wish to be associated with the sister of a . . . a murderer.' She remembered how angry and humiliated she had made him feel and stumbled to a halt.

'Tell me one thing: did you always mean to refuse me even before Davenport began his insidious blackmail?'

Helena could hardly believe her ears. 'I . . . I . . . don't understand,' she faltered. 'Why should you think . . . ? You never asked me before . . . when we were in London that is.'

'No,' he agreed. 'I was arrogant enough to think I could guess your answer and I wanted to do what was proper and speak to your father. I never imagined that you would relegate me to the ranks of all your other unsuccessful suitors.'

'Oh, Tom, I'm so sorry. I should have been honest and told you, but I had not the courage . . . I was so frightened of Davenport's threats . . . Please forgive me.'

She stopped abruptly. 'And suppose Richard is guilty? I thought I was doing the best thing at the time, you see.'

'Oh yes, I see very well.' He smiled for the first time. 'I see that Percy Davenport is about to have a lucky escape. He is not aware of it yet, but the fortunate fellow is about to be relieved of the problem of a spirited and difficult marriage partner and that I, dear

Helena, am, on the contrary, sentencing myself to a lifetime of difficulty with the most beautiful and adorably difficult wife in the world.'

Helena couldn't help a little gurgle of laughter at this and Lady Lavinia positively beamed.

'That's better,' he said encouragingly. 'And now here's what we will do. As examining magistrate for Wintham and Kesthorpe, I shall request a meeting with the Runners pointing out my own meeting with Rudd and setting them on a completely new line of enquiry. Then I shall go down to Bath for the horse race and intercept both your brother and Davenport to get to the bottom of this whole affair.'

'But just think of the trouble and danger I'm putting you in! Oh why did I ever apply to you? I cannot think what made me do it. I had no business to embroil you in my troubles.'

Her voice faltered and she stopped, dashing a hand across her eyes as the tears threatened to start again.

Tom moved swiftly across the room and drew her to her feet. Under the bright eyed gaze of his grandmother, he took Helena firmly in his arms and kissed her with satisfying thoroughness, much to the delight of Lady Lavinia who observed all this with undisguised approval.

'Do not talk such fustian, Helena. Dry your eyes and reassure your papa that I will return Richard safely as soon as is possible.'

'Well, at least take Stubbs with you. He knows Blueboy thoroughly and can handle Richard when he is in his strange moods.'

'Very well, Helena,' Tom agreed. 'And now, my dearest love, we will take our leave,' he said, holding her away from him and smiling into her eyes. 'I shall send word to let you know of my progress. Until then, try not to worry. Come, Grandmama, I have a great deal to do and must make a start.'

Lady Lavinia kissed her gently and followed him out of the room, leaving Helena in a daze.

14

Tom decided to travel to Bath in his own chaise. There was already a half-formed plan in his mind as he ordered his groom to ride down with his own favourite black hunter, Tantalus. He stood in the stable yard, bare-headed and gently stroking his horse as he bade farewell to the groom. Tantalus had staying power as well as strength, but Bob Bingham was more than a match for him and well the horse knew it. He stood now with his velvety muzzle on Tom's shoulder while the two stable lads, fussed and scurried around him adjusting his harness and polishing his glossy coat to a high sheen of perfection.

Tom stroked the proud arching neck and patted the black powerful haunch affectionately as the lads tightened his girths and offered him a last drink of water. Tantalus began to toss back his shapely head, snuffing the mild September air, impatient to be off while Bingham sat respectfully awaiting Tom's final instructions and keeping a firm hand on the reins.

'He's looking in excellent form, Bob.'

'Aye, sir, and he's even better than he

looks. A ride'll extend him, sir. Give him a proper run like.'

'Yes, surely, Bob. But take good care of him for me. Stop for rest at the Crown in Marlborough and see he gets good stabling. I don't wish for a lame horse when I arrive in Bath.'

'Was you minded to race him yourself then, Sir Thomas?' Bingham asked, with a shrewd look at his master.

'Good Lord, I haven't decided yet.'

This was not quite true, but he wished to keep his plans to himself. In fact, Tom's ideas were beginning to firm up. One way to absolutely finish the Honourable Percy Davenport, financially and personally, would be to beat him so thoroughly at his own game that he would be utterly ruined. Tom decided that he would indeed ride Tantalus in the race and back his horse very strongly for a win. He laughed with joy at his magnificent hunter and his own youthful strength, with pleasure in the crisp morning, and delight in the fact that his beloved Helena returned his love.

'Don't rule out the possibility of my competing entirely,' he told Bob Bingham, 'and take good care of him.'

'Very well, sir,' his groom replied gravely. 'We'll meet tomorrow in Bath then, sir.'

'Yes indeed. At the York House Inn.' He

gave Tantalus one more pat and then nodded farewell to Bingham and turned to seek out his valet.

Strang didn't even bat an eyelid when Sir Thomas announced that he would be bound for Bath within the hour and would take only the under groom with him.

'Certainly sir,' he said smoothly. 'And how long will you be staying, Sir Thomas?'

'Well, not more than two or three days. No evening wear, Strang. I shan't be attending any assembly balls and such.'

'Very well, sir. A portmanteau will suffice then, Sir Thomas. Your dressing-case will no doubt go in the chaise, will it, sir?'

In less than half an hour, Strang had expertly packed sufficient shirts, neckcloths, toiletries and changes of outer wear for his master's journey and had ordered the cook to prepare such refreshment as was needed on the first stage of the road to Marlborough. These viands were entrusted to the small sixteen-year-old under groom, a boy of exceptional thinness who was nicknamed Little Wonder, by the rest of the staff on account of his prodigious appetite and emaciated frame.

'And mind you don't eat all the victuals,' was all Strang had to say to the lad about the proposed expedition. Although Strang would not dream of discussing his master's private affairs with any of the other servants, he felt he knew Sir Thomas intimately enough to know that this gentleman had fallen head over heels in love with the parson's daughter and that the visit to Bath was somehow connected with this. In Strang's opinion a gentleman in love was particularly in need of the right sustenance and his stern look at Little Wonder held the threat of retribution if the lad failed to look after his master.

So all was ready and Tom's final task was to send a message to the two Runners who were putting up at Kesthorpe, to the effect that he would like to speak to them forthwith and that they might learn something to their advantage. These two gentlemen were soon striding across the yard and were invited to an interview with Sir Thomas in his library. As the magistrate for the area, he was able to ask them what was their interest in pursuing investigations in Kesthorpe.

'Why, as to that, Sir William,' Pridding, the taller of the two runners answered mildly, 'we're enquiring into the murder of a London gent. Name of Jonah Rudd. Might you have been acquainted with him, sir?'

'Not closely,' Tom answered. 'But I had occasion to visit him with regard to the discharging of a personal debt.'

Clegg, the smaller of the two men who had listened intently to what Tom had to say, asked very pointedly, 'And would that have been in connection with Mr Richard Steer, Sir Thomas?'

'Yes, that is so.'

Pridding carefully knocked out his pipe on the back of the firegrate and said gently, 'You see, sir, we're trying to ascertain who was the last person to see Mr Rudd alive.'

'As to that, I cannot know. Mr Rudd had several fashionable gentlemen as clients who will all be well known to his clerk.'

'Yes, we're aware of that, Sir Thomas, and are following up leads in the City.'

'What is your opinion of Mr Steer's character and integrity, Sir Thomas?' asked Clegg suddenly.

'Well, as to his character,' he said cautiously, 'he is the son of Wintham's rector. Respectable as far as I know. He's at present in Bath. In my opinion it would be far better for you gentlemen to pursue the list of Mr Rudd's other clients which I know you could obtain from his former clerk. Of course, I will be available if after that you would seek to interview Mr Steer in my presence.'

'Yes, we have such a list, sir. What were his dealings with the aforementioned Mr Rudd, do you know, Sir William?' Pridding asked quietly.

'Why as to that,' Tom said coolly, 'he had some debts in London, as I believe most young fellows of his age do. They were only trifling in comparison to the usual Bond Street blades who patronized Rudd's services.'

He spoke so firmly and with such knowledge of the law that they were impressed by his authority and seemed content.

'I believe that the Honourable Percy Davenport, a friend of Mr Steer's, is also at present in Bath, sir,' said Clegg.

'Yes, that is so.'

'And are you intending to travel down to Bath yourself, Sir Thomas?' Clegg asked.

'Yes, I shall be travelling there today.'

The Bow Street Runners seemed content and expressed their intention of returning to the White Hart, where Tom's gamekeeper, who happened to be in the taproom, overheard them settling their account with the landlord before they departed for Bath on the Mail coach.

Tom was now ready to set off on his journey himself and although it occurred to him that Bingham might not find it so easy to get accommodation at such short notice, he decided to trust to luck. He was a very healthy young man and not easily tired. The chaise was fairly new and very well sprung and they made good progress. Little Wonder was punctilious in drawing his attention to the refreshments available to them on their first comfort stop and they both enjoyed the food and wine in the open air. Tom also enjoyed the company of the young boy who, shy at first, opened up to provide him with some amusing anecdotes and even imitations of the more pompous of the Capley Hall staff. They set off again and reached Bath shortly before nine the next morning. By this time Tom was somewhat weary of having to concentrate for so long on the rather boring drive and by the way that the chaise bounded over the inequalities in the road and swayed with every curve. He had not enjoyed his stay at the Crown in Marlborough and hoped Bob Bingham had been able to procure a comfortable room for him at the York House Inn.

In spite of his tiredness when he reached his destination, he was restored by a most substantial breakfast washed down with some cool ale. A very superior private parlour had been reserved for him by his faithful groom and Little Wonder gallantly heaved the portmanteau and dressing-case up to his bedroom for him. Having changed his clothes, Tom went to make sure that all was well with Bingham and Tantalus, leaving the lad to help the ostlers uncouple the horses from the chaise. Then he set forth in search of Richard. It was a day of bright September sunshine with just sufficient breeze to make it feel invigorating, and under these conditions he saw Bath at its best. George Arnold and his father were putting up at the Queen's Hotel as planned, and he quickly established contact with them. Over convivial tankards of the best home brewed the three of them decided on a plan of action when Tom revealed his intention of entering the race himself.

'In that case you must approach the Furnace Club stewards without delay because you must know, old fellow, that the race is set to take place this afternoon after two o'clock. The officials are based in the taproom here at the Queen's all morning. They have to be informed and give permission by twelve noon for any outsiders and also-rans,' George Arnold advised him.

There was no problem with this and Tom duly registered Tantalus and himself as its rider and was able to place a substantial sum to back his own first place at the winning post.

The race was to start in the north of the town, out towards the London Road and a large field had been prepared as a starting point. Well before noon, all the members of the Furnace Club as well as the smart set of Bath were parading about the riders' enclosure with many of the *ton* wearing the colours of their favourites. All were intent on promenading in front of their peers showing off beautiful clothes, elegant companions or magnificent horseflesh, particularly as His Royal Highness was hourly expected. Tom looked in vain for Richard and Blueboy, but they were nowhere to be found. Squire Arnold and George were much in evidence with Whirlwind being led round and round by his groom and being much admired by Miss Chamberlain and the other onlookers. Tom was introduced to Sir Marcus Tetley and Captain Pegg of the Guards who was riding Regency Buck, a handsome chestnut, and he stood chatting to them while they waited. It wasn't until a bare half-hour before the race was due to begin that he caught sight of Richard on the familiar Blueboy and there was hardly time to exchange a hurried greeting before Squire Arnold and George paced up to them.

'George,' said the squire, looking up at his son with love and affection, 'it will be a punishing race for all concerned. Both horse and man will be under extreme duress.'

'Yes, sir.'

'But you will do your very best, won't you, George? And remember, dear lad, I've only one son, eh George?'

'Indeed, sir,' smiled George. 'And I'm going to do my damnedest to do you proud, Pa.' He reached down and shook his father's hand.

Richard had now moved away and was chatting unsmilingly with Percy Davenport who was mounted on a magnificent grey, his famed Desert Fox.

'Mr Steer is looking very pale, sir.' Bob Bingham looked towards Richard with some concern. 'Do you think he'll be all right, Sir Thomas?'

'Who knows?' Tom answered soberly. 'I shall keep a weather eye on him, circumstances permitting. But it's anybody's race, Bob, and Blueboy is a strong, reliable mount.'

'So is Tantalus, Sir Thomas. I've got five guineas on you and him, sir.'

'Why, Bob, do you mean to say that you've wagered five guineas on me . . . to win?'

'Aye, sir. Five guineas is all I've got in the world, do you see?' Bob said simply. 'They're layin' forty to one against you, sir.'

'Well, I'm ready to prove them wrong, Bob.

I'll do my best not to let you down.'

'Only ten more minutes, sir.'

All the riders were now mounted and moving slowly out of the enclosure and towards the starting-post. Tom got a glimpse of Richard looking very stiff and pale and caught the malevolent stare of Davenport, who was wiping a languid white finger across his thick lips before replacing his riding gloves. The horses pranced nervously as the riders all looked towards the great pavilion which had been set up in honour of Prinny. Flags, banners, bunting of every colour flew in the slight breeze as well as His Highness's own Royal Standard. The Prince Regent himself was seated on a gold and scarlet chair beneath a huge silken canopy. His plump legs reposed indolently on an embroidered foot-stool and he was surrounded by his richly dressed friends and admirers.

There was much tossing of heads and shaking of manes as the horses took their places and their owners directed respectful bows in the direction of Prince George.

Tom adjusted his cravat and made his own bow to the Prince Regent and then became aware of Davenport sidling towards him, alternately bowing gracefully towards the pavilion with an air of easy confidence and at the same time glaring sideways at Tom.

Beyond Davenport was Captain Pegg, who laughed softly at some remark by his neighbour on the other side. Momentarily distracted, Davenport allowed the highly strung Desert Fox to fidget sideways and barge Tantalus who immediately reacted by rearing up and baring his large teeth angrily. Davenport reined in his mount just in time and glared at Tom harder than ever.

'Oh, it's you, sir, I might have known it,' he hissed, between clenched teeth. 'And the Wintham outsider, to boot. Why cannot you control that animal of yours?'

He attempted to strike out at Tantalus, but Tom deflected the riding whip with his own and Davenport was almost unseated.

'Shame,' whispered one or two of the gentleman riders who had observed Davenport's regrettable behaviour and he was reduced to impotent fury. Tom returned his glare with an angry frown, but at that moment there was a murmur in the crowd which gradually swelled to a mighty roar of, 'They're off!'

The line of riders surged forward and almost immediately spread out into tightly knotted little groups. The Furnace Club Gentlemen's Race had begun.

Tom was aware that Blueboy was up with the leaders. Richard, looking pale and tense, was leaning forward in his saddle, but seemed to be remaining calm.

Tantalus galloped half a length behind Davenport's powerful grey, Desert Fox, who seemed to provide the inspiration for Tom's magnificent black mount. His eye was fixed angrily on the horse in front of him as he tried to lengthen his stride against Tom's deliberately short rein. As the riders swept along the first twenty-five yard level and up a slight incline, Davenport glanced behind him with a scornful look as he kept his lead, but in spite of the fact that he increased his speed, Tom still continued to keep Tantalus half a length behind him all the way.

Captain Pegg on Regency Buck was now far in advance of the rest of the field but being pressed closely by Viscount Kingston on Slipper and Sir Marcus Tetley on Bucephalus. Tom had lost sight of Richard at this point but he heard the main body of the racers thundering behind him as they approached the first jump. This was quite a low hedge but with a substantial trough of water beyond it. As it loomed nearer and nearer, the first horses were well over and Davenport's horse made it easily with Tom close behind, but he heard the muffled cries and curses of a couple of riders who had fallen at the first hurdle, Lord John Dexter among them. With some relief, Tom saw Blueboy gallop forward and clear the hedge easily. He turned his head and saw George Arnold's Whirlwind coming up close behind him.

'Bit of a bender, that one,' George yelled, above the noise of the horses. He was grinning and out of breath. 'Told you it would be a good race,' he shouted. 'Five of 'em out of the running now. Water got 'em you know, Tom. Sorted out the real nonpareils already, eh?'

Inch by inch, Tom was creeping up nearer to the leaders and was able to shout some encouragement to Richard, who still looked taut, but was nevertheless keeping well up with George Arnold and the other front runners.

'Come on, Tom. Tally ho, old chap.' George flourished his riding crop and urged Whirlwind to an even faster pace, sending up a spattering of mud and clods of earth as the riders advanced across open fields, over hedges and ditches towards the next serious jump. This time there was a very wide stretch of water. Now, as he rode with Tantalus still well in hand, Tom became aware of the huge grey with its flaring nostrils and sweating flanks as Davenport went past him, yet again urging his mount with quite immoderate use of the whip. Tantalus saw him as well and snorted loudly in his efforts to overcome the restraining bit and chase after his rival, but Tom was biding his time. The formidable water jump loomed gradually nearer and nearer. A quarter of a mile. Two hundred yards. Then even less! Yard by yard it drew ever closer. They all raced together with Davenport once more only slightly in front of him. Richard and Viscount Kingston riding knee to knee were still with the leaders and off into a rolling gallop. Tom marked his take off and, just as he steadied Tantalus for the jump, Davenport's grey suddenly swerved in front of him. Tom swung Tantalus aside but only just in time. Halted in mid stride, the horse made a gallant attempt at the jump, floundered into the water and Tom hurtled over his head on to the opposite bank.

Stunned and covered in slime, blinded by the spattered mud of the other riders, Tom crawled to his feet, dazed and almost crushed by the thundering hooves of the horses racing past him. He saw as in a dream that Tantalus was scrambling up the bank and leapt after him, grabbing the dangling reins and heaving himself painfully back into the saddle. There was no way now that he had the strength to restrain Tantalus any further. He had to give him his head and, as though sensing this, the horse set off at full speed after the others. Bruised and bleeding, filthy from head to toe, all Tom could do was concentrate on staying on his horse. He crouched low in the saddle. His hat and gloves had disappeared as had his riding crop. He felt numb and almost unconscious as he mechanically made the jumps over fences and ditches. It seemed that Tantalus was running the race for him while he was still in a dream. They rode hard past stragglers and riderless horses and finally caught up with the rest of the field. Captain Pegg was still going strong as was George Arnold, but Richard and Blueboy had fallen back. Tom was aware that Richard's face was now quite a ghastly colour and that he was swaying alarmingly in his saddle.

'Can't go on, old fellow,' he gasped. 'Wind's gone. Blueboy's still in with a chance, but I'm done for. No hope of retrieving my fortunes now, old chap. You go on, Tom. I've done my best, but . . . not good enough . . . unfortunately . . . I've tried . . . '

He swayed over completely this time before Tom had a chance to stop him and various stewards ran from the sidelines to help him. The survivors of the race thundered on and Tom bent his energies to the last and hardest part of the struggle. Davenport was still level with the Viscount and George Arnold, but with Tantalus always close behind. They raced down a last slope where an almost impossible wall jump awaited them.

Viscount Kingston saw a narrow gap and prepared to be first to jump but Davenport was neck and neck with him and refused to pull over.

'Give way, Davenport!' yelled the viscount at the top of his voice.

'Give way yourself, damn you,' shouted Davenport, and gave an exultant roar as he leapt in front of him to try and take the advantage. There was a terrible scream and the next moment an awful thud as the magnificent grey lay in a twitching, kicking heap, with Davenport pinned helplessly beneath him.

'Ride on Capley, Desert Fox is done for,' urged the Viscount and George Arnold added his encouragement.

'Just the stake fence, one more ditch and then the home run, dear old fellow,' he gasped. 'Come on, we can make it!'

At the fence, Tom was still behind the Viscount's Slipper with George now bringing up the rear. At the last ditch, the big black horse seemed to summon up hidden reserves and the crowd around the winning post began to murmur; quietly at first, but then louder and louder: 'It's Slipper, Kingston's

Slipper!' But the cries sank to a murmur again as the huge black horse ridden by a bare-headed rider, wild and filthy with mud and bleeding from a head wound, began to inch forward into the lead.

As they came down the home stretch the murmur in the crowd began to change to Tantalus, softly at first, but as Tom's horse, panting and spattered with mud and sweat, pulled away from the other riders and galloped towards the winning post it grew to a mighty shout of 'Tantalus! Tantalus!' until he was past the raving crowd and Bob Bingham had hold of his bridle and brought him to a halt at last, the great horse shuddering and sweating uncontrollably, with his supreme effort. The Viscount and George Arnold, Squire Arnold, the stewards of the course, Captain Pegg and all the members of the Furnace Club, came to congratulate him. As if in a dream, Tom was ushered up to the royal personage himself and bowed low over the chubby white hand, while he received the congratulations of the future King of England.

'Well done, sir,' murmured the Prince Regent. 'A magnificent race. You must make it down to Brighton soon, Sir Thomas. Such a pleasure to meet you. On behalf of the Furnace Club, it gives me great pleasure to present you with the winner's purse.'

He was still in a dream when he climbed stiffly out of the saddle and saw Richard Steer, his shoulder strapped up and leaning on Stubbs's arm as he was helped back to his lodgings. Tom gave a brief wave and continued slowly and painfully through the crowd back to York House with a jubilant Bob Bingham. As the throng parted for a moment, he saw two men carrying a makeshift stretcher made out of an old barn door. On it was the pale, still figure of Percy Davenport.

They paused in the shade of a huge oak tree and laid the improvised stretcher down for a few moments while they mopped their sweating foreheads. Davenport struggled onto one elbow and looked up at him.

'Oh, Capley,' he said mockingly. 'I must congratulate you on your magnificent win. What a triumph for you. I, alas, am the loser, doomed to remain an honourable for ever. I shall never be Viscount Davenport now.'

Languidly, he wiped a finger across his lips in his habitual way. 'I am done for, Capley. Lady Luck has proved a bitch today. But . . . *c'est la vie.*'

Tom stopped abruptly and looked down at him. 'And what of Jonah Rudd?' he asked urgently. 'What of Richard Steer's creditor. The promissory notes?'

'Destroyed, sir.' Davenport said faintly.

He tried to smile, but only succeeded in twisting his lips into a deathly grimace. He wiped his mouth again and the bright sunlight seemed to drain all the colour from his eyes.

'Destroyed? By whom?' Tom demanded urgently, and bent over the broken figure.

Davenport leaned back wearily, and gave his usual mocking smile. This time his voice was a faint whisper. 'Both of them. Both the man and the IOUs . . . destroyed by my own fair hand, Capley.' He stumbled on, almost inaudibly, 'With my winnings, I could have made a fresh start, perhaps even won the hand of the divine Helena . . . Dame Fortune thought otherwise.'

Tom became aware of two silent onlookers and saw that Pridding and Clegg were also close by. Pridding was writing in a small notebook while Clegg watched the dying man like a cat watches its prey.

'The race went to you, Capley . . . and . . . the rule is . . . winner takes all.'

Davenport's mouth sagged open and he closed his eyes wearily for the very last time.

15

Tom stood still, head bowed as the men picked up the stretcher once more and bore it across the field to a waiting horse and cart. He was finally roused from his thoughts by a touch on his arm.

'You can do no more, sir. He is beyond even the Runners now. We have taken down his confession but would still like to speak with you further, Sir Thomas.' Pridding was speaking in an unexpectedly soft and gentle voice and Tom nodded as the Bow Street Runners melted into the crowd and were gone.

He had no further chance of conversation with either Richard or the Arnolds but made his way back to the York House Inn. Much restored by the copious hot water provided for his bath by the innkeeper's wife, he requested a meal in his private parlour and was much amused to discover that Little Wonder had taken Strang's strictures to heart to such an extent that he had insisted on trout followed by mutton chops and red currant jelly, with a custard tart afterwards. All these were dishes that he knew his master liked for his dinner and he had bullied the landlord and his wife into making them available. The warmth of the day had now passed and the September evening was cool enough for a cosy fire as Tom lounged at his ease enjoying a glass of claret and thinking of the events of the day and inevitably, the effect that Davenport's confession would have on Helena. Surely there could now be no more impediment to their marriage. His thoughts drifted to their last meeting when he'd responded to her desperate appeal, her tears as he'd held her in his arms, the open and loving way that she'd returned his kisses. One thing he was sure of, to have his love returned by a woman so proud, so admired and self-reliant as Helena Steer, made him feel a king among men. He would do his utmost to deserve her love, he thought. Never by thought, word or deed would he do anything to hurt her. His whole body burned with his raging need of her, of the longing that her kisses had unleashed. He wanted more than anything to please her, not merely to take pleasure for himself in her lovely young body, but to give her such joy in their lovemaking that she would never want any one else. He'd never felt like this before. The few women he'd experienced in London, had been prepared to have sex in return for a price, never for love's sake. It would be different with Helena. It would be like making love for the first time. He would be dedicated to soothing away all her anxieties, protecting her from every burden that life might offer. He longed to have her nestling trustingly in his arms again, to rest his cheek against her soft hair, and to hold her in an intimate embrace, feel the texture of her skin, not just the shape of her body through her clothes. His longing for her was well nigh unbearable and it was almost a relief when at nine o'clock, there was a tap on the door and the landlord's wife announced Squire Arnold and his son.

'I know you're relaxing, sir,' she said apologetically, 'but there's two gentlemen to see you and it ain't my place to say 'em nay.'

'No, of course not,' Tom said, courteously. 'Ask them to come in, and bring two more glasses if you please.'

'What a pleasure,' Tom smiled at them. 'I hadn't thought to see you two before my departure tomorrow. Sit down, do. Have a glass of wine, sir. How are you feeling after the race, George? For my part, I must confess to feeling so languid that I plan to remain pretty quiet here until morning.'

'I understand, Tom, and we wouldn't have invaded your quiet for the world except . . . '

'Except? Nothing wrong, I hope?'

'Well the fact is, Tom,' George said slowly, as Tom poured out the wine. 'Well, I hope it's nothing, but the fact is we're deuced worried about Richard Steer.'

'Richard?'

'Yes. He's not at all the thing, Tom. Perhaps the tumble he took this afternoon has affected him more adversely than we thought.'

'I saw the stewards aiding him and I thought he had made a safe landing. He seemed recovered afterwards.'

'Yes that's just the trouble. He put his shoulder out you know and they strapped it up for him, but the pain seems to be making him quite feverish. He's lying in his lodgings at James Street, tossing and turning and raving like a madman. His injured shoulder seems to be plaguing him more than is usual in these cases.'

'Wondered if we should send for Doctor Quick,' Squire Arnold said.

'I think that's a capital idea, if he is so troubled,' Tom said.

'Yes he seems quite knocked out this evening. Not in plump currant at all. Unable to get up from his bed, poor young man. If he goes on at this rate, he'll not be up to snuff for the ride home in the morning.'

'In that case, gentlemen,' Tom said, forcing

his weary limbs into action. 'Be so kind as to wait for me. We will send Little Wonder to summon Dr Quick and seek an expert opinion on the young man.'

The under groom was duly despatched and the three men made their way to Richard's lodging. When they arrived, the door stood open on to the street with a flight of worn oak stairs leading up to his room. While they hesitated at the door, they were confronted by a stout, red-faced woman who glowered at them, hands on hips, and demanded to know why they thought that she, Liza Greensmith, should be in charge of the invalid.

'This 'ouse ain't an 'ospital and I ain't a nurse. He's only paying normal bed and board dues and I won't take responsibility for 'im.'

At this point, Tom advanced towards her with a pleasant smile saying, 'No, of course not. Why should you indeed? I should like to stay with him until the doctor arrives. I intend that he shall leave tomorrow for home and not incommode you any further, Miss Greensmith.'

Liza Greensmith was momentarily overcome by the onslaught of his open smile and attractive charm, but it was for one moment only. She recovered immediately and resumed her offensive.

'I'm not an unfeelin' female I'm sure, but I ain't in the business of nursing sickly tenants, so you needn't think as I am. I'm sorry for the young man, and he seems quite a gent but I must beg to have matters settled and I'd like him out by tomorrow noon, doctor or no doctor.'

'Quite so,' Tom murmured soothingly, and then even more quietly, 'May I go in?'

She sniffed resentfully but let him pass and Tom was able to see for himself how Richard was. He was lying in a low-pitched room in a four-poster bed with crimson curtains which had once been brocade but which were now worn to a nondescript uniformity of texture and were somewhat faded. The bedclothes were damp and disordered with his restlessness and fever, his breathing heavy and uneven.

Looking down at the thin body and handsome, sensitive face, Tom was overcome by a wave of compassion and tenderness as he saw the image of Richard's sister. He observed that the stewards had strapped up Richard's injured shoulder, but it seemed to bring the young man no ease and he threshed and moaned constantly in his sleep. He licked his parched lips all the time as though he had a terrible thirst and muttered incoherently.

Tom knew nothing of nursing the sick, but

when he felt the heat of Richard's forehead, he was thankful that the doctor would soon be on hand to advise him.

In a low voice he conferred with George Arnold and his father. 'Tomorrow, we must somehow contrive to get him home, where he can receive proper care and nursing. If you agree, I will accompany him in the carriage with the two ladies, if you could manage my chaise, George, and the grooms can see to the rest of the horses between them.'

It was agreed in an instant and Squire Arnold and his son returned to the Queen's Hotel just as Dr Quick arrived. Tom felt a considerable lightening of his anxiety as the doctor's gig drew up at the front door and the aggressive Miss Greensmith announced him in resentful and truculent tones.

'I'm very grateful for your prompt attendance, sir. I observed Mr Steer's fall from his horse during the race, but afterwards, he seemed fully recovered.'

The doctor was unfastening the binding put on by the stewards and gently felt all around his neck and shoulder.

'Broken collar bone,' he said briefly. 'Send the woman for a draught of lemon barley water. I'll strap it up again and drug him sufficiently to allow him to rest properly. The cut on his forehead will have to be stitched which I shall do now.'

Doctor Quick supported Richard's head and got him to swallow some barley water and administered a heavy dose of laudanum. He proceeded swiftly and expertly to stitch the cut in Richard's forehead and laid him back gently on the bed.

'Tomorrow we plan to travel to Wintham. If he wakes, shall I send for you again?'

'He won't wake, sir,' he said, and began to pack his medical bag. 'I shall call in the morning to advise on whether the patient may travel. He's in shock and needs to be kept quiet.'

He fastened the leather straps on his bag and stood up. 'Good evening, sir.'

So Tom prepared to make himself comfortable for the night on Richard's bedroom chair and the ungracious Liza Greensmith even unbent sufficiently to bring him an ancient patchwork quilt and some mulled red wine. In spite of himself, Tom slept the night away and woke up early to find the bright sunlight shining through the tiny mullioned window. Miss Greensmith grimly brought him some steaming coffee and even invited him to step downstairs for some breakfast. Observing how deeply Richard still slept, Tom declined and hurried back to the York House Inn to wash and shave and give instructions to the men about the journey home. The portmanteau was packed much less expertly than when it had been done by Strang, but Tom soon explained the travel arrangements to Bob Bingham and Little Wonder heaved the luggage into the chaise while Tom settled his account. He managed to write a brief note to Helena and entrusted it to Stubbs before going back to Richard's lodgings to await the doctor's visit.

Doctor Quick frowned heavily at the patient and said, 'If you move the young man today, it will be against my advice. However, if you're adamant on this course of action, send for one of your local practitioners just as soon as you reach home. Here is my written medical diagnosis of the patient's condition and the course of action I have taken so far to alleviate the same. Keep the patient as warm and quiet as possible on his journey and encourage him to drink as much lemon and barley water as he likes. I have made up a sleeping draught for him if he should prove restless when he wakes.'

He paused and gave Tom a keen look from his small brown eyes which were like currants in his large bun of a face. 'I take it you are going to remain with him throughout this journey?'

'Yes, although I have no experience in nursing the sick.'

'Well, the main thing, as I have said, is to keep him calm and use whatever means you can to soothe him if he should become distressed. The sleeping draught should help and a hot brick at his feet with a blanket around him in the coach. He also needs to have sufficient cushions to soften any uneven motion of the carriage. So, God speed to you and good day. I shall forward my bill to Capley Hall in due course, sir.'

With a final kindly smile at the oblivious Richard, Dr Quick departed. Almost immediately, Squire Arnold and George arrived and with the help of their servant and the stalwart Stubbs, the patient was conveyed down the oak staircase with as much tenderness as if he had been delicate Sèvres porcelain. Tom settled him into the Arnolds' carriage and tucked a rug around him. Liza Greensmith grimly carried out a hot brick wrapped in an old piece of blanket and a large jug of home-made lemon and barley water. Then she unsmilingly received the settlement of the tariff and a handsome tip and returned to the house with a satisfied sniff.

Once Mrs Arnold and Miss Emma Chamberlain were inside the carriage, they were able to make good progress back to

Marlborough and had a good rest for refreshments. Richard remained in the carriage and Tom didn't leave him for a moment. He was punctilious about administering little drinks when Richard needed them and earned both ladies' approval by the care he took over having the brick replaced for the next stage of the journey. Fortunately, there was no alarming change in Richard's condition, but because of the care they were taking over their speed, it was very late at night when they finally reached Wintham Rectory. Stubbs had returned much earlier with Blueboy and Helena had been hourly expecting them. The two younger girls clung anxiously to their father as Richard was carried upstairs to his room and Helena and Tom had time only for a short embrace and a brief word about Dr Quick's advice before they parted and he went thankfully to seek his own bed.

First thing in the morning, Charlotte and Eliza came to help and Dr Jones the family physician was sent for. He had known Richard from his earliest youth and had heard some of the local gossip about the young man's fast lifestyle in London, but no mention of this passed his lips as he gravely felt Richard's forehead and his pulse. He approved quietly of Dr Quick's treatment and medicine, but gave it as his considered opinion that Richard's fever was due to pneumonia brought on by the shock of his injury. He left further medicine for him and instructions about the nursing care he was to receive and promised to call again.

'Try not to worry, my dear,' he reassured Helena. 'Master Richard has always been a robust lad in spite of his delicate appearance. He'll pull through, never fear. Good day to you, Reverend,' he said to Francis Steer, who had hovered anxiously by the bed throughout the consultation. 'Keep the patient quiet. I'm sure we'll rear him, sir,' and with a smile and a wave he was gone.

Francis Steer gratefully disappeared about his parish business and left his daughters to their sick-room duties.

Tom did not visit until after six o' clock and had in the meantime been able to have a good night's sleep and check on the horses. He made a point of seeking out Stubbs and pressed some money into his hand to thank him for his assistance. After a brief word with the Reverend Steer he went up to the sick-room and opened the door quietly. The curtains were drawn to shut out the late-afternoon sun and Richard was still restless but at least he was asleep. As his eyes became accustomed to the gloom he saw that

Helena was standing by a little table, wringing out some flannel in a bowl of lavender water.

She came towards him, drying her hands on a cloth and whispered, 'He's just gone back to sleep.'

She glided out of the room on tiptoe and he followed her onto the landing. 'It's so good to see you,' she breathed. 'I was never able to thank you adequately last night for all your kindness to Richard. You saved his life you know.'

'Nonsense,' he said caressingly. 'But are you content with the local man? Would you rather I sent for a London doctor?' He took both her hands in his firm grasp. 'I would be more than happy to go personally and bring a specialist back to him if that is what you want.'

'No. Indeed. Doctor Jones is more than competent and has known Richard since we were children and Charlotte is good at calming Richard. He was particularly restless this morning and babbled incessantly of Jonah Rudd and Percy Davenport.'

'Ah. Davenport, of course. Did you know that he has died as a result of his riding accident in the Furnace Club race?'

'No. I didn't. This explains a lot of things.'

'The Bow Street Runners were present

when he confessed to the murder of Jonah Rudd.'

She shuddered as, immediately, an image of the dead Rudd, flashed into her mind, but she continued bravely, 'Richard raved on about Davenport and gambling debts in his delirium. I was unable to calm him for a full hour.'

'Well, you may impress upon him that Davenport is no more.'

He saw her stricken look and took her hands, saying softly, 'His horse fell at the final hurdle, but he lived long enough to exonerate Richard from any blame over Rudd's death.'

He wondered if she had any idea of how vulnerable she looked and what effect her devastating blue gaze had on him. He could feel her fingers trembling in his and he turned her hands over and gently kissed the pulse point on each of her wrists. He looked down at her. Her full lips were slightly parted, her eyes soft and luminous. Tom was utterly lost in his desire for her and lowered his lips to hers, overwhelmed by the seduction of her willing mouth.

He released her hands and she twined them around his neck pulling him closer until they were body to body, so close that even a sliver of tissue paper couldn't be placed between them. So close that it stopped any words and made even breathing difficult. He clasped her waist, lifting her slightly until she fitted so closely against him he could feel her heart pounding against him, or was it his?

Tom was the first to draw back, drawing a deep breath before his desire overcame the steel of his self-control. He framed her face in both his hands, tilting up her chin until their eyes locked.

'When are we to be married, Helena? God knows, I love you to distraction. I suspect the whole of Wintham knows it and as soon as Richard is on the mend, I want you for my own.'

Impulsively, she reached up and drew his mouth back to hers and answered him with a deep and intimate kiss. Her own reservations were at an end. The more she saw of him the more she loved him and Helena had never in her life loved any man before. She had always been on the receiving end of admiration and passionate desire, never knowing what it was like to love unconditionally. Tom had so significantly overturned the calm pattern of her life as the rector's daughter and Wintham's beautiful breaker of hearts, that she had been in a state of some confusion, not sure of what she really wanted. Now all her doubts were resolved. She acknowledged to herself that she wished to spend the rest of her life with him. He was the perfect man she had never hoped to discover.

As Richard gradually became better and began to gain strength every day, it was no longer necessary for Helena to always remain on call. Francis Steer and her two younger sisters good-humouredly provided as much amusement as Richard needed when he was awake and bored with his invalid state. Although he was painfully thin and white he was soon able to play cards for an hour or so and have Charlotte read to him a little before becoming fretful again and demanding to have his pillows rearranged.

After a few days, Tom was visited by the Runners and he interviewed them in the library at the Hall. They were greeted hospitably and treated as courteously as though they were honoured guests. Finally, when some claret had been poured and pipes had been lit, Tom brought up the question of Davenport's involvement in Rudd's murder.

'We know that it was the Honourable Percy Davenport, sir, the son of Viscount Davenport of Miston, who purchased the promissory notes for Richard Steer's debts from Jonah Rudd last August. He paid a high price for them in more ways than one. As to the sum involved, it was the debt plus twenty per cent, but he was hopelessly in debt himself, unbeknownst to his father of course. He wagered heavily on his horse, Desert Fox, but he was unable to recoup any of the money and, as you know, sir, died in the attempt. Viscount Davenport is left to grieve for his only son.'

He coughed disapprovingly. 'And when I tell you that the old gentleman is in queer street himself and has been these last twelve years, you can understand how desperate Davenport had become.'

Tom was silent for a moment remembering the elderly viscount, who was already quite advanced in years when his son was born and who had proceeded amiably and thoroughly to indulge Percy from his earliest childhood.

'A sad circumstance,' he said soberly.

'Sad, is the word, sir. When Rudd's papers were examined, Davenport was not only deep in debt, but the clerk and others of the moneylender's clients have all testified that he was the last person to interview Rudd in his chambers on the day he died.'

'Do I take it then that he is unquestionably responsible for Rudd's death?'

'Exactly so, and he would have been arraigned for murder, if he hadn't fortuitously died himself. On the day of the murder, his clerk overheard an altercation between Rudd and Davenport, because Rudd wanted to sell the promissory notes to yourself, sir, but Davenport refused to sell them back and finally was driven to attack him.'

He cleared his throat again and said, 'But we will need to question Mr Richard Steer in your presence, when he is strong enough of course.'

'Of course,' Tom agreed.

The second Runner volunteered, 'During the course of our investigation, it was revealed by several of Jonah Rudd's acquaintances that Davenport was something of a . . . a . . . ladies' man. It seems he has tried two or three times over the past few years to compromise various young ladies of means or with expectations, with a view to making an advantageous marriage and resolving his problems.'

'That gives me no surprise,' Tom said, thinking of Davenport's blackmail of Helena. He stood up, indicating that the meeting was at an end. 'Well, thank you for your kind attention, gentleman. Let us hope that the whole sorry episode is now closed.'

Apart from Helena and his grandmother, there were few people Tom held in affection, but he was becoming increasingly fond of Richard and meant to foster his career. He realized it wouldn't be easy. Even when he and Helena were married, he would hold no responsibility for the young man who, after all, had a father to look out for him. For all his absent-mindedness, Francis Steer loved and needed his family. If Tom were to help Richard, he must do it with a light touch. Subtlety would be his watchword. In spite of her obvious love for him, Tom knew that Helena was overwhelmingly concerned about her brother and sisters. That such a beautiful, exciting, passionate and self-willed creature could at the same time, be such a mother hen to the three of them, beggared belief. And yet, it was a twist in her character that he adored with all his heart. She seemed to take it for granted that he shared her concerns and because he loved her, he did share them.

Tom was nothing if not determined and resourceful. Without wasting any more time, he paid his respects to the Reverend Steer and asked to be allowed Helena's hand in marriage. Francis Steer, merely blinked at him vaguely and shifted any decision-making on to his eldest daughter.

'For you must know, Sir Thomas,' he said apologetically, 'that like Solomon, Helena makes her own decisions and will answer to no one but herself, but if she agrees, my dear chap, I will offer my felicitations.'

Tom was content with this. It was clear that the momentum for their union must come from him and he made his plans accordingly. He sought out Richard and chatted awhile and then disengaged Helena from her brother by asking if she would care for a walk.

Richard offered his encouragement. 'You're too much with me, dear Sis'. I make a monopoly of your time and I'm no longer an invalid, you know.'

'Yes, do, Helena dear,' Charlotte urged. 'It is such a fine day and will bring colour to your cheeks.'

Charlotte had been the greatest surprise to Helena, since Richard's return. She seemed to blossom under the responsibility of helping to nurse him and the former disagreement between the sisters appeared to be forgotten. Alfred Carty was no longer mentioned and had returned to Oxford. The prospect of a season in London, with new clothes for the come out parties and balls seemed to have driven him from her mind. She had confided ingenuously to Helena that although she would never forget him, she would wait a year or two before thinking of an engagement.

Now, Helena laughingly ran to get her bonnet and pelisse and she and Tom set off, but not for a genteel turn round the garden. It was indeed a fine day and Tom took her on one of the rambling walks they both loved so well. He deliberately led her to the little clearing in the woods where they'd first met and they stopped to gaze into the stream.

'Helena,' he said, 'now that Richard has plucked up so well in the last two weeks, I feel he should seek some restorative treatment at a Spa. Doctor Jones recommends Harrogate as the best resort for his convalescence.'

'Oh do you think so, Tom?' she asked, turning to him. 'I hadn't thought of it myself, but you may be right!'

Her eyes were glowing with the deep azure that he loved so well. She was still too slender for a woman of above average height, but her face was as radiantly beautiful as ever in the bright autumn light.

'I'm sure I'm right,' Tom said firmly, resisting the impulse to take her in his arms and kiss the beautiful, mobile mouth. 'And once it's arranged, your father has agreed that we should make plans for our wedding, Helena.'

'Yes. But . . . the girls . . . '

'No 'buts', my dear love. Charlotte is too young to be thinking of marriage. Eliza has still not completed her education. We should be planning Charlotte's come out and once we're married, it could be arranged from the London house. Miss Rosling's Academy for Young Ladies in Bath, I'm sure would suit

Eliza and provide her with the company she needs. But first things first, Helena: When will we be married? I want you to be truly mine. You're the only woman I've ever loved — ever wanted. I never thought I would ever find such a love.'

He put his hands on her waist and felt that she was trembling.

'Oh it's not possible at the moment ... Richard ... Charlotte ... I'm still needed ...'

'That, my darling,' he said firmly, 'is twaddle. We are going to be married very soon and there are arrangements to be made. We will make them together. I have decided on October the seventeenth as the happy day. If you are prepared to carp at this, beautiful Miss Steer, I shall throw you over and you will then be at your last prayers, ma'am, condemned to be an old maid forever.'

She was torn between laughter and tears. 'Oh no, Tom. We can't ... Can we? Your Grandmama ... ? What will Papa say?'

'Yes, we can. Very easily,' Tom said catching her into a suffocating embrace. 'I have the licence. I have your papa's approval. It's all arranged. Now we must get on with it. I shall rent a house for your brother and his sisters may join him. I can hire some hacks so that the young people can ride every day if they wish. My grandmother would be delighted to accompany them and she knows Harrogate well.'

It wasn't merely Tom's voice which was persuasive. His lips were more so. They pressed seductively against her own, exerting a subtle dominance which robbed her of all power of protest. Helena was lost and she knew it. She returned his kiss with undisguised passion and, as if in a dream, agreed to all his plans.

All the villagers of both parishes turned out for the wedding in Wintham Church, as well as the fine guests from London and Kesthorpe. Charlotte and Eliza, in pretty new dresses, were bridesmaids. Sophie Malpass, was a brilliant attendant on the bride. Everyone was in high good humour as they gathered to wish the bride and groom well.

When Tom finally slipped the ring on her finger, Helena felt a happiness and contentment such as she had never known before in the whole of her life and when he raised her wedding veil to kiss his radiant bride on the lips, there was such a deep and complete devotion in their embrace that every member of the nuptial party was silent. Even the shuffling crowd of villagers who had overflowed into the old Norman porch were utterly still, recognizing that the commitment

348

in this kiss was as serious as their solemn vows at the altar.

The awesome silence lasted until the triumphant peal of wedding bells sounded across the green peace of Wintham and the two of them walked triumphantly towards their new life.

THE END

We do hope that you have enjoyed reading this large print book.

Did you know that all of our titles are available for purchase?

We publish a wide range of high quality large print books including:
Romances, Mysteries, Classics
General Fiction
Non Fiction and Westerns

Special interest titles available in large print are:
The Little Oxford Dictionary
Music Book
Song Book
Hymn Book
Service Book

Also available from us courtesy of Oxford University Press:
Young Readers' Dictionary
(large print edition)
Young Readers' Thesaurus
(large print edition)

For further information or a free brochure, please contact us at:
Ulverscroft Large Print Books Ltd.,
The Green, Bradgate Road, Anstey,
Leicester, LE7 7FU, England.
Tel: (00 44) 0116 236 4325
Fax: (00 44) 0116 234 0205

Other titles published by
The House of Ulverscroft:

DEAR MISS GREY

Shirley Smith

When beautiful Lucy Grey and her brother, William, become orphans, their futures are organized by hard-nosed Aunt Esther. Whilst Will is sent to Oxford University, Lucy is found a post in London as governess to Lord Hallburgh's two motherless children. However, Lucy soon senses a strange and threatening atmosphere in the household, run by Edmund Hallburgh's much older sister, the autocratic Honourable Caroline Hallburgh, who is physically disabled. She sees the growing friendship between Lucy and Edmund as a threat to her own position and is determined to break Lucy Grey . . .

LORD WHITLEY'S BRIDE

Sharon Milburn

Edith Backworth, daughter of the local parson, leads a tranquil life in rural Northumberland until the tragedy of Waterloo propels her into London society. Charles, Lord Whitley, is still mourning the loss of his fiancee and friends when he is thrust into the unwelcome role of exeuctor. His life is totally disrupted by the new Lady Edith's outspoken behaviour. He would like nothing better than to throttle her! But when Edith's murderous cousin, Bertram, covets her father's new title and kidnaps her, only Charles can come to the rescue . . .